Bridge
Over
Troubled
Water

Hannah,

Enjoy the reading!

L. C Sim

L.C. Simon

ISBN 979-8-88851-380-4 (Paperback)
ISBN 979-8-88851-381-1 (Digital)

Covenant Books
11661 Hwy 707
Murrells Inlet, SC 29576
www.covenantbooks.com

Introduction

Shaken Baby Syndrome usually occurs when a parent or care-giver severely shakes a child in frustration or anger, often because the child won't stop crying. Permanent brain damage or death may result. Symptoms include irritability, difficulty staying awake, seizures, abnormal breathing, poor eating, bruises, and vomiting.

> Treatment will vary depending on complications related to Shaken Baby Syndrome. In rare instances, breathing support or surgery may be needed to stop bleeding in the brain. (Mayo Clinic)

Although this novel is fictional, the dangerous effects of Shaken Baby Syndrome are undeniable. This book is in memory and dedicated to the silent victims of Shaken Baby Syndrome.

My thanks to the Washington County Child Protection Team, Washington County Attorney's Office, Washington County Sheriff's Office, Washington County Child Protection Services, Bureau of Criminal Apprehension, Midwest Children's Resource Center, and CornerHouse.

CHAPTER 1

My footsteps echo as I walk down the seemingly endless white hall-way. I seem to be walking through a fog, but I know I am inside. I seem to be the only person in this space, wherever I am. And then, the fog clears. There is a person in a white coat ushering me into a cubicle with glass walls, and curtains pulled over the glass. The person in the white coat disappears. I look over my shoulder to see where she went, but no one is around. I turn forward, and there she is. A baby is lying on a full-length exam table. She barely makes a bump under the blanket pulled up to her neck. She is dead. There is no movement. Her little chest is motionless under the blanket. Her eyes are open. They would have been beautiful if the hemorrhaging in them hadn't turned almost all of the whites red. Dried tear tracks were running down her nearly colorless face. I reach out to touch her face when suddenly, she turns her head to look at me. I am frozen in place. I want to look away. But I couldn't. Her eyes are crying tears of blood that follows the old tear tracks down her tiny face. Her little mouth starts to move, and she says, "Why didn't you help me? Isn't that your job? Why am I dead?"

I deliberately pulled myself out of the nightmare, snapping my eyes wide open. The dim light seeping through the crack in the blinds was crossing over my bare legs. *My covers must be on the floor,* I mused, as I struggled to recover from the nightmare that had been plaguing me for months, eventually making me decide to retire four years shy of my target date. I sat on the edge of my bed, rubbing my face between my hands. I didn't know what time it was, but there was no way I was going back to sleep and into that nightmare again. I got up, pulled on a pair of well-worn jeans, and headed to the kitchen. Leaning over the kitchen sink, I stared out the window and remembered.

1

It was her eyes that haunted me. The sparkling-blue eyes were so unusual for a baby that age. They were so big and haunting, with red blood flares streaking them. They seemed to stare right through me, silently asking, *Why didn't you help me?*

Her cheeks had been so pale, with pathways from tears dried on her face. Her tiny bow-shaped lips had already had most of the color leached from them in death. She lay on her back, staring, lifeless, gone before she had a chance at life.

Her name was Mary.

The patrol officer and paramedics had been simultaneously dispatched to an unresponsive baby, followed by a callout for me from my residence. Her mother reported that she had gone into the baby's bedroom to check on Mary in the middle of the night and found her dead. Sudden infant death syndrome (SIDS) was her explanation. Upon checking vitals, the patrol deputy found a weak pulse. Upon the arrival of the paramedics, Mary was transported to Ramsey Hospital and placed on life support.

She had been a perfect baby but hadn't died from SIDS. Somebody had shaken her to death. Out of anger or just the simple frustration and exhaustion of a new mother, it didn't matter what the triggering mechanism was. Her mother had snuffed out a perfect little precious life in just seconds.

Running my hand over my face, I reached for the cold water faucet and turned it on. I lowered my head, splashed cold water on my face and hair, then grabbed a nearby towel. I paused briefly, thinking about drying my face with the towel that I dry dishes with but thought, *What the hell*, and did it anyway.

Turning from the sink, I crossed the room to the fridge. Opening the door, I grabbed a can of beer, unlocked the back door, and stepped out onto the porch of my duplex. I sat in the old rocking chair that had been gently rocking in the early morning breeze. Setting the beer on the nearby table, I pulled my feet onto the chair in front of me and laid my forehead on my knees.

Would it ever stop? I thought in something close to despair. I had many abuse cases, some much more violent than Mary's. So many in seventeen years, they had stacked up. That last one had just broken me, and I couldn't rebuild the barricade to my feelings. The only way to handle these cases was to have a solid, impenetrable barrier between your personal feelings and the job. That baby had cracked my shell, and it just wouldn't heal.

I started my career in law enforcement twenty-seven years ago. All those years, I had been serving and protecting the citizens of Washington County, Minnesota. Washington County is 384 square miles, with a population of 235,000. The county is made up of small towns, bigger cities, and many rural and township areas. During my years as deputy of the Sheriff's Office, I performed almost every duty that a deputy fulfilled in the department: communication center, jailer, court security, civil process, patrol, patrol sergeant, and, finally, investigation.

I was assigned the night shift or the dogwatch in my earlier years. That is the last shift of the night and the first of the next day. On the night shift, you worked while the rest of the world should be asleep. I patrolled North Washington County; it was primarily rural and nicknamed the *Corncob Jungle*.

We were the only two-deputy squad in Washington County. A two-deputy team was considered safer for the patrol deputy since backup could be up to a half-hour away. It was not uncommon for either one or both deputies to be pulled off the road to replace a sick dispatcher or replace a county jailer for vacation. I wouldn't say I liked the jailer job. There were often nights when there would be only one deputy in the north squad or, on occasion, no squad—just another night in the *Corncob Jungle*.

Once promoted to sergeant of patrol, I saw county law enforcement during the day. Then I was transferred to the investigation division. I had worked on all types of major crimes before being assigned to focus primarily on child abuse investigations.

WSTP-I Team aired an investigative report on a Minnesota case that focused on the sexual abuse of children and the Scott County attorney who had charged twenty-four defendants in an alleged child sexual abuse ring.

As a result, child abuse cases, specifically child sexual abuse cases, were brought out of the closet, and reports came in from all directions. Teachers, nurses, therapists, families, and victims began calling in.

Washington County developed a protocol for child abuse investigation which is used statewide today. Besides myself, a team of social workers and county attorneys made up the team of county professionals who managed a report of child abuse, from the investigation up to and through court proceedings, and beyond if necessary. We had advisers from the medical and psychiatric fields on call as well.

Most law enforcement professionals want nothing to do with child abuse investigations. Not because they don't care, but precisely the opposite. They care too much and find it almost impossible to be dispassionate when dealing with the accused. I was uniquely qualified in this particular field of investigation. I was the low man in seniority, and so I got the assignment. I developed the necessary detachment. It didn't come naturally.

Child abuse investigations are unique because your victim is always young and often dependent on the person abusing them. The victim is almost always in imminent danger, and we almost always have a suspect. The very nature of the crime calls for immediate action. It could cut you to your core if you don't learn to compartmentalize your feelings. You have to be able to file those feelings away and act professionally.

And here I am, a dried-up cop, retired, with no sense of purpose and haunted by nightmares. Great.

I sat up and popped the top on the beer can. As I pulled that first sip out of the can, I heard the creak of the door adjacent to mine.

"Jackie, is that you?" The whisper came from my neighbor, Adeline Hoglund. She had rented from me for the last ten years. She liked to mother me. We were a perfect match: a motherless man and a childless woman. We had developed a bond.

"Yes, it's me, Ms. Adeline." The door snapped shut, and she leaned over the fence that separated the decks to peer more closely at me.

"The dream again?" she asked.

She had found me one night in this same chair. I had been having a rough night. I remember crying; she had pried the dream out of me at a weak moment. Later, I made her promise never to share it with anyone. She had agreed. In the months since, I had found it somewhat cathartic to be able to talk to someone about it if she was around. She made a point of being around. She had radar or something. She always seemed to know when I was having a rough night.

"Jackie, you need to get out of this house, and don't tell me you go fishing! That gives you more time to brood. You don't even bring fish home. You go out there for a change of scenery and brood on the water. You will never be able to move on until you fill your time with something else."

It was a familiar refrain. Ms. Adeline had been trying to get me interested in something else since I retired in May. I didn't feel like having this discussion. "Do you want a beer?" I asked, trying to distract her.

"Don't mind if I do," she replied as she sat down in her rocking chair.

We had spent many such late nights and early mornings in the last few months this way. She was the closest thing to a date I had had in a long time. I thought as I went back into the house to grab her beer.

Popping the top and handing the can across the fence to her, I said, "I know you are probably right, but I don't feel like making an effort to reach out to anyone. I think I will know when it is time. For now, I want to work on the duplex, work out, and fish."

"Jackie, I don't mean to nag. I want what's best for you, and I don't think it is good to brood for so long. God knows that little girl's death was not your fault. There was nothing you could have done. I wish you had known how close to the edge you were so you could have avoided this mourning."

I looked over at her, silently questioning the word *mourning*.

"Yes, I meant mourning," she said, reading my thoughts. "I know what mourning looks like, and *you* are mourning the job. You poured yourself—heart and soul—into being a cop. It was more than a job. It was your identity. Now you are lost. You don't know who you are or what to do with yourself. And I don't think you will find yourself on the river. You are too young to sit in that chair and rock the rest of your life away."

Dawn was beginning to break with a thin line of orange on the eastern horizon. The St. Croix River was down there. We couldn't quite see it from our back porch. The rooftops of the little town of Bayport lay between the river and us.

"You're right," I said, not wanting to carry this conversation any further. "As long as I am awake, I am going to grab my bag and head down to the gym. It shouldn't be too crowded. Why don't you go back to bed for a few more hours."

Ms. Adeline reached over and patted my cheek. Standing up, she crossed to her door, leaving the nearly full can on the railing between us. Pausing before opening her door, she looked back at me and said, "You worry me, Jackie." Opening the door, she went inside.

*****

It was well after sunrise when I returned from the gym, sweaty and tired. I was heading for the bathroom and a shower when my home phone rang. My landline didn't ring much these days, so it surprised me. I didn't recognize the number. I answered, "Hello?"

"Detective Janssen? Judge Lord calling."

CHAPTER 2

I reflected on twenty-seven years of police work while traffic crawled through downtown Stillwater on a balmy September afternoon, northbound to Judge Vivian Lord's estate.

The historic lift bridge, built in 1931, spanning the scenic St. Croix River, was up, allowing boat traffic to pass beneath it. At the same time, the day shift for Anderssen Windows, a leading window manufacturer in Bayport, was clogging up traffic on Main Street. It is a perfect traffic storm for the people at a dead stop in their cars.

Sitting in traffic had always driven me crazy. No matter how hard I tried to relax, calm was always just out of reach. Allowing my mind to wander was the only way to deal with the frustration of Chestnut and Main on sunny late-summer days. My mind wandered back to the inevitable—the job.

I had never taken a life with my duty weapon. A tough guy I wasn't, but I had carried the caseload of the most challenging crime that ever faced a cop for most of my career—child abuse.

I allowed my mind to travel into my past as the traffic before me stood still. A glance at the traffic behind me in the rearview mirror told me many people were doing the same thing.

Stillwater is the birthplace of Minnesota and the county seat of Washington County. Every one of the fifteen thousand residents of the area knows to avoid downtown in the summer, making room for the swarm of tourists. The charming river town has also attracted movie producers who have filmed several movies here, including *Beautiful Girls*, *Grumpy Old Men*, *Grumpier Old Men*, *The Cure*, *Overnight Delivery*, and *Fargo*.

The population of this expanding river town and the sister city of Somerset, situated across the river in Wisconsin, should have resulted in a new bridge being built years ago. However, because of political ineffectiveness, city officials have been hamstrung in constructing a new interstate bridge and easing the severe and increasing congestion.

As traffic moved slowly forward, I could see that a semitruck attempting to negotiate a turn from Main Street East, onto Chestnut Street, toward the lift bridge, had toppled the traffic light on the corner. This frequently happened when large trucks tried to avoid the weigh scales on Interstate 94, six miles south of Stillwater, adding to the congestion. *Serves him right*, I thought. I was settling into my seat for a prolonged wait.

It seems not so long ago that I began my career at the Historic Courthouse and patrolled the gravel roads of the *Corncob Jungle* of Washington County. My height of five-foot eight just edged me above the height requirements, which have long since vanished. Similarly the muscles on the lean physique of the graduate from the Bureau of Criminal Apprehension Rookie School had also disappeared, I thought, as I adjusted my seat belt in my lap. *My blond hair has turned gray, but my eyesight is pretty good, and my eyes are still blue,* I thought with a chuckle. Bloodshot debriefings at Geister's Bar and the occasional jab from a suspect should have resulted in more tired, older-looking eyes.

My two-inch stainless steel Smith and Wesson .357 Magnum revolver looked old and tired, giving away my age more than my appearance. Younger deputies carried county-issued .40 caliber Smith and Wesson semiautomatic. Some of them had never even seen a revolver up close.

Marriage had always been on my mind, but I never found someone who truly understood my stressful lifestyle and was willing to tackle my baggage. My one long-term relationship had been with an assistant county attorney, LaVonne Williams. We had dated for quite a while. It hadn't worked out. According to her, I visibly carried my stress across my shoulders, and she didn't want any part of that lifestyle. I let the idea of marriage go after that.

A horn behind me brought me out of my reflection. Looking back, I saw a package delivery driver urging me to move forward with some rather graphic hand signals. Mumbling "asshole" under my breath, I continued northbound along with the now-flowing traffic, turning onto Arcola Trail, where the Honorable Judge Vivian Lord resided.

Judge Lord had invited me to an early dinner, which was intriguing. She had said it was because she missed my retirement party, but that was almost four months ago. Something was up.

As a detective sergeant, I had been to Judge Lord's residence on numerous occasions for her signature on search or arrest warrants for suspects in child abuse cases.

The bulk of my investigations were sexual abuse cases. However, months before my unexpected retirement at the age of fifty-one, I had investigated a shaken baby case in Lake Elmo. This city contracted with the Sheriff's Office for law enforcement services.

Classified as Shaken Baby Syndrome, a caregiver vigorously shakes an infant, resulting in the baby's head jerking back and forth uncontrollably. Consequently the baby's brain will also move back and forth, striking the skull's interior. The results can cause bruising, swelling, tearing, or bleeding of the brain tissue, resulting in permanent brain damage or death.

Shaken baby cases are tremendously complex investigations involving medical documentation and definitive history of who had contact with the baby victim when the injury occurred. These cases are emotionally demanding of Child Protection Services and police officers because of the age, condition, and vulnerability of the non-verbal victim, often on life support in a hospital.

In the Lake Elmo case, not only did the investigation contain documentation that placed the biological mother with the baby victim when the injury occurred, but the mother had also confessed to shaking her infant daughter, which resulted in severe brain damage.

I will never forget the mother's terror-stricken eyes. When she demonstrated on an anatomically correct doll the force she had administered to her baby. Resulting in the brain damage found on her expressionless little face and the flame-shaped hemorrhages in her lifeless eyes.

Three days before the Lake Elmo mother had shaken the life out of her baby, a family member had filed a report with the Sheriff's Office. The information contained allegations of physical abuse and shaking. The assignment commander decided to delay assigning the case until I returned from a scheduled long weekend off. That decision delayed the investigation and assessment by Child Protection Services. This decision may have contributed to the brain death of a Lake Elmo baby.

Law enforcement officers are trained in first aid and quickly learn that emergency responses are bleeding, breathing, and poisoning. Criminal investigations involving children are often not given priority assignments.

I struggled after the Lake Elmo case emotionally. I couldn't continue with child abuse investigations or law enforcement. I submitted a written notice to terminate my employment without disclosing my true reasons.

Turning onto Arcola Trail, I admired the posh houses along the drive and wondered who lived in the exclusive homes, speculating how much money one would have to make to live in such an affluent house. "Certainly more than a government pension," I mumbled to myself.

Judge Lord lived in a ranch-style house with a lower-level walkout that overlooked the St. Croix River. The Lord's estate had a black ornamental iron gate. Carefully manicured shrubs framed the long concrete driveway. *Nothing as mundane as asphalt in this neighborhood*, I thought.

The expansive serpentine driveway concluded at a grand circle entrance surrounding an island. The drive accented by aprons of brick, making a design like spokes on a bike tire, running between plants and flowers, coming together in the center, where a flagpole majestically stood.

A short brick walkway brings guests to the stately double-doored entrance of the residence. The beautifully manicured lawn was free of additions that grace the yards of the more common homeowner. Dandelions or crabgrass wouldn't dare show up here. The Lord's estate was as prominent and picturesque as any Arcola Trail estate. They all had two things in common: prosperity and Buster Greeley, a meticulous groundskeeper.

Buster was omnipresent on Arcola Trail; a large solid man in his midseventies, with thick gray hair, a sun-dried tomato complexion, and a gracious smile. I presumed Buster had completed his duties and was long gone from the estates this afternoon.

Judge Lord was not only an extraordinary judge for Washington County; she was the most sincere person on the bench. Unlike most of her fellow judges, she was unafraid to preside over a child abuse case.

Judges and public defenders would rather face a firing squad than take on one of these cases. I thought she was one hell of a woman.

Judge Lord was in her late forties and married her husband, Charles, after a three-year law school romance at William Mitchell College of Law. Judge Lord's career path followed the way of public service, unlike her husband, who joined the corporate world as a lawyer.

Judge Lord had a distinguished career as an assistant county attorney who specialized in child protection matters before her appointment to the bench by the governor. Although the judge herself was not politically discerning, her husband was a steadfast Republican with connections.

Charles Lord might have been appointed to the federal bench if not for his untimely death from a heart attack on Christmas Eve morning over three years ago. Charles Lord's overweight frozen body was found at the end of his driveway.

That morning, he had been attempting to free his Silver Mercedes Benz Coupe from a two-foot snowplow drift. A St. Paul Press news mobile carrier had discovered the body. I had been dispatched to the Lord's residence to assist another detective and to locate Vivian Lord for the death notification.

The Lord's residence was secure, and Vivian Lord was not at their residence or her chambers at the government center. It had been common knowledge that the judge and I had a professional friendship for years, some even speculating a romantic connection.

I remember approaching the Lord's residence on that frigid, lifeless morning and hearing the tires crunching in the snow. It had been nineteen below zero. Not even close to the record of thirty-eight below zero for December 24.

The squad cars and medical examiner's vehicles were running and emitting a cloud of steamy exhaust. At the same time, emergency lights flashed and reflected red on the snow at the scene of a death investigation.

Before my arrival, the medical examiner and investigators had erected Charles Lord's frozen corpse. Charles Lord was wearing a red plaid jacket, tan corduroy trousers, black driving gloves, and a black driving cap. Charles Lord's stone-white face and frozen solid body stood upright in a two-foot-deep snowdrift. Charles's right arm was extended and his left arm at his waist.

On this penetrating cold morning, Charles had the grotesque likeness of a cast-iron lawn jockey greeting visitors at the gated entrance to his estate. As I pulled up, I saw a couple of flashes from a camera.

The expressions of amusement immediately fell from the deputies' faces as my unmarked navy-blue Crown Victoria Ford stopped at the Lord's driveway. They quickly turned and assisted the medical examiner in placing the body on the stretcher.

Vivian Lord was at her sister's home in Bloomington, where she traditionally spent the night before Christmas Eve, decorating the house and preparing for the family Christmas feast. Her day usually involved a final dash through the Mall of America to complete her shopping.

Together with a Bloomington police officer, I delivered the tragic news of Charles's death. I had learned that Charles was going into his office early on the morning of December 24, and the couple had plans to connect for an afternoon Christmas party.

At precisely four o'clock, I parked my deep-green Jeep Wrangler in front of the first of four single-garage doors closest to the residence. As I was exiting my vehicle, the garage door opened. Judge Lord was standing inside.

Every time I went to the Lord's home, this routine happened without fail. I had often thought about parking in front of an alternative garage door, but my compliance with protocol and her position prevented me from such a rebellious maneuver.

I met the judge at the entrance to the garage door, and she greeted me with, "Detective, come in." She gently grasped my hand, adding, "You are right on time!"

My relationship with Judge Lord has always been friendly but official, in and out of the courtroom. I didn't know what to expect from this dinner engagement, as we didn't travel in the same social circles.

The entry was the location where I removed my deck shoes. I had removed my shoes—at Judge Lord's request—the first time I came out for a warrant to be signed, and I have done it every time since.

I followed the judge through to the solarium that overlooked the St. Croix River, a view only Arcola Trail residents or hot-air balloon enthusiasts could enjoy. The solarium was quite large, with a wall of windows, a vaulted ceiling, and a fireplace for winters.

There were imposing vases filled with beautiful cut flowers, which I presumed were from her many gardens. The southern wall had a watercolor painting of the historic aerial lift bridge, with a background of trees and foliage in beautiful autumn colors. Most likely bought from one of the many local Stillwater artists that sell their art at various festivals along the levee during the summer months.

"Can I bring you a beverage, Detective?"

Feeling a little uneasy and not knowing if the judge enjoyed a cocktail, I asked for an iced tea.

Judge Vivian Lord was a tiny woman. Every feature was perfect, in my opinion, with her brown eyes, hair, and standout features. Her auburn hair framed her classically beautiful face, always styled in an elegant twist at the back of her head. Her eyes were a beautiful penetrating brown. It appeared as though she could read people's minds when she looked at someone in court. She had a delicate build, but she didn't look weak. The muscle tone in her arms was proof of a regular workout routine.

She was wearing a flowing black dress with black sandals and the most prominent gold necklace I had ever seen. I felt like the hired help in my beige Dockers and green golf shirt, even though I had worn my dress deck shoes.

In a few minutes, she returned with an iced tea trimmed with lemon and, I presumed, a tonic and lime, maybe with gin—I wasn't sure—for herself.

Still anxious about this dinner engagement, I said, "Judge, you can call me Jack. You know that I have been retired for almost four months."

"You're right," she replied, "but I still can't believe you have retired! You have been there for my whole career, first on the Child Protection Team when I was with the County Attorney's Office, then as a judge. I presided over so many of your cases. It's hard for me to believe you aren't there anymore."

She looked down at her drink for a moment before raising her eyes to look at me again and said, "You're a fixture in my professional life."

Turning toward the table behind me and taking a few steps away from her, I took a minute to wonder what exactly that meant. I sounded like a piece of furniture that came with her office.

Setting my glass on the table, I just turned to her and said, "It was time to retire, Judge. I have been enjoying time away from the courthouse, and the fishing on the river has been pretty good."

She settled gracefully into a white rattan chair behind her and indicated I should take the matching one. "Yes, I heard that you have an interest in fishing. Charles enjoyed fishing, and we had many good times on the river. I rarely venture out on the river myself these days. The boat seldom leaves our—" She paused and corrected herself, "My dock."

My comfort level was moving from mildly uncomfortable to highly uneasy. *What am I doing here?* I thought to myself. *Why did she ask me out here?*

After a brief pause, Judge Lord took what looked to be a bracing swig from her drink before she set it down. Turning slightly in her chair, she was almost facing me. She folded her hands, looked at me, and began. "Detective, Jack, I always considered you a compassionate and very competent investigator, one I could call upon if I were a victim of a crime. You were such a comfort to me when Charles died. I don't know what I would have done without you. And here I am again. I need your help, your advice. I don't know where to start," she said with a sigh.

I could see that the judge was beginning to tear up. I leaned in closer to her, with my forearms resting on my knees but still keeping a respectful distance between us. "It has you pretty worked up. Judge, you know I will help you in any way possible. Tell me, what's going on?"

"Jack, I've received some taunting letters at the courthouse, really nothing new. You're going to think that I am crazy, but I have also been finding evidence that someone has been in my house and searching through my belongings."

"Did you file a report with the Sheriff's Office?"

The Sheriff's Office provides police protection to the residents on Arcola Trail since it is well outside the city of Stillwater's boundaries.

The judge leaned back in her chair and closed her eyes. Sighing, she replied, "I haven't told anyone. I don't know if I'm scaring myself. I keep thinking it is the courtroom stress, and I am still not accustomed to Charles being gone."

"Do you have a security system?"

"Yes, but it only covers the exterior doors and is quite old. Charles was always more diligent about setting the alarm than I was." She gave me a sheepish look.

I continued, "Who else has access to the house?"

"I have a housekeeper, Madel. She works for me four days a week. Of course, Buster, who does my lawn, and an assortment of delivery people. I certainly don't suspect any of them!"

I attempted to alleviate her fears and asked if I could have a friend at the Sheriff's Office conduct a security survey of her residence. She responded, "I would like that very much, but please promise me there will be no formal report. I don't want everyone in the courthouse to know about this."

"I will ensure that only the three of us know anything about it," I assured her. She seemed much more relaxed as we headed into the kitchen.

The kitchen was less formal than the dining room and had a relaxing light atmosphere for people having dinner together, engaging in easy conversation with instrumental piano music flowing from concealed speakers. Judge Lord seated me to her right.

The kitchen appliances looked rather industrial in size, and I had never heard of a Vulcan range or a Sub-Zero refrigerator. Still, I could envision the Lords entertaining guests with a glass of champagne, white-collar conversation, and delicious hors d'oeuvres prepared by a caterer in this kitchen.

The judge looked quite at home in the kitchen and served a mixed green salad, always suspicious to me and never very appealing. Especially with a vinaigrette dressing, but I did my duty and ate it. I enjoyed the tortellini and prosciutto ham dish, complemented by a red wine that was probably more expensive than my clothes.

"Is the wine from your vineyard?" I asked as I took another appreciative sip.

Laughing a little and wrinkling her nose, she replied, "Confidentially it is not the best wine. I lease the land to Somerset Winery. My favorite Cabernet is from the San Sebastián Winery in St. Augustine, Florida.

Our dinner conversation centered around our interactions and involvement in the Child Protection Team before her appointment to the bench. We handled some pretty bizarre cases over the years.

The years had given us distance from the emotions we experienced during the active cases. However, the second bottle of wine had us open up a little more and share some of our emotional difficulties. For my part, it was the first time I had shared some of my private demons with anyone other than Ms. Adeline. I was left wondering why I was doing it now. Here. With Judge Lord. I blamed it on damn good wine.

We didn't get around to dessert until well after 8:00 p.m. The crème brûlée was delicious, and we shared a couple of cups of fantastic coffee at the same time. We both felt very relaxed and comfortable in each other's company.

I finally felt like I should be wrapping up the evening. Rising from the table, I said, "I enjoyed myself this evening. I will have a friend at the Sheriff's Office contact you on Monday and schedule a security review. Her name is Anne Reed. Have you met her?"

"I don't think so." As she rose from the table, she said, "Is she a new deputy?"

"Anne isn't a sworn officer. She is a CSO—Community Service Officer. She is good. She has the most progressive training in community policing. A good officer with good instincts has always used the same methods. They have a fancy title and are now used to teach citizens good home security and personal safety."

As I started walking toward the service door to the garage, I saw a portrait of Charles Lord towering over a pearl baby grand piano in the formal living room. "What a beautiful piano!" I exclaimed. Pausing in the hallway, I turned to ask her if she played.

"Charles played. I enjoyed it so very much." She ended in almost a whisper. Visibly forcing herself to take control of her emotions, she said, "I'm sorry, Jack. It is still difficult for me to talk about Charles. I still can't believe he is gone."

I wanted to tell her that not only did I enjoy piano music, but I also played the piano. Pretty well, if I do say so myself. Now didn't seem to be the best time for that reveal.

Judge Lord was looking so sad that I wanted to give her a supportive hug. Suddenly she put my thoughts into action and hugged me. You know, the kind of hug you would give someone at a funeral. "Thank you so much, Jack. You have been a real friend to me."

While leaving the Lord's residence and driving out the gate, I thought, what good is a gate that doesn't lock and is always open?

It was dark as I drove home; dark was preferable to the afternoon traffic. I thought that I recognized what Judge Lord was feeling. I think all of us who work in law enforcement, in one way or another, worry about our suspects or defendants coming back to take revenge on us. Many people sent to jail or prison think that they are dealt with too harshly. Some will even threaten retaliation. I never like seeing a former suspect in a public place. I always keep my eyes open and take every means to avoid someone I have arrested.

I have dealt with threats before; some overt, some veiled, and either one is unsettling. I have never personally had a threat acted upon me. One of the people that Judge Lord has sentenced may be involved in the letters and her fears of someone being in her home.

One thing was for sure—I wasn't going to dismiss either one.

CHAPTER 3

It was another beautiful day with a light breeze in the valley, and I thought a day on the river would do me good. While gathering my fishing gear, Ms. Adeline came out with a brown bag in her hand. I could smell her apple strudel.

"You baked already this morning?" I said with a smile.

She smiled at me and handed me the bag. Ms. Adeline was in her eighties, slightly overweight, with a pale almost-white face, a perennial smile, and too much red lipstick.

Ms. Adeline's husband had been a retired Anderssen Windows employee. Anderssen Windows, a local company, had a great pension plan, and they had lived comfortably in retirement until his sudden death, just before she had moved in next door.

Mr. Hoglund had fallen through the ice and drowned. Ice fishing on the St. Croix River was always a little dangerous, particularly near the Allen S. King Electric Plant. The plant is two miles north of my duplex in Oak Park Heights. It is a coal-burning power plant that discharges clean warm water into the river. The water surrounding the discharge point rarely freezes, and the ice around the warm water pond is fragile and dangerous.

Despite the danger and signage warning against it, the excellent fishing and open water draw many die-hard fishermen. The fishermen dragged their boats across the ice into the open water and rowed into the "pond" to fish.

Mr. Hoglund was the safety officer for Anderssen Windows and always took extra care. While he walked alongside his small duckboat wearing a personal flotation device, he took small steps until arriving at open water. Tragically Mr. Hoglund slipped on the ice near the water opening, hit his head on the aluminum boat, and fell to his death facedown in the St. Croix River.

He had always taken pride in his safety officer position with the company. Ironically he would issue a memorandum every winter requesting employees not to travel across the frozen river on the renowned Winter Ice Road that led to Hudson, Wisconsin. Though it was time-saving for employees who lived in Wisconsin, it was dangerous.

Every year, employees disregarded the memo, even having a running betting pool annually for the first and last car to cross the river on the ice road. That Mr. Hoglund drowned in the river when no one had reportedly perished crossing the ice road was not lost on anyone. Several cars had gone through the ice trying to win the bet, but no one had died.

Ms. Adeline had moved into my recently rehabbed rental shortly after her husband's death. She often relaxed on the porch in nice weather. She would give me her bright smile and tell me to be careful when I went to work. In those early years, though her smile was bright and her voice cheerful, her gentle blue eyes were sad. She had been missing her husband, Clarence.

Over the years, she resumed some of her local activities and kept the flower boxes on the porch railing looking perfect. In a way, we were family. She was a widow, and I was an orphan. We filled a space in the other's life.

Ms. Adeline must have believed the empty space in my life was my stomach. She loved baking cookies, bars, and pies. In the fall, she would bake apples with butter, brown sugar, and raisins in the middle. Her chicken and wild rice soup was always a contender at the Minnesota State Fair. It was a good thing I worked out regularly.

Thanking her for my treat, I headed down to where I slipped my fishing boat during the summer, Bobber's Bait and Marina, located on the south side of the I-94 bridge, on the Minnesota side of the river. My boat was a sixteen-foot red aluminum Lund with a fifty-horse Mercury motor and a trolling motor. The bait shop's owner always told me to upgrade, but I was happy with my little boat. Even though I didn't follow his advice, he liked me and gave me a discount on the slip fee. He called it a law enforcement discount. He called my boat the *Coffee Can* because it was so small. He said it made him think of a Folgers coffee can.

I headed north. I passed under the Stillwater Lift Bridge and continued. I planned to take a close-up water view of Judge Lord's property as I cruised to one of my favorite fishing spots. As I approached the Lord's property, I slowed down to look at the beautiful estate. The view from the river did not capture the elegance or market value of the Lord estate. Judge Lord's forty-two-foot Carver was moored on her aluminum manufactured dock and was christened *Courtship* after two lawyers who had fallen in love.

Although I never boarded *Courtship*, the pristine white yacht was one of the most elegant on the Upper St. Croix River. Most boats the size of *Courtship* travel the St. Croix River south to Prescott, the confluence of the St. Croix and Mississippi Rivers, then continue south to the warm waters of the Gulf of Mexico in the fall.

Lock and dams make traveling to the aqua-blue waters of the Gulf of Mexico for the winter season possible. *Courtship* spends winters on a specially designed bunk, expertly shrink-wrapped at SunShine Marina, in much colder temperatures.

I continued north toward one of my favorite fishing spots, just south of the little riverfront village of Marine on the St. Croix. A small historic town with only 689 residents. Also, the location of the first retail sawmill on the St. Croix River. I sometimes stop for coffee at the Marine Landing. The little café had a pleasant atmosphere, a river view, and great food.

My fishing strategy today was to drift from Marine on St. Croix with the current and occasionally cast near shore, but the wind was picking up, and fishing may not be possible today. An alibi I often used. I was content drifting with the three-mile-per-hour current and enjoying the calm and peaceful sights along the river, where eagles soar and kingfishers were plentiful.

Southbound on the river, I was approaching the historic Arcola Railroad High Bridge, with its beautiful arches. At 184 feet high, the bridge creates a breathtaking moment as boats pass beneath. Many St. Croix River Valley locals, primarily teens and young adults, often visit the bridge. The bridge spans almost one mile over the St. Croix

River, from Arcola Trail to Wisconsin. It is considered the most haunted railroad bridge in the Midwest. The scenic bridge is not only beautiful to the eye, but it is also perilous to traverse if your courage overcomes your fear. To my knowledge, other than railroad construction workers, only a single death had been reported. A twenty-year-old woman had been crossing the bridge at night with a friend and plunged to her death.

Summer weekends always bring out partygoers near the bridge for alcoholic beverages, campfires, and ghost stories.

No activity was happening here today, and heading south for a few minutes will bring me to the Lord estate for another water-access security review. The river has more prescribed No Wake Zones south of Stillwater than north of Stillwater. However, I am always cautious around islands for swimmers. I only saw one Park Service boat pulled up to a large island. The green pontoon with a distinctive white stripe was very recognizable. I throttled down upon reaching the Lord's property again. Vulnerable areas on the riverside of the property may be compromised by boats pulling up to shore or the dock itself. Security cameras in conjunction with floodlights are certainly needed. The bathhouse could use a closer look as well.

As the south side of the Lord's property passed, I relaxed and thought about the evening spent with the judge and the spark of attraction that I had felt. I never entertained anything but professional admiration for the judge in our past, but seeing her in her private environment as a widow made me see her differently.

She looked beautiful, with her shiny dark-auburn hair twisted up in a casual bun at the back of her head, more relaxed than her usual style, and for some reason, the red-painted toes sticking out of her sandals struck me in the gut with feelings I should forget. *You jerk. Suddenly painted nails turn you on? Well, forget it,* I scolded myself. A second dinner with the beautiful judge was probably not in the cards. Or maybe it could be.

Shaking myself out of that particular fantasy, I returned to enjoying my solitude and my memories of fishing with my parents. Memories were my usual companions while fishing on the river.

With a smile, I thought about coworkers who thought I would retire and become a fishing guide on the river. What most didn't realize is that unlike a fishing guide, who has a goal of actually catching fish, more often than not, I never filled my live well with fish or water, for that matter.

I passed the area known as the Boom Site, where the early loggers tended to the log jams that occurred at this location. The logs flowing downstream met up with the log backup floating down the river toward Stillwater. The resulting collision would make a loud echoing boom.

The St. Croix Valley Bluffs were now blocking the winds. I accelerated the *Coffee Can* south toward Paddy's Marina for breakfast.

I entered Paddy's and saw Bubbles seated near the rear of the restaurant with his back against the wall for a full view of the river and the entrance. Uniformed officers preferred this location in any restaurant, or room for that matter. No one could sneak up on you in this position. With a nod and a smile, I joined him.

Bradford "Bubbles" Hagen was a stalwart and seasoned law enforcement officer assigned to the Sheriff's Office's Parks and Water Patrol Division. As the sergeant assigned to water patrol, he was responsible for multiple boats and the deputies that patrolled the various bodies of water within Washington County. Besides the St. Croix and Mississippi Rivers, the county also included 251 pristine lakes under their authority and protection.

Hagen was the summertime envy of both male and female deputies. Patrolling the river allowed him to enjoy the natural beauty of the river and all the slightly clad, darkly tanned beach bodies up and down the river on day patrol. The envy would evaporate quickly when the water patrol division had the duty of recovering a body from the waters of Washington County.

Hagen had a darkly tanned complexion despite the gallons of sunscreen he applied. He was clean-shaven. He kept his dark-brown hair in a military haircut that the wind couldn't affect when his hat was off on the river. His physique concealed his forty-three years of age. At five-foot ten inches, Hagen could take control of every situation faced by law enforcement. Brad could effectively and persuasively administer the use of force continuum in an area where most officers got into trouble. The UFC is a standard that provides law enforcement guidelines on how much force an officer can use against a resisting subject in a given situation. Brad was a patrol officer's first choice of backup.

Water patrol isn't a year-round division in Minnesota. If lucky, water patrol is active for six months of the year. However, recreation in Minnesota is year-round. Before the ice forms on the lakes, boats are winterized and stored away, and the snowmobiles are taken out and prepped for the winter season. The lakes and trails attract snow-mobilers from all over.

Recreation was Brad's department, you could say. The Sheriff's Office has a fleet of snowmobiles that patrol the 140 miles of trails in the county. Brad was every bit as comfortable on a snowmobile as in a boat. As fun as it sounds to patrol on a snowmobile, there are genuine dangers and challenges, as Brad knows all too well.

Brad's handsome face has a conspicuous six-inch zipper scar on the starboard side of his face. One of those dangers put that scar on Brad's face. He was involved in a high-speed chase, attempting to nab a stolen snowmobile in rural northern Washington County.

Brad's high-performance polished-brown snowmobile, equipped with Sheriff's Office graphics and flashing red and blue lights, came to a sudden almost-deadly stop at 2:30 a.m. on January 1. The accident report classified as personal injury, snowmobile versus barbed wire fence.

The sheriff's officers recovered the stolen snowmobile. However, no arrests were made. Brad healed, with the visible scar as a warning of the dangers of high speeds on a snowmobile at night.

Meeting up with coworkers after my retirement was on my agenda. Paddy's on the River, a favorite coffee cop stop, was a prominent place to run into Brad. I could see Brad carrying his water patrol Smith and Wesson .357 stainless steel revolver four-inch with his after-market enhancements.

After losing two of his guns in the river, Brad installed an eighteen-inch nylon cord onto the wooden pistol grip of his .357 with two wood screws and secured the line to his gun belt. Brad had patted the handle of his gun and said, "Problem solved."

It was the only similarity that we shared in law enforcement. Our Smith and Wesson .357 magnum stainless wheel gun. We both like the ease and safety of the revolver, old school.

Brad also carried the title of master scuba diver with countless dives under his weight belt, where he had gotten the nickname Bubbles. Only his close dive friends and coworkers knew that Bubbles received this moniker when a fellow scuba diver realized that Brad could pinch his nose and exhale air around his eyes to equalize ear pressure. One standard ear-pressure equalization method is pinching your nostrils and blowing through your nose. The resulting overpressure can force air through the Eustachian tubes. When Hagen performs this technique, bubbles appear around his eye sockets. Fellow divers report that this is unique.

Statewide, whenever a seasoned water recovery team was required, Brad Hagen was the first officer who got the call for assistance.

"Hey, Bubbles. Good to see you," I greeted him as I approached his table.

With a big smile across his face, he returned the greeting, "Hey, Jack, have a seat and tell me about retirement."

"Couldn't be better," I said as I pulled out a chair and sat down. "More time to fish. I've been thinking of heading south this winter. Maybe Naples, Florida." I don't know why I said that other than to try to make my aimless last few months of retirement look better than it was. "Maybe I'll take up golf."

The waitress set down two cups of black coffee and menus, then left without conversation or a friendly good morning.

"I guess I could learn, but I have no desire to take up golf," I continued with a questioning glance at the waitress's back.

"Jack, you are too young to join the senior crowd looking for the early bird specials in Florida. It would be best if you had more hobbies, like wood carving. I think you would like to carve wooden ducks or loons. It would also give you a cash flow."

The waitress suddenly appeared. "Can I take your orders?"

Brad ordered a short stack with fruit—no butter—and I ordered two eggs—basted—hash browns, bacon, and sourdough toast. She turned and, without any questions, walked away.

"What's her problem?" I asked. "She acts like we just gave her a subpoena to appear in court."

Brad lowered his voice and leaned over the table. "Patrol busted her for DWI last week. She blew a .23, and she puked in the holding cell. It wasn't pretty."

Rolling my eyes, I replied, "Thanks for telling me. Who knows what I will find in my hash browns."

"No, don't worry. Patrol did a really nice report, saying she was cooperative and always helpful to the Sheriff's Department. She will be fine."

"Oh yeah, Brad? What about that cook at the diner? Remember the asshole spitting on our hamburger buns? I still get checked for HIV! I suppose I won't be able to have breakfast here anymore." Just the thought was depressing for me. The food was cheap, and you couldn't beat the view. Plus, I could stop in from my boat.

"Jack, you worry too much. Seriously, Jack, you need to have a hobby. Look at all the retired cops who eat their guns. Why? No hobbies! Christ, look at Farnsworth and that state trooper, Samuelson. They were retired for less than a year, and bang! They're dead. Sometimes I wonder how McCloud is doing. In my eyes, he would be a good candidate. Family hates him, and I have heard he is pretty sick."

I didn't like to hear Brad talking about Scott in that manner. Brad probably wasn't aware of how close I was to Scott. "Never happen, Brad. Scott's doing well and living in a senior home on Lake Superior, watching the ore ships coming into port. He thinks the Aerial Bridge looks like the Stillwater Lift Bridge. He loves the place."

The waitress set our plates of food in front of us. I started to ask for more coffee, but the waitress had already left. I picked up my fork and began to pick through my hash browns. Brad looked down at his pancakes loaded with butter, looking for anything suspicious.

"Didn't I ask for *no* butter?" he asked me. "I suppose we will have to make this place off-limits. Damn it. I like this place." Scraping off any butter that hadn't already melted, he said, "Say, Jack, I heard that you had Reed do a security review at Judge Lord's house. What is that about?"

So much for keeping it quiet, I thought to myself, and reluctant to discuss the judge's business, I replied, "Just routine, Brad. She lives out there alone. She wanted to beef up her security. Just helping out a friend."

"I was grabbing a coffee in the ME's office break room, and they still have the picture of Lord's frozen body in a snowdrift." He made a face and said, "Grotesque, Jack."

I was mad as hell. I could feel my face getting red. I set my fork down, my appetite gone. "How could the Medical Examiner's Office be so unprofessional? It pisses me off! They cannot display a potential crime scene photo like a trophy catch."

"Oh, settle down, Jack. You know how we cope with all the blood and guts we encounter doing our jobs. I probably see more than most. Those bodies that surface after a couple of weeks, man, they are not pretty." He waved the waitress down. "Julie, could we please get some more coffee?" Continuing, he said, "Coping mechanisms, Jack, it is how we keep our sanity."

As the waitress filled our coffee cups, I smiled and gave a pleasant thank you. Brad didn't miss a beat, and he continued to talk.

"Take for example, young Thompson. Remember last month, he was in Hugo, on a suicide. The guy put a twelve gauge in his mouth. Thompson said that one of his eyes was falling out when he arrived. I guess the eye fell out in the body bag. The next day, Thompson came to roll call with those glasses with eyeballs on springs falling out. Or how about the Afton drunk who you were investigating for child abuse? He fell asleep in his sauna and was found three days later. I was at that crime scene. He looked like a piece of seasoned beef jerky. There wasn't even any smell. So the next day, someone brought beef jerky from Norell Farms to roll call for everyone. Jack, it is just how we cope with tragic events."

"Brad, you call it whatever you want. I think this is a little different. I call it unprofessional conduct, and I might stop by the ME's office and talk to the good folks about that photo."

"You like the judge, don't you, Jack?" he asked with a big smile. Then more seriously, "Jack, this is kind of on the QT. The public hasn't been told of this, but if I had a lady friend that lived alone, I would be sure to tell her." Leaning in a little closer to me and dropping his voice down to a quieter level, he continued, "There has been a rash of rapes in the county lately. I don't have all the details, but they have a task force working on it with several other counties involved. Last I heard, they are pretty sure they have a serial rapist on their hands. Let the judge know to be extra careful. Good thing she is getting her security updated. The slime breaks into the victim's residence in the early morning hours."

"Well, Brad, between that, our tasteful conversation, and the suspicious waitress, if I don't get indigestion from this breakfast, it will be a miracle, but thanks for that tip. I will be sure to let the judge know."

I stood up, and the waitress handed me a check and placed Brad's bill on the table.

"Brad, for the record, I do like Judge Lord, and that's where it ends."

As I walked to the cash register, I heard Brad mutter, "One seventy-five, excellent."

As I was paying my check, I saw the waitress had charged us one dollar seventy-five, the tourist price for coffee. The remainder was discounted as a police comp.

While pulling into my slip at Bobber's Bait, I saw a National Park Service (NPS) pontoon on the other side of the marina. Once I secured my fishing boat, I walked to the Park Service boat to look closer.

The customary NPS watercraft, painted green with a diagonal white-stripe graphic, looked abused and seriously needed new paint. The entire service boat needed reconditioning. It was in bad shape. In my mind, I speculated that this pontoon couldn't be part of the NPS fleet. Not in this condition. I reasoned somebody privately owned it. When I saw the Minnesota boat registration numbers displayed, I knew it was a private boat. I speculated that it was probably a fisherman that had bought it at auction. He probably likes the space that the pontoon affords when he is fishing.

Walking to my Jeep from the dock, I thought again of Scott McCloud and the good times we had shared on the river. I decided a trip to Duluth was in order. McCloud's health necessitates frequent visits.

Sooner than later, Jack.

CHAPTER 4

Two and a half hours north of Stillwater, on the Southwestern edge of Lake Superior, was the city of Duluth, which had always been a favorite spot for the retired commander of investigation, Scott McCloud.

McCloud, a seventy-four-year-old with a curmudgeon personality, was drawn to Lake Superior for its excellent fishing and pristine beauty. We shared a passion for fishing.

McCloud began his career standing a beefy six foot five with his fiery red hair proclaiming his Irish heritage. In his Minneapolis police uniform, at the department's most challenging and dangerous precinct, number 6, known as the Model Cities Precinct, McCloud rapidly moved through the ranks. Not because of his education or the customary internal politics, McCloud advanced due to his keen sense of human behavior and interaction with minority communities and peers, but because of his uncanny street-tested common sense. Although a white officer, he was befriended by his minority counterparts and was voted Police Officer of the Year on three occasions.

An article about Scott in the *Minneapolis Star* caught the eye of the Washington County sheriff, who desperately needed to find a commander for the newly created Felony Investigation Division.

The small-town sheriff had been elected to serve and protect the *Corncob Jungle*, had found himself with significant city crimes, inadequate clearance rates, and, most importantly, dissatisfied voters. McCloud was just who he needed.

He approached the inspector with his proposal that very day.

McCloud turned in his Minneapolis police inspector's badge and blue uniform for a gold star badge and brown uniform. Scott

McCloud was in command of a felony investigative unit that became a statewide county model for Sheriffs' Offices.

As commander of investigation, the rank and file welcomed McCloud's streetwise administrative style. He kept up with the times and recognized that a professional force in the next century would require more than good instinct. The cops of tomorrow would need an education in more than the streets. They would need what the books could teach them as well.

We instantly became lifelong friends and shared hours of fishing, inexpensive cigars, good bourbon, and, most importantly, war stories. McCloud was an inspiration to me and guided me during my investigative career.

Although his retirement at sixty-seven was anticipated, his failing health that followed was not. McCloud's love of alcohol and his weakness for tobacco—both unchecked throughout his life—combined with his passion for trans-fatty foods, resulted in a diagnosis of an aggressive case of diabetes. He had been diagnosed shortly after his retirement. The doctors explained a combination of genetics, neglecting his medical care, and lack of physical activity, all combined to the point that this giant man was shrinking with each surgery that removed parts of his legs little by little. Diabetes was a mean SOB.

I found myself driving to Superior Shores Care Center in Duluth at least once or twice a month to share government center news, local crimes, and department gossip with a man who has been like a father to me for more years than I care to think.

I usually planned to keep my visits to about fifty-five minutes; although on many occasions, more time passed with laughter, jokes, and memories only two retired cops could enjoy.

Scott had lost both legs above the knee and much of his graying-red hair, but he still loved stories of the arrest.

Like a father, I shared my deepest thoughts and emotions with Scott, who always afforded me respect, support, and advice.

According to my driving schedule, I should arrive at Superior Shores at noon, just in time to be with Scott during his lunch. There wasn't a day that passed that I didn't think of Scott at lunchtime, wishing I could be there for him.

I arrived in the parking lot of Superior Shores Care Center. The large solid red stone facade, with numerous fireplace chimneys, had a North Shore appearance.

Exiting my Jeep, I paused to look at the breathtaking view of the harbors of Duluth, Minnesota, and Superior, Wisconsin. I recalled fondly the many times I had fished for salmon from Duluth to the Brule River in Wisconsin over the years. The centerpiece of the view is the Canal Park Aerial Lift Bridge, which allows traffic and pedestrians out to Minnesota Point when it is down. The bridge enables boat traffic—both large commercial vessels and tall-masted personal sailboats—into the safety of the harbor when raised. Scott even recalls riding the lift bridge upward in a caged compartment for fifty cents in the 1960s. Scott often called the Duluth Aerial Lift Bridge the sister bridge to the Stillwater Lift Bridge.

Walking to the entrance of the building always made me apprehensive, so my melancholic hesitation was familiar. Seeing Scott in such a frail condition was disheartening. I walked along the portico, which, today, was absent of staff and residents. Often residents who used a wheelchair were positioned along the walk with expressions of delight on their faces, enjoying the scenic view as I passed. Or maybe it was the absence of the fragrance of eau de bleach that permeated the hallways of the care center that they enjoyed so much as they sat outside.

I entered the information requested in the visitors' logbook—date, time, patient's name, and my name. I retrieved a plastic numbered badge and pinned it to my lapel.

Inside the door of Superior Shores Care Center was a typical residence for the elderly, with all the sights, sounds, and fragrances that calls to mind. An occasional outcry for a loved one or the volume of the *Wheel of Fortune* escalated for all to hear was normal. Silence from a resident's room was commonplace as well. Many residents may not have appreciated the grandeur of the care center's exterior, but the greatness, beauty, and character continued inside.

Appreciating the grand view of Lake Superior was only the beginning of this hillside treasure. The beautiful architecture inside and outside was a marvel. Crystal chandeliers, marble-faced fireplaces, a circular dining room with built-in buffets, chair rails, and crown molding. An elegant setting for aging in comfort and dignity, and called to a past era.

Pausing momentarily outside room 102, I observed an older woman, fully dressed and lying on top of her nicely made bed. The purple walls had pictures of what appeared to be family, all black-and-white photos, except for an older man standing next to a black ore ship entering the canal with the aerial bridge lifted against a blue sky background.

A vase of artificial white, pink, and purple flowers stood on the nightstand next to a porcelain white candy dish mounded with Hershey's Kisses for her guests or that grandchild arriving for a visit. Her room was tidy with a lilac fragrance, demonstrating how much care she took to keep it that way.

What puzzled me was the apron she was wearing. She had it pulled over her upper torso and face in a tentlike fashion. The older woman was quietly mumbling and poking her finger upward from under her apron, as if she was typing an escape plan.

"Can I help you?" a young voice questioned. The voice belonged to an attractive staff person whose name tag identified her as Wanda, RN. She appeared to be sizing me up as a potential intruder.

"No, thank you. I'm here to visit Scott Mc Cloud."

"His door is the next one on the right. I will accompany you."

As we walked toward Scott's room, I asked, "Wanda, could you tell me what is wrong with the lady in room 102? She had her apron covering her face."

Wanda interrupted, "Sir, we must maintain a sense of privacy here at Superior Shores. Could I bring you a cup of coffee for your visit?"

"I'd like that. Thank you. Black, please, Wanda."

I arrived at Scott's room, 104. Scott thought it was good karma to have his last residence the same as the badge number that he had retired with, 104. Commander of investigation.

As I knocked on the partially opened door, I called, "Hey, Scott. It's Jack."

"Hey, kiddo, so good to see you!" Scott sat in his wheelchair facing east, looking out the only window in his room. I walked over to Scott's left side and hugged him, a little cumbersome with a tray of food between us.

"How have you been, Jack?" Scott's right hand grasped mine with such strength it was difficult to believe he was in a weakened condition.

"I'm good, Scott, enjoying retirement. Getting out fishing."

"Jack, you need a woman. A good woman who will occupy your time and thoughts. Then you won't need to fish all the time." Avoiding the subject of women altogether, I suggested he finish his lunch.

"This? Lunch? What I wouldn't give for a greasy hamburger with fried onions and bacon bits. You know, like at Geister's Bar?"

Geister's was a longtime local hangout in Stillwater that served up some of the best burgers in the world. They were total artery cloggers, but, man, they tasted good.

The baked chicken on Scott's plate, with the oversteamed broccoli and red potatoes, didn't look too exciting. While shaking my head and somewhat at a loss for words, Wanda walked in with my cup of coffee and handed it to me.

"Have you met my son, Jack? Wanda, are you busy tonight? Jack drove from the Twin Cities to visit his old man and needs a dinner companion. I'll buy!"

Wanda was smiling and doing her best to make a clean exit from the room. As I said, "My dad is always trying to set me up. I'm sorry. Thank you so much for the coffee."

"Maybe next time Jack comes, huh, Wanda?" Scott said with a wink of the eye.

Wanda walked out of the room smiling and partially closed the door behind her.

"Thanks, Scott, for that embarrassing moment. You probably scared the girl. Besides, she must be ten years younger than me."

"Jack, age is a nonfactor nowadays, as long as they are legal age. Hollywood sets the standards, and ten to fifteen years is nothing these days."

"Okay, Scott. Next time I come, I'll give her a smile and let her know I'm interested."

"That's my boy. Now I have two requests—actually three. The first is, could you take this food tray over to the door? Just leave it on the table."

I wheeled the tray table over to the door.

"I need your assurance that you will help me with these requests. My health has turned sharply south, and I need a few things."

I could tell that Scott's demeanor had changed from jovial to somber. As I pondered what Scott was aiming at, he said, "Are you listening, Jack, or thinking about jumping Wanda's bones?"

Grinning, I told him I was listening.

"Okay, Jack, I have a storage unit in Columbia Heights owned by a cop from my Minneapolis years. I need to have my shadow box from Minneapolis. Can you bring the box up next time you visit?"

"Not a problem," I replied.

"I also need the brown Washington County duffel bag." He continued, "It's like a workout bag. It has my dress uniform from the county in it. It looked pretty good on me. It may be a little bit big, but it should fit."

"Where is this storage unit anyway? Did you say Columbia Heights?"

"Yeah." Thinking a minute, he continued, "It's on Central Avenue, just northeast of Minneapolis. I think it's on Forty-Seventh. I will give you my buddy's number, and he can give you directions. Shit, it might be in Hilltop. It's a small shithole trailer park city. You don't even know when you go through it. Here, take my buddy's card and give him a call. He can give you better directions than I can."

Uneasiness and fear filled my mind. I could hardly ask Scott, "What's with the shadow box and uniform?"

He looked at me for a few seconds. It felt like minutes before he responded. "Well, bud, I've been thinking about my life, the good times with Minneapolis, the day I received that gold badge, and want to hang the shadow box next to my closet door. It would look perfect there, and I could see it from my bed."

"So what about your uniform? Are you going to wear it to impress Wanda?" Desperately trying to lighten the mood that had suddenly gotten heavy.

"Hell, Jack, I want to be buried in it. My final duty as a cop. You know it is going to happen sometime, bud." His voice was uncharacteristically gruff.

"Scott, is there something you're not telling me? Because I have a right to know?"

"No. Nothing immediate. Just planning for the future, that's all. The doc is talking about the progression of diabetes. It sounds like they want another slice of my legs. There's not much meat left on my thighs before they reach my balls. I gotta draw the line somewhere." We shared a laugh, which served to lighten the mood.

Hearing that the uniform was for his funeral was a hard punch in the gut. My only thought right then was to humor Scott. So I said, "So what is your third request? A Geister burger?"

Scott made a face and replied, "God, no. I don't think my stomach could handle one anymore after all this white shit they call a meal around here. I want you to have a drink with Wanda. Do you think you can handle that?"

"Yes, Scott. I can have a drink with Wanda."

After a little more talk, I gave Scott a big hug, which he returned. I walked to the door, turned back, and said, "I love you, Scott."

He gave me a wink and a nod, and that was it. I walked down the hall to the entrance to return my name tag and log out. Walking out the door, I saw Wanda had just pushed a single wheelchair resident outdoors for fresh air. I walked over and asked her if she had a minute to talk.

"Sure I do," she replied, indicating we should move slightly away from the resident who uses a wheelchair.

"I'm sorry about that embarrassing conversation with Scott. He isn't my dad, more like a foster dad."

Wanda interrupted, "I have seen your name on Mr. McCloud's contact list. It records you as a relative. What is important to me and all of the staff is that you continue to be Mr. McCloud's regular and trusted visitor. He enjoys your visits and looks forward to them."

"I enjoy them as well...," I replied while I wondered how many more visits I would have with him.

Like she was reading my depressing thoughts, she continued, "Mr. Janssen, I want to impress upon you the importance of maintaining our patients' privacy. Mrs. Reynolds, in 102, had her apron pulled up to cover her face while napping. A little habit of hers. She was poking at what she believes are flies but were floaters in her eyes. They are age-related and don't hurt, but she insists they are flies. Now that is just between the two of us."

As she finished, she reached out and patted my arm. I knew she was trying to take my mind off Scott, and I appreciated her effort. She was a lovely lady.

"Sorry for being so nosy. I'll try to resist it in the future. It is an occupational hazard, I'm afraid. Cops are nosy," I said a little sheepishly.

She smiled at me. She had a beautiful smile. Then cautioned me to drive safely back to the cities. She turned and started walking back toward the door. She looked pretty good from the back, too, I thought. Then suddenly, she turned around and caught me watching her. She smiled again, and I waved with a big smile.

Driving home from Duluth would be even more depressing than my travel to Superior Shores Care Center. I needed some time to decompress after I visited Scott. Suddenly the knowledge that I was losing him had to be faced. It would be the second time that I lost a father. Looking back, I had spent more time and had a stronger bond with Scott than my dad.

I decided to head down to Canal Park. I walked while kicking a stray rock off the boardwalk and watching the gulls fight over the popcorn kernels on the ground. Unlike the pleasure craft passing under the Stillwater Lift bridge, the Duluth Aerial Lift Bridge has Great Lake ships, lakers, and salties passing under its raised bridge.

I recognized *Walter J. McCarthy Jr.*, a three-hundred-foot laker pulling through the canal and under the bridge. The loud foghorn from the bridge tender barely made a dent in my mind as the reality of my impending loss settled in.

I wanted to head over to Grandpa's Saloon, a watering hole beside the bridge, and have a few stiff drinks. I knew I would have coffee, but I would have preferred the drink. I purchased a coffee from the to-go cart outside Grandpa's and sat on the retaining wall surrounding the flagpole outside the Maritime Museum.

I watched the children feeding the sometimes too-aggressive gulls. They hovered over the children in a flock, waiting to dive when they dropped their bags and ran. It usually made me laugh. Not today. The sky was a beautiful blue. Some gulls glided above on the brisk breeze. It didn't match my mood. With their colorful sails, the Windsurfers were almost an insult in my current state.

Rolling waves, big enough to take down ships, would have been more appropriate, but they came in November. Maritime records reveal 350 ships have fallen prey to the waters of Lake Superior, the most famous being the *Edmond Fitzgerald.*

Scott loved to watch the lake, especially those gales of November. The winds that all Duluth residents talk about. Would he see them this year?

My cell phone rang, and for a few minutes, I forgot about Scott. I answered and was talking with CSO Anne Reed about my request for a security survey of Judge Lord's residence. Reed was a striking thin black five-foot-nine-inch woman who usually wore civilian clothes rather than a uniform.

Reed possessed a bachelor of science degree in criminology and an abundance of common sense. A powerful crime-fighting arsenal. Reed had completed her internship at the Sheriff's Office and was immediately appointed to a community service officer position until a vacancy occurred in the patrol division. Reed was a trusted friend who always did the most comprehensive security survey at the Sheriff's Office.

"Hey, Jack, I received your security survey request, and I'm more than halfway finished. I will meet with Judge Lord next week and provide her with my findings."

"Do you think she is sincere about complying with your recommendations?" I asked.

"Jack, she is terrified. Something is going on there. Jack, the water access to the property is troubling. I have some concerns. However, it's been years since any significant crime was reported up there, especially compared to the lower St. Croix area. Afton and

Lakeland have high numbers of small outboard motor thefts, break-ing into boathouses, and thefts off boats. Stealing liquor, cigarettes, and breaking into the larger boats, that sort of thing, but the upper St. Croix to Marine on St. Croix is pretty low in criminal activity."

"Thanks, Anne. We can connect after you meet with Judge Lord. I'll talk to you then. See you soon, bye."

I stopped for another coffee at the to-go cart for my return trip home. I wouldn't make it home till after dark. As I walked to my car, I reviewed my conversation with Anne. The open gates, the dark areas of the property, the water access, and so on. I wondered what else Anne would find. I wanted the judge to feel safe in her home. Everyone should have that comfort, but more importantly, I wanted her to *be* safe at home.

CHAPTER 5

Heading home down Interstate 35, I kept thinking about Scott's mental state. I believe *depression* is too strong a word for what I saw in Scott. It almost seemed like his personality was fading before my eyes. He was quieter and slower to smile. His once-startling bright-green eyes seem to have dulled. He was struggling with this phase of his life, the last one.

I wanted to help relieve some of his fears, but what could I say? I certainly had no experience in this area. There are no rules. We each find our way. I was hoping my visits helped keep his spirits up. I guess the duffel bag, with his uniform and his shadow box, was, maybe, part of Scott's process. He wanted to look at the shadow box and relive the actions that were the reason for all his awards I had seen in the shadow box. The next time I visited, I wanted Scott to share those memories.

Law enforcement has had a long tradition, more like a culture of solidarity, that honors the proud employment of all city, county, and state officers with a shadow box for their years of service. It is not uncommon for officers to work at two or even three different departments throughout their careers.

Each department would have its shadow box to display the officer's career in that department. Families take pride in memories of the service they have all shared. Police work is a family culture, and all members share the commitment. All the items displayed are symbols of pride for the whole family to enjoy.

Scott had two agency boxes to display: one from Minneapolis Police and one from Washington County Sheriff's Office. Blue and brown, respectively. The uniforms for Minnesota State Patrol are maroon, and the Department of Natural Resources is green. These are state of Minnesota standards, not national.

Making a deliberate left turn out of my depressing thoughts, I started to think about Judge Lord. Just south of Forest Lake, my phone rang. *Wow*, I thought as I looked at the display on my phone. My mind must have sent out signals to her. The call was from Judge Lord.

She started talking before I even said hello. It sounded as if she was crying.

"Judge, are you okay?" I asked.

"I'm fine. Jack, a sheriff's deputy just left. The garage had an alarm, but they didn't find anything." Her voice sounded shaken and afraid even though she claimed to be okay.

"Would you like me to stop by?" I asked. "I'm in Forest Lake on my way back from Duluth. It wouldn't be a problem."

"Yes, yes, yes, Jack. Please come." She sounded relieved at the idea.

"I'll be there in thirty minutes," I replied and disconnected.

Automatically shifting into urgency response mode, I changed my route—Highway 97 to Highway 95 south, the quickest way to the judge's home. I turned off 95 onto the north entrance of Arcola Trail and began traveling southbound.

When I reached the Arcola Railroad High Bridge, I noticed two cars parked on the dirt road leading down to the bridge. I paused long enough to jot down the license plate of the first vehicle, a newer white VW Jetta with a Wisconsin dealer plate, WI7900SF. The second vehicle's plate was obstructed but appeared to be an older red Ford pickup, possibly an F150. Probably lovers or kids daring each other to walk the bridge, but you never know, I thought.

Judge Lord's estate was only a short distance from the bridge. I remembered the judge describing the many evenings during the summer; she could hear the people partying around the bridge. She even has partial views of the bridge during the day from her gazebo. A little further down the road, I turned left into the estate. The gate was standing open, maybe left open by the deputies. I pushed the call button and announced my arrival.

The judge indicated that she would open the garage door for me, which I presumed would be the first door, the same one I had used the last time I was here. I hadn't even gotten the car door shut when Judge Lord came flying out the door and threw her arms around me and began crying.

"I am so scared and so sorry to have called you," she said in a rush.

The hug was one of desperation, and we both sensed it. Would Vivian do that to anyone? I put my arms around her to comfort her and let her cry for several minutes.

Lifting her head from my chest, she said, "Please come in." She pulled away from me, allowing me to look at her for the first time. She looked pale and frail. Very uncharacteristic for the Honorable Judge Vivian Lord that I had known.

Entering the kitchen area, I began, "Judge Lord—"

"Oh, for god's sake," she interrupted with her more authoritative voice, "will you please stop calling me Judge? I think we have gone beyond that, haven't we? My name is Vivian."

I paused for a moment, then said with a bit of a grin, "Well, okay then, Vivian, what happened this evening?"

Vivian took a moment to compose herself and to get the details straight in her mind.

"I was preparing to sit down and have a bite to eat. Madel had prepared a lovely salad dinner when I thought I heard something from the direction of the river path and looked out the window. I saw someone with a flickering light, like a glow, like the tip of a cigarette, walking toward the cart path. I immediately went to the living room window to check if the gate was open, and it was, but there was no vehicle."

I interrupted, asking, "Are you leaving the gate open all the time?"

"There is a problem when it closes, Jack. I have to do it manually with the remote. I suppose that Madel didn't close it when she left."

"When did you call the Sheriff's Office?"

"I was getting to that," she replied with a bite. "As I was looking out the front window and before I had a chance to make the call, the alarm company called. They explained that an alarm had been tripped in the garage area and asked if I needed an alarm tech or the Sheriff's Office. I told them the Sheriff's Office. Immediately!"

"Try to relax a little. You did what you should have done, and now I am here. You're not alone anymore."

"Oh, Jack, I haven't even offered you a beverage or anything. You must be tired after your drive from Duluth. Would you like coffee or something stronger?"

"Something stronger would hit the spot. I think you could use something too," I answered. "How about I bartend?"

Vivian replied, "The job is yours." Waving her arm in the direction of the bar cabinet. "I want a bourbon, Bullet Bourbon, over ice."

The grand size and design of the mahogany-looking cabinet were impressive. It cleverly concealed everything a bar needed—a wine cooler with divided sections for white and red wine, a beer cooler, a small Sub-Zero freezer for ice, and a complete selection of excellent liquor for cocktails.

My liquor stock at home consisted of a twelve-pack of beer—whatever was on sale—and a bottle of Bullet in the cabinet beside the coffee. Another connection between us. We liked the same bourbon. Reaching overhead, I took down two glasses, opened the little Sub-Zero freezer, dropped a couple of cubes in each glass, and poured a generous amount of bourbon. Carrying them over to the table, I placed one in front of Vivian before sitting down.

We sat at the small table between the kitchen and the great room where we had eaten together the last time I was here. Somehow a toast together didn't seem entirely appropriate on this occasion. I waited for her before I took a sip.

Vivian lifted her glass toward me and said, "Thank you."

After we both took a bracing swallow, Vivian began, "I have two more concerns, more like requests."

"Judge—" She glared at me. I continued, "Vivian, you know I will do anything I can for you."

She gave me a shaky smile, her eyes filled with tears. Getting her composure back, she reached for my hand. I looked down at our hands but didn't pull away, then I looked back up, and she began. "Number one, my office has continued receiving threats through the courthouse mail. Probably not serious, but it is of concern."

I asked if the Sheriff's Office had been made aware of the letters, and she said, "No, I have not filed a formal complaint with the Sheriff's Office, and it has caused some animosity between my assistant, Gail, and myself. So, Jack, I hope you can resolve this quickly without involving the Sheriff's Office and courthouse chatter. I am beginning to question some of my decisions and the thought process behind them. I don't want anyone else to criticize them. My assistant, Gail, has discussed her concerns with me. A state of indecision is not a characteristic that elicits respect. I think between the letters, someone in my house looking through my things inside my closet and drawers are—"

"Wait," I said, interrupting her. "When you told me you thought someone had been in the house, you didn't mention the details. I thought going through your mail or something. Rummaging through your personal effects raises this to a more disturbing level. I think it's time you tell me the whole story. Don't leave anything out this time."

"That's just it. I don't know what the whole damn story is! I didn't overthink the letters at work. They were easy to blow off, even though Gail thought I should report them. It feels more threatening now since someone has been in the house when no one should have been there. Madel only works for me four days a week, and Buster generally has no reason to go in the house and always calls me before he goes inside. I thought maybe I had moved things, put a skirt in with the shirts, or something like that."

I just looked at her. No, I didn't understand that. Her closet was much more organized than mine. So without replying to that, I asked her to continue.

"There isn't much else to tell. It has just started to occupy all my waking thoughts, keeps me up at night, and affects my work. Honestly I am not sleeping well and am exhausted when I go to work. I have never felt uncomfortable here alone after Charles died. Now I almost hate to come home. I hate that."

"Vivian, have you had any other alarm trips?"

"Well, yes, but that was before I felt someone was in the house. In the last month, I've had multiple trips. I figured it was wind or an electrical problem. I had the alarm service out several times to check it out. It hadn't happened in a while till tonight."

I sat still for a few minutes, thinking, unconsciously making little circles on the back of her hand that we were still holding. She was quiet, waiting for me to talk. I looked down, realized what I was doing, and stopped, but she didn't release her hand. It seemed like the contact was comforting to her. Finally I looked up and said, "What I would like to do is meet with the alarm company tech here at your home to understand your system better."

"That's no problem, Jack. I can call them in the morning to let them know you will be calling."

"You had another thing on the list, Vivian. What else can I do for you?"

She squeezed my hand tighter and paused. For a minute, I thought she had changed her mind about asking anything else. But bracing herself visibly, she said, "Yes, I did. If it's not too much to ask—" And she paused again. She started again, "If it's not too much to ask, could you please spend the night here with me?"

I must have looked shocked. Judge Lord's cheeks turned pink, and she hastily said, "I have a guest suite downstairs for you if it wouldn't be too inconvenient. I know I won't sleep very well if I'm alone in the house tonight."

Smiling at the additional explanation, I said, "That is no trouble. We can talk more in the morning about the alarm company. Maybe you can relax and get some sleep tonight."

Vivian rose, walked around the table to give me a heartfelt hug, and said, "By the way, my niece Mary will be here in the morning. You will get a chance to meet her. I bet you are hungry. Let's see what Madel has in the fridge for me. As I mentioned, I planned to have a salad, but she usually has several choices for me."

There were several salad choices, so we each had one. Vivian had the salad with chicken mixed in. I chose the one with delicious steak slices and a Caesar dressing. The baguette that Vivian pulled out of nowhere was also fresh and delicious. I could use a Madel of my own.

We sat at the table and talked about lighter things. I told Vivian I had gone by her house on the river the other day. Vivian briefly discussed the current case she was hearing. We talked of mutual acquaintances, mainly from the courthouse, since we didn't travel in the same circles.

Before long, it was time for Vivian to show me the guest suite. It was located just down the hall from the kitchen and down a few steps. Vivian opened the door and made a gesture indicating I should go down the stairs first, so I brushed past her, walked down the stairs and into the room, then turned to look at her. She had followed me down the stairs. Vivian was standing just outside the threshold of the room.

"You will find juice in the fridge upstairs, and the coffee maker is programmed to be ready by six thirty." She made a little face. "Not all of us are retired. Madel will be here by eight or so, and Mary will come around eleven. Maybe I will see you before I leave, but if you sleep later, don't worry. I will leave a note that you are here. No one will bother you."

"Vivian, I don't sleep much later than you do. I will see you in the morning."

"Jack, thank you so much for everything. Good night."

I retraced the few steps I had taken into the room. I was leaning against the doorjamb, very close to Vivian. I gently kissed her on the forehead. I'm not sure what compelled me to do it, but what was done was now out of my control. "No worries tonight," I said quietly. "We will talk in the morning." Giving me one last smile, she walked back up the stairs and closed the door.

The guest suite was more like a five-star hotel room than I expected. Looking at the wall across from the door where I stood, I discovered that the basement was a walkout with a sliding door opening to a lower patio. I had carried my second glass of bourbon downstairs with me, and walking toward the door, I momentarily thought of Scott. He would have gotten a kick out of this.

That reminded me that I needed to call Erin McCloud, Scott's oldest granddaughter, in the next couple of days. Although I had never met Erin, I knew she was a Minneapolis police officer and the executor of Scott's last will.

A second item on my list was the alarm company. I need to clean up their quality control of Vivian's alarm system, which, from my perspective, was unsatisfactory.

I should have been getting ready for bed, but I was too restless to do that, so I wandered around the room, checking out the amenities. I discovered a minibar with a bottle of Bullet. So splashing a little more bourbon in my glass, I walked back toward the sliding glass door. The riverside door opened toward the backyard and the St. Croix River.

I decided not to try to open the door. It was probably alarmed, and I thought Vivian had had enough excitement for one night. From the door, I could see the cart pathway as well as the silhouette of *Courtship*.

I was confident that I would be able to clean up the security for Vivian's protection and peace of mind. I walked back to the recliner and settled in. But my mind was far from settled. It was going a mile a minute. The letters that were doing a pretty good job of scaring Vivian and beginning to impact her work were disturbing, but the thought that someone had access to her home was now qualified as a problem. Start with what you know, Jack. So wide awake and staring at the ceiling, I began to put the puzzle together.

The sun was rising as I opened my eyes. I hadn't slept long but was supercharged to begin my day. I could finally see a picture starting to merge. Rising from the recliner I had slept in all night, I was surprised I had no aches or pains to show for it. I could hear some activity upstairs, so I jumped into the shower.

I found a new toothbrush and travel toothpaste in the vanity, along with a dispenser of small paper cups. Instantly I had a memory flashback that made me smile. My mother handed me a small cup of water from a similar dispenser. You don't see them very often anymore.

With a shrug, I put yesterday's clothes back on. It wasn't as if I hadn't ever done it before, and I went up the stairs, closing the door loudly so I wouldn't surprise Vivian or Madel with my appearance.

It was Madel Martinez in the kitchen. She was the housekeeper and nanny for Vivian's niece.

"Good morning, Detective Jack. You will have coffee, yes?"

"Yes, ma'am, black, please. Thank you."

I have heard good things about Madel but hadn't met her until this morning. Madel is in her early sixties, I guessed. She had light-brown skin and a friendly smile. She had a solid Hispanic accent and wore a white top and turquoise scrub pants.

As I looked out the door toward the backyard, Madel approached me and handed me a cup of black coffee.

"Did Judge Lord leave for the courthouse?"

"Yes, Detective, she left fifteen minutes ago. The judge had a couple of stops to make before court."

Damn, I had wanted to run my plans by her before she left. I will talk with her about my progress later in the day.

While I drank my coffee, I got the number for the security company out. Vivian had told them to expect a call from me because I had no trouble making an appointment to meet a technician here. I learned a technician in the area could meet with me before his next assignment. So helping myself with another cup of coffee, I moved back to the windows to enjoy the view.

Madel busied herself in other parts of the house. A short while later, a tone sounded, indicating that someone was at the gate entrance. I responded. It was the technician from the security company. I buzzed him in and called down the hall to tell Madel that the technician was here, and I would meet him outside, then went out the door to the garage.

The technician and I walked the entire property and discussed updates for the existing system, additions Anne had suggested, and others I thought were worthwhile. I asked him to send Vivian a copy of the plans and pricing as soon as possible.

I thanked the tech for such a quick response, and he said that Arcola Trail had kept him busy. He was heading to North Arcola Trail to increase the security of a residence because of a recent attempted break-in. As the alarm tech drove away, I ensured the gate had closed after him.

I let myself back into the house by way of the garage. Madel was again in the kitchen, hard at work making something wonderful, I assumed, and keeping an eye on Mary, sitting at the table outside the kitchen window on the patio. Keeping my distance from the window so I wouldn't startle the little girl, I watched her and her cat with something approaching fascination.

I had never seen a cat so attentive to a human before. The cats I had seen were aloof, too good to associate much with their owners except for mealtime. This cat couldn't seem to get close enough to the little girl.

Mary had climbed up on one of the cushioned deck chairs surrounding the table to color. The cat jumped up right beside her and settled in. Mary absently patted the cat's head and began to color. Amazing.

Feeling awkward just standing there, drinking my coffee while Madel made herself busy in the kitchen, I decided to begin a conversation. I asked what Mary's cat's name was.

Madel said, "Ms. Vivian's cat's name is Tabby. Ms. Vivian buy Tabby for Mary, but Tabby lives here."

Hell, I hadn't even known a cat was in the house! Amazing.

Madel interrupted my thoughts by saying, "Detective Jack, I'm bringing out a snack for Mary. Would you like to meet my *niña?*"

"Yes," I replied, "very much. And also the cat named Tabby."

"Detective Jack, my niña, she no talk, but she has other ways to tell you what she is thinking." Before I could ask any questions, she smiled at me and said, "You will see."

I reached around Madel at the door and opened it for her since she was carrying a tray with muffins, glasses for juice, and a bowl of fruit. Next to this delicious fare was a small bowl of cream for the cat.

Setting the tray down beside Mary, Madel put her hand on Mary's shoulder and said, "Mary, this is Detective Jack. He is friends with your auntie. Can you say hello?"

Mary stared at me with her big blue eyes, not moving a muscle. I said, "Hello, Mary, you have a beautiful cat." Mary made no sounds or movements.

Madel spoke into the silence, saying, "Mary, I have snack for you and Tabby's bowl of cream."

At the word *cream*, Tabby roused herself from beside Mary, jumped up on the table, and began to lap up her cream. I laughed at the cat, but Mary continued staring at me without blinking.

Madel offered me a muffin that I accepted. Mary continued to stare at me. It was a little unsettling. I wasn't sure she had blinked. I thought, *Now is a good time to say my goodbyes and start my day.* I thanked Madel, waved goodbye to Mary, and headed to my Jeep.

CHAPTER 6

I had spent the night in the recliner going over all of the cases that Vivian had presided over. The list was long, but I was confident that I had remembered every one of them. It was early morning when I hit on the name of a rapist I had arrested several years ago.

I didn't usually investigate crimes against adults by that time; my workload was almost exclusively child abuse, but because of the sexual nature of the crimes, the sheriff had felt that I would be better suited to taking statements from the traumatized victims.

Sandy Jo Pittman was his name. He was scum and the bottom of the barrel of humanity. He just rang the bell for me. His MO was precisely like the rapist currently under investigation by the task force. When I combined his modus operandi with the harassing letters that Vivian had been receiving made me consider that she was on this new rapist's list, she was not in the age demographic, but everything else fits.

Everything except Sandy Jo Pittman was in jail. Vivian had sentenced him to a long term in Stillwater Prison and had many years of his sentence left. Was it possible that Pittman had an accomplice with whom he had shared his brand of terror? An apprentice he instructed while in prison, who had completed his sentence and is now out and applying the instructions Pittman had given him?

In my years of investigation, I learned there is no such thing as a coincidence. I knew I was right. Pittman was a connection to the unusual activity going on here—at Vivian's as well as the current serial rape case.

Maybe he had family that had moved to the area since his incarceration so they could visit often. Many families have made such a move. Some of those families were upright, respectable members of their new community, but some were more similar to the inmates they visited and just added to the job of the local police.

Most importantly, the prisoners newly released from the correctional facilities often remain in the area with family. In my particular area of investigation, I have found that their newfound freedom, more often than not, added to my caseload. I don't think the residents of Stillwater, Bayport, and Oak Park Heights think about that. These situations may be one of those times when having a prison in your community makes the residents more vulnerable than most.

Pulling out of Vivian's driveway on my way to a face-to-face conversation with Sandy Jo Pittman, I thought there couldn't be two places more different than the one I was leaving and the one I was going to. The aging Stillwater Prison, built in 1914, bore no resemblance to this affluent rural neighborhood on Arcola Trail.

The entrance to the historic building was an attractive two-story white-stone facade with two large white Roman columns that looked rather impressive and even welcoming. It just shows how outside looks can be deceiving. You can't see most areas of the prison building from the main entrance.

The only part of prison activity visible is the outside recreation yard. Fencing with razor wire along the top and armed guard towers positioned strategically around the perimeter keep the inmates in the yard from having any thoughts of escape. At some point, all 1,622 inmates have time in the yard.

In its earlier years, inmates could work on a farm adjacent to the prison. There, vegetables were grown and used in the prison kitchens. A dairy farm was also in operation. To the casual observer, it had looked like a hobby farm. When citizens were concerned about the safety of the residents of the small town of Bayport, some areas outside the prison walls were eventually closed down. The state now uses that property for government storage and auctions several times a year.

St. Michael's Cemetery is located just outside the grounds of the prison. I thought a cemetery was a good use of property next to a prison as I drove down Highway 95. The cemetery residents aren't likely to complain about their neighbors. Or so you might think.

Grieving loved ones visiting the cemetery became aware of the Par-Three golf course adjoining the two properties. Golf balls would fall at the visitor's feet while at the cemetery visiting the grave of a loved one. The golf course was open to workers at the prison and minimum-security inmates. After slicing a ball and sending it over the fence, golfers would call for their balls to be thrown back to them, further disturbing the cemetery visitors. Not surprisingly, this little enterprise was closed as well.

Stillwater Prison was the only state prison when I started working at the Sheriff's Office, but by 1982, Minnesota had built another prison in nearby Oak Park Heights.

The supermax facility serves as a model nationally for maximum-security prisons. To date, there has never been an escape from this facility. Unlike the imposing structure of the older prison, the supermax facility is barely noticeable to its neighbors and people who pass by the facility. The parking lot and administrative offices are the only visible parts of the facility as you drive by. It looks like a very well-maintained business.

The property is on 165 acres, between suburban and rural settings, protected by an early-warning fence alarm system and contingency plans not known to the public. It even has a plan for an attempted escape involving a helicopter. It has never been tried here but has happened worldwide in several countries.

At supermax, there is nothing left to chance. They have a thoroughly modern approach to incarceration and rehabilitation. The inmates are cared for in a modern medical facility with no need to go outside for treatment, as well as a mental health facility, educational programs, and the like.

I wouldn't say I liked going into either of them. Over the years, I have been in both, and walking through that first visitor threshold and hearing the door close and lock behind me always gives me an instant feeling of claustrophobia. Not having the trigger of my weapon on my belt triggered my anxiety—contact with inmates, who would give them great pleasure in taking me out. A cop killer tends to achieve dominance over other inmates in a prison yard. I have never gotten used to it.

Pulling into the parking lot for the Stillwater Prison, I sat for a moment, considering what my second step would be if I didn't make it through with my retired ID. I was determined to talk to Pittman but wasn't sure if it would go smoothly. A former Sheriff's Office ID probably won't carry much weight, but I was hoping it would get me through the ID inspection.

Sandy Jo Pittman has been a resident of Stillwater Prison for two years and three months for predatory sexual assaults of women between the ages of sixteen to twenty-four. Prison authorities classified Pittman as a serial rapist.

Pittman is forty-three years of age, white, five-foot ten inches in height, with a medium build. His face is acne-scarred. He has brown hair and blue eyes. He was born to a mother who had given birth at the Minnesota Women's Correctional Facility in Shakopee, Minnesota. His mother, Shirley, named her baby after her cellmate, Sandy. The women were both convicted of welfare fraud and drug trafficking. The women bonded in prison and moved in together when they were released.

Law enforcement officials became familiar with Pittman at an early age when he began window peeping and stealing woman's undergarments at fifteen. Pittman had been a thorn in the side of burglary detectives and sexual assault investigators when he lived with his two moms in Wrightstown, a small river town outside Green Bay, Wisconsin.

The Fox River flows through this predominately agricultural community and is known for supporting the Green Bay Packers football team.

Pittman had been in and out of prisons, jails, and halfway houses for most of his adult life but had squeezed in enough time to get a bachelor's degree in psychology from the University of Minnesota. While in prison, he studied law and became very knowledgeable about the courts, probation agencies, and police.

Like many other inmates, Pittman used his acquired knowledge of the court system to file civil lawsuits in Washington County. No attorneys are necessary for civil court. Some inmates have filed as many as twenty-five civil suits while incarcerated. The lawsuits filed were mostly dismissed by the magistrate for being frivolous, but for the inmate, it was still a win. Having to appear in court allowed them to get out of the prison walls for a while, albeit under guard, and they were usually able to pick up lunch before heading back to the prison.

The cost of this activity eventually prompted the prison to create a video courtroom for this purpose. The new technology also was used for arraignments of county jail inmates. The new technology improved the safety of the magistrate and the people in the courtroom. It also prevented the occasional inmate from deciding to make a speedy exit from the courthouse while in custody.

Pittman's timing always seemed to work in his favor. Wisconsin was late in registering sex offenders and collecting a DNA sample to be kept on file for registration. Pittman completed his sentence in Wisconsin at Waupun Prison in 1996. One year before, the Wisconsin legislature had enacted the DNA Convicted Sex Offender law. No one was tracking Pittman when he walked out of Waupun.

An unsupported résumé, including an official certified copy of Pittman's bachelor's degree in psychology, was all he needed to land a prestigious job at a medical supply company in St. Paul. A career path that brought Pittman inside homes and apartments to evaluate prospective targets for his vicious attacks.

Pittman had left a string of shattered lives from Woodbury, Oakdale, to Forest Lake and Somerset, Wisconsin, until his arrest in Wisconsin. Law enforcement agencies, county attorneys, and courts have labeled these fractured lives as victims for efficiency and documenting purposes. Still, each number represents real human life—convictions in Washington County total nine.

Pittman had a very distinctive modus operandi for committing his offenses. He would choose his victims with well-established criteria. His first step was to conduct window peeping in a lower-level apartment building. Upon identifying a potential candidate for his attention, he would meticulously and patiently plan his attack. He would find a protected staging area, crouch nearby out of sight, and watch his prey like a spider on a screen.

He would first determine if anything would indicate a male presence in the apartment—a shirt over the back of a chair, shoes tossed in the corner, wallet on the nightstand. If any of these items were present, he would scrub the plan and move on to his next candidate.

He would surveil his potential victim for several nights before settling on one and long before the night of his visit. Weekday versus weekend was considered and logged, as well as the information regarding the surrounding houses and escape pathways.

Pittman never found a locked window to be an obstacle. If Pittman determined that an entryway had lights and might expose him, he would do something straightforward, like unscrewing the lightbulb.

Pittman would come equipped with what he fondly called his bag of tricks, containing proper tools, duct tape, and a pair of handcuffs. The police, on the other hand, called those items burglary tools. According to his study of human behavior, he would wait until 3:30 a.m., when he believed his victims were in their deepest sleep. Then with a practiced finesse, Pittman would enter through a window or door with gloved hands, holding a flashlight and wearing a ski mask over his face.

Sound asleep, lightly clothed, and completely vulnerable, Pittman would awaken his victims with a hand pressed over her mouth. The terror in her eyes would send the blood circulating, pulsing, and throbbing into his now fully erect penis. The power that was his, the complete control he now held over another person, made him feel superhuman.

Law enforcement officials, off the record, feared that if the rapist wasn't apprehended soon, his need for additional satisfaction would escalate to murder, the ultimate act of control. The local police were under intense pressure from the community and their fears, to finding him and removing him from society.

Courtroom testimony from his Wisconsin convictions indicated that Pittman found pleasure in his victim's struggles and was nearly orgasmic when she screamed against the duct tape across her mouth. His victim's eyes displayed her terror. He would bind her, then position his flashlight to illuminate her face as he raped her. Eventually he watched her eyes go blank as she sank into herself, trying to avoid the horror of what was happening to her.

In a Washington County case assigned to me, there had been a critical twist in the modus operandi. Pittman entered a lower-level apartment by a sliding glass door, child's play for Pittman.

When Pittman entered the bedroom, he was confronted with a challenge: two women, not one, in the bed. The two women almost overpowered Pittman, tearing off his mask, causing facial injuries for Pittman, and a broken arm for one of the victims. Pittman had appreciated that; besides handcuffs, he carried heavy-duty plastic zip ties in his bag of tricks.

The arrest of Pittman in Somerset, Wisconsin, with a similar MO, was made while the Washington County investigation was barely underway. Somerset was located across the river from Stillwater, eight miles away.

I quickly went to Somerset to review the evidence and consult with St. Croix County, Wisconsin, authorities. The modus operandi in our cases was similar to the suspect in Somerset, but we could not physically place Pittman at the crime scene in Washington County. A crucial element of the crime.

Law enforcement utilizes photo lineups in criminal investigations. However, the victims never saw Pittman's face due to the darkness, the mask, and the light he shined in their eyes, blinding them.

He was a chatty attacker; the last two victims thought they could recognize his voice. I arranged to have five officers and Pittman record several of the statements Pittman had made to the victims. Both victims, independently, were able to pick out Pittman's voice from the audio lineup.

He was subsequently convicted on the Washington County charges. According to the County Attorney's Office, this was the first occasion of a voice identification in Washington County.

As I walked into Stillwater Prison, I went through all the facts of Pittman's case, preparing myself for the unpleasant task of coming face-to-face with Pittman again. Something I had fervently hoped I would never again have to do.

Entering the prison visitors' area, a correctional officer I remembered but couldn't recall his name greeted me. I displayed my retired WCSO identification. Since he knew me, he barely glanced at the ID.

I requested a visit with Sandy Pittman in the conference room. The officer made a phone call and instructed me to leave my firearm and any metal in a locker before I passed through the metal detector. It was the first time I had used my retired ID, and I was pleasantly surprised by the results.

I walked to the conference room that appeared like a library, except for the heavily reinforced metal door.

This interview was the first since Pittman's conviction and my first time at the Stillwater Prison since retirement. I firmly believed that Pittman, or Pitts, his nickname, would cooperate and not be hostile toward me. Ironically the defendants have always treated me respectfully in the bulk of my caseload, and I anticipated Pitts would be the same.

I was pulled out of my musings when I heard the large metal door open, and Pittman was escorted to my table with a giant grin wrapped across his face. Handcuffed in front and wearing his standard khaki uniform, he took his seat across the table from me. The correctional officer handcuffed Pittman to the metal table, which is standard procedure.

The officer said, "This is Sandy Jo Pittman, sir!"

I thanked the officer while watching Pittman's smile evaporate from his face and be replaced with a harsh and rigid stare.

"Hello, Pitts. How the hell are you?"

"I'm doing great, Detective Janssen. Thanks for asking. To what do I owe this visit from you? I haven't done anything against the law for a couple of years now."

I explained to Pittman that Judge Lord had been receiving threatening letters at the courthouse and wanted to know if he knew who was sending them.

"Now, Detective, you know all my correspondence is screened before it's mailed, and I am under constant watch day and night. The state monitors my phone calls. You are looking at the wrong person," he said smugly, leaning as far back in his chair as his handcuffed hands would allow.

"I appreciate that you didn't send the letters yourself, Pitts," I replied patiently. "I just thought you had an idea who might be sending them. I know that you have regular visitors. Anybody you can think of who might be sending them?"

Pittman was trying to display casual indifference to me, but his reclined position with his arms extended in front of him looked pretty ridiculous. He sat there and just looked at me, finally saying in a rather petulant voice, "Detective, I am disappointed that you would think I would have someone correspond with the judge that sentenced me. My attorney would take care of any letters I request and certainly wouldn't be threatening. Detective, you are wasting my time today. I think we're finished here."

I sat for a minute, just staring at him, seeing a trace of the smugness he was trying so hard to conceal. Did I imagine it because I wanted my instincts to be correct? We continued with our staring contest, neither wanting to be the first to break eye contact.

I just wanted a little crack so I could know for sure he was the seed for all of this. For him, it was just a game. It had always been a game for him. Pittman is a sick SOB and should never have his freedom again.

I raised my arm, indicating that the guard could come over and take him back to his cell.

"Okay, Pitts. Thanks for your help. I'll let you get back to your busy day."

Getting out of the prison took longer than it did to drive the short distance to my home. Pretty much a waste of time, I thought as I got out of my car. At least I can let Vivian know about my conversation with Pitts and what I thought.

Switching gears, I began to think of much more pleasant things, like spending the evening with Vivian. Vivian has become more and more present in my thoughts and my heart. *That could spell trouble for you, Jack.*

I shrugged off the negative thoughts and focused on the evening with Vivian.

CHAPTER 7

Driving through the gates at Vivian's was beginning to feel like coming home. It wasn't the beautiful home and grounds that made it feel that way, though. It was the woman who was waiting for me just outside the garage door. She looked adorable. She was wearing some long denim shorts just above her knees. She had a plain white shirt knotted at her waist, and much to my surprise, her hair was in a ponytail.

Getting out of the car and smiling, I took her hands as she approached me. I held her away from me to take a good look. "You look amazing! I just realized that I have never seen you with your hair down, so to speak." And then, to my surprise, she laughed and flipped her ponytail. I loved the sound of her laugh. It was soft, not quiet—soft, almost like a purr. It was a very enticing sound.

"Jack, I don't always dress like a stuffed-shirt judge. I relax like everyone else. Now come with me. I have a surprise for you."

As she pulled me into the house, I responded, "I have never seen you looking like a stuffed shirt. You look pretty amazing in your suits." Who am I kidding? She looks hot in her work suits. "What is going on? Where are you pulling me?"

"We will partake of a simple charcuterie board for dinner and a very nice bottle of wine. On the patio." She continued to pull me behind her out the door to the patio. There was this beautiful assortment of cheeses, meats, fruit, and bread on the table, artfully arranged on a wooden platter with natural edging. I had never seen anything like it before.

"I guess that is the charhooter—whatever board you were talking about. I got worried when you said we had a board for dinner."

She was laughing again and indicating that she wanted me to sit down. "It is such a beautiful evening. I love this time of year, when summer and fall decide whose turn it is. It's so good to have someone to share it with. I want to put aside all the worries for tonight. I want us to relax, talk, nibble through some delicious food, and drink a lot of wine."

And with that, she sat beside me so we could see the river, and we spent several incredible hours talking. We had known each other for years but had never delved any deeper than the surface. Over this extraordinary selection of food, we met each other again yet for the first time. It was incredible.

As the evening waned and became dusk, I didn't want it to end, so I suggested we take a stroll along the paths that led out to the vineyard and along the riverbank. Agreeing, Vivian refilled our wine glasses and stood.

It was a beautiful evening to walk through the vineyard on the stone path. The air was crisp, and fall was beating summer back as darkness fell. Illuminated by solar lights, the trail ended at the screened gazebo. The gazebo had an unobstructed view of the St. Croix River Valley. The steeple of St. Michael's Church, the rotunda of the Historic Courthouse, where my career began, and the aerial lift bridge.

They were all illuminated, creating a fairy-tale horizon for our viewing pleasure.

We walked up the few steps into the gazebo. Vivian took my hand and led me to a porch swing perfectly placed to enjoy the river view. Nightfall captured the romantic beauty of the St. Croix with the flickering red and green navigation lights of the boat traffic. We could enjoy the glittering lights of the St. Croix paddlewheel and hear the sounds of their Dixieland music playing. Tourists and residents alike loved the Dixieland music cruises. As the paddlewheel passed below us, a golden glow encompassed its luminescent wake as it traveled north to the Arcola Railroad Bridge.

It was a panoramic display before us and felt very intimate and personal. Few words were spoken between us, and I could sense Vivian relaxing beside me. With a sigh, she pulled her legs on the swing beside her and settled her head on my shoulder.

She spoke quietly, "I haven't been out here at night since Charles died."

I began feeling needle-pin numbness in my tongue, which may have been from the wine, but I thought it was probably nerves. It was the first time for me to tap into delicacies from a charcuterie board. I hadn't ever heard of it before, but I sure did enjoy the selection of cheese, meats, fruit, and sweets. It filled me up just fine. Jack, you are a clod. Filled me up just fine. Sure glad I didn't say that out loud.

I had put my arm across the back of the swing, and she curled right into me as she repositioned herself and lay her head back on my arm. I didn't want to say anything and break the mood. Vivian was a perfect pairing with a glass of San Sebastián Cabernet. I was just fine with the subtle romantic buzz in the air. Vivian finally broke the silence with a softly whispered question.

"Jack, what happened to your parents? I heard a drunk driver killed them."

This subject was always difficult for me. It was a raw wound that had never healed, but if I couldn't share it with Vivian, I couldn't share it with anyone. So I just let the emotions roll, as I knew they would. My eyes tear up every time. "My parents were killed in an accident in Prescott, Wisconsin."

"How old were you?"

"Seven," I replied. "It happened on my seventh birthday."

Vivian said, "Jack, I am sorry. I can see this isn't something you want to discuss. Let's go inside."

She began to rise, and I grabbed her hand and pulled her back down to the swing. "I want to tell you."

She returned to her comfortable position without saying a word, and I began.

"We were coming back from fishing on the Mississippi River. It was a trip celebrating my birthday. My dad just loved fishing. It was late in the evening, and I had fallen asleep in the back seat. My mom always made a bedroll for me. She never fished. She always said being with us was enough for her. Anyway I remember waking up with a wet face. It turned out to be blood. I was in pain, and I thought my father was already dead. He never made a sound or movement.

He was twisted around the steering wheel. My mom called for me. She said my name. She always called me Johnny. Her voice sounded funny, gargled. I tried to move closer to her and found her hand wet with blood. My five little fingers clutched her wet hand. I think she squeezed my hand. At least, I like to think so. I later learned that the Wisconsin State Patrol was chasing a drunk driver at high speeds and broadsided my parent's station wagon. The state trooper was killed in the accident."

Vivian interrupted, "Oh, Jack, I'm so sorry."

I barely heard her. I was back there, reliving the trauma. "Vivian, I could never understand why they transported the state trooper by helicopter, and my parents were both taken by ambulance to the hospital where they died. All the emergency response team attended to the trooper, and my parents were secondary. They didn't even know I was there. I hated the police. I hated all police. I was lodged on the floor between the back and front seats and wasn't discovered until the tow truck driver removed the vehicles. I must have passed out. I woke up feeling sick from the smell of antifreeze or something from the crash. With all my strength, I grabbed the tow truck driver by the arm as he reached into the car. I remember him jerking away and yelling, 'Jesus Christ!'

"I lost everything that night. My mother, my father, everything. They are buried in a cemetery off Highway 10 in Denmark Township."

"And you lived with your uncle?" Vivian asked in a low voice.

"It was just the three of us—my uncle, his wife, and me. I don't think she ever liked the idea of taking me on. My uncle did his best with me, but I knew it wasn't easy. He died in an airplane crash on their ranch when I was twelve. His wife shipped me back to Minnesota into the care of the state. I was placed in a foster home in Stillwater and stayed there until I graduated. My foster parents were wonderful people, the Anderssens."

"Jack, do you want to continue to talk about this?"

"Actually," I said, taking a little inventory of my feelings, "I feel good. Talking about my parents is new for me. I guess talking to you about them is good for me."

Getting up and pulling her up from the swing, we began to walk toward the house. Just before we reached the steps for the deck, Vivian paused, turned toward me, and hugged me, laying her head on my chest. I felt a warm glow spread through me and felt comforted. It felt good. I hugged her in return. We stood like that for a minute before she began to pull back. I took hold of her hand and pulled her closer for a kiss. What would she think? First kisses were potential land mines. I wasn't sure what her reaction would be, but it felt right.

Vivian dropped my hand and moved closer yet. The empty wine glasses clinked together as she reached up with her open hand and caressed my neck with her soft delicate hand. Tilting her head slightly for a better angle, Vivian pressed her lips to mine. She tasted like the wine that we had shared. The glasses clinked, and I paused to take them out of her hand and set them both on the steps behind us. Reaching my arms around Vivian was very natural. Enjoying our first kiss became a permanently recorded event in my mind. A very long kiss that gave me an indescribable rush. A natural pause occurred as we nibbled at each other's lips. I moved my arms up from her waist, brushing the sides of her breasts, as I moved to draw her back into another kiss, but she stepped back and said, "Let's go inside for dessert."

Wanting nothing more than to continue right where we left off, I joked, "I thought we were having dessert. Is there more?"

She chuckled and said, "Jack, let's move forward with this—whatever it is—slowly, okay? These feelings that I have for you are pretty sudden for me. They are quite a surprise. A welcome one," she continued as she must have seen concern on my face. "A very welcome one," she said as she raised her hand and touched my face. "Do you understand?" she asked in a pleading tone.

I gave her a smile and a kiss on the tip of her nose and smiled as I said, "As long as you say slowly and not stop, I'm okay with it. Let's go in and have dessert." Bending down and picking the empty glasses up with one hand, I motioned for her to go up before me.

After Vivian dimmed the bright lights and turned on soft piano music, she served fresh apple pie and a scoop of cinnamon ice cream. "Don't get excited, thinking this is my doing, Jack. Madel made the pie with orchard apples. Would you like coffee?"

"Your coffee? Yes, please. I think I am addicted to it. The pie looks delicious."

The dessert conversation was pretty light. Finishing, Vivian moved her plate out of the way, leaned across the table toward me, and smiled.

"Oh, I'm not sure what that look means." I said, "I think every man instinctively knows it can't be good, though." I reached over the table and began to gently tap her forehead. "What's going on up there?"

"Well, Jack, I wanted to ask you, every year, the St. Croix Valley Doctor's Association has a fundraiser for breast cancer awareness month. I purchase two tickets every year." Vivian seemed uncharacteristically flustered. I liked the look on her. "I haven't attended since Charles passed," she continued. Now she was playing with my fingers on the table that had somehow come to be holding hers.

"I was wondering if you would join me this year. No pressure," she added hastily. "It will be on the *Majestic Lady*, a new boat on the river."

"Well, sure, I would love to." I paused and smiled. "I always love being on the river."

Laughing at the implication that the boat and the river were the main draws, Vivian visibly relaxed and continued, "I'm sure it will be a lovely evening. There will be cocktails, dinner, music, and, Jack, I hope you don't object. It is a formal affair, which means you need a tux. Are you okay with that?"

"Sure, not a problem." *Oh shit, a tux*, I thought as I took another bite of the enormous piece of pie she had cut for me. A charcuterie board—a first—now a black-tie event on a yacht with the Judge. Scott is going to get a laugh out of this.

CHAPTER

8

I woke from a familiar nightmare, soaked in a cold sweat that almost felt like I had broken a fever. Each night always seemed like the first time I experienced the night terror that was haunting me. My left hand had clenched so tightly in my sleep, it was hurting. I began stretching my fingers in an attempt to alleviate my discomfort. It would seem unlikely that I was having a heart attack, although left arm pain is one of the symptoms. People had suggested that maybe I had PTSD. I was starting to think perhaps they were right.

Suddenly my cell phone rang, and I could see it was LaVonne. "Hello?"

"Hey, Jack, it's LaVonne." Without waiting for a response from me, she started in, "I need your help with a situation involving a local federal judge's daughter. Could you come by my office this morning?"

"Pretty early for a phone call and a favor, isn't it, LaVonne?" When she didn't respond, I said, "I was up anyway. How does forty-five minutes sound?" I was still flexing my left hand.

"Forty-five minutes will be great. Let's meet in the cafeteria. I'll buy coffee to make up for the early call."

"Sounds good," I replied as I hung up. Well, so far, my retirement hasn't been too dull. Loss of purpose in my life and boredom has not been a problem lately. I've heard from coworkers who retired and reported they were more active than when employed. How true.

Looking back, as I took a quick shower, I thought my career had been one I was proud of. I enjoyed most of it. I had always felt a passion for my work. Most of my relationships had grown out of the job. During business hours, I had an excellent professional relationship with the County Attorney's Office personnel that had often flowed into celebratory gatherings at local watering holes.

It did seem professional lines were drawn between law enforcement and lawyers. LaVonne has been the exception, and we have become quite close personally. We had dated for almost a year but had broken it off about a year ago. Our personal goals were radically different, and I wanted what my parents enjoyed in marriage. She wanted the bench, the supreme court. Serious relationships weren't in her plans; however, we stayed good friends.

Waiting for her near a window in the cafeteria with a vending machine coffee, I stared out toward a little brown-log tavern called Club 36, and reminisced. Club 36 wasn't one of those places that separated the ranks. All government employees enjoy meeting there for drinks, meals, and camaraderie. Club 36 is the hot spot for all professions before, during, or after work. This establishment is where dispatchers, deputies, lawyers, judges, and jailers congregate for all purposes.

It began when Washington County was much smaller in population with a small-town feeling. Club 36 became the place for government employees' quick lunch. After work hours, dispatchers would gather to discuss traumatic 911 calls. Patrol deputies would share pitchers of beer and decompress after a suicide call involving a shotgun and a faceless victim. Defense and prosecuting attorneys dropped the adversarial nature of their jobs to share a plate of cheese curds and cocktails. Judges would occasionally partake in the festivities, polishing their political skills while benefiting from an occasional complimentary drink. And let's not forget correctional officers. Jailers have the most difficult, dirty, and disgusting job of any county government job that comes to mind.

I discovered this jewel during my first year at Washington County Sheriff's Office. Dispatched to Club 36, the manager met me at the door of this rustic-looking brown log cabin restaurant. The manager indicated that Judge Sandgren would like a ride home as he had too much to drink. Judge Sandgren sat slumped over a drink at a table near the enormous rustic rock fireplace. I didn't want to start my probationary period with Washington County having a conflict about the subtle differences between taxis and squad cars with a judge, so I complied, helping the staggering older man to my squad. I opened the passenger door and began to drive the judge home.

It wasn't until the intoxicated Honorable Judge Sandgren started ranting about the Sheriff's Office and me personally, whom he had never met, I realized I didn't know where His Honor's residence was, and worse yet, neither did he.

After driving around the historic residential area of Stillwater near the river bluffs for twenty-five minutes, listening to the judge rail against my incompetence, I began to lose my patience. The last drop of patience evaporated when he barfed in the front seat of my squad car. Enough was enough.

I took action. Said action colored my relationship with some judges for years to come. I contacted communications by radio and requested that Detox be advised I was bringing one adult male to their location. The smell of the puke was beginning to make me sick. At least the judge had passed out and wasn't calling me obscenities anymore. Judge Sandgren never signed a criminal complaint for me after that.

I was smiling over my recollections when LaVonne arrived. She sat down at the private table I had chosen and began without a hello or a how are you? "Jack, I need your help with a family matter involving Judge Magnuson. He's a federal judge who lives here in Stillwater."

I interrupted to ask, "Just so I understand correctly, is this a favor, or will I be working on behalf of the County Attorney's Office?"

"That is a fair question. Let's see if you can help find this young woman first. I will make it worth your while. The judge's daughter's name is Josie." She handed me a picture of Josie and a statement she had taken from a friend who had gone with her to the Washington County Fairgrounds.

"Jack, this girl may be a runaway, but it doesn't feel like a runaway to me. The Sheriff's Office reluctantly took a missing person report but didn't seem enthusiastic to continue with any follow-up. Could you review the statement and call me this afternoon? I need to be in court now. Please see what you can do. Her parents are beside themselves."

With that, she turned and hurried from the cafeteria. I hadn't said a single word, let alone the cup of coffee she had promised. Watching her leave, I smiled a little and considered her motives.

LaVonne Williams is a beautiful woman in her early forties, fair complexion, brown eyes, and short dark hair, who has promised never to marry and so far has kept her word. She is a very bright and competent prosecutor with future aspirations for the bench. She is petite at only five foot two inches but has shaken many defense attorneys after sparring with her.

She has many connections on the bench statewide and is understandably anxious to help out this federal judge. While I knew that was not her only motive, it couldn't hurt either.

The statement said Josie and a friend were dropped off at the Washington County Fairgrounds with a scheduled pickup at midnight. Josie's friend last saw her at eleven thirty near the horse barns and admitted they had both been drinking beer provided by two adult men described as cowboys.

The two men had a large white horse trailer with a black sign that said "Show Horses." The friend could not provide license plate information, truck description, or a good description of the two adult males. The friend said that she believed the owner of the trailer's name was Troy, and he had a missing or deformed thumb on his right hand. She had noticed the deformity as he was clumsy when handing cans of beer to them.

Statistically it is a fact that teenagers are the most common age for abduction. While it is also the age of most runaways, possible kidnapping should not be discounted by police before an investigation. The patrol commander should have assigned a deputy to do a cursory search of the county fairgrounds, where the girl was last seen, after receiving the telephone report and entering Josie into the computer as a missing person.

One last sip of the coffee I purchased before dumping the cup in the trash, I headed for the fairgrounds to search the horse barn area for Josie.

The friend was at the closest entrance to the horse barn and picked up by her older sister, who was upset about the girls drinking and refused to wait or search for Josie.

The county fair manager was unavailable, but I saw the horse trailers were gone, and talked with a friendly young man cleaning the barns. He was unable to provide any information regarding Josie. However, when I asked, he confirmed that a team roping competition had been at the fairgrounds.

Most sports have an inherent risk of injuries, such as ice hockey and missing teeth. Team roper's inherent injury is losing a thumb. Ropers have a dally maneuver in which they wrap the rope around the saddle horn. The inexperienced roper will get their thumb wrapped into the rope, resulting in a severed thumb.

I recalled this from living with my uncle on his ranch in the San Rafael Valley in Arizona. Two cowboy brothers who worked for my uncle were both missing thumbs. I was young at the time but curious. I asked my uncle if they were born that way, but my uncle told me that they were professional ropers, and explained how they lost their thumbs.

I thanked the young man, made several phone calls, and learned that the next team roping competition was in Sioux Falls, South Dakota.

I knew that the Sheriff's Office had a volunteer-mounted posse and thought they could cover more territory than I could, and faster. I didn't have the authority to call them out to sweep the area around the fairgrounds. Finding a body was the last scenario I wanted for this family, but I had to cover every possibility.

I contacted CSO Anne Reed, explaining the situation. I asked her if she could have a couple of riders check the fairgrounds and surrounding fields on horseback for our missing girl or any evidence. Anne had two mounted posse riders in mind and would take care of my request.

CSO Anne took the opportunity to tell me that she had done a walk-through of Judge Lord's residence and property and would meet with the judge upon concluding the survey. She also said that the river access to the Lord's estate may be problematic but will keep me appraised.

I left a message at the County Attorney's Office for LaVonne to call as soon as she returns from court. Very important.

Arriving home and awaiting a callback from LaVonne, I packed an overnight bag and grabbed lunch. Sioux Falls is a four-hour drive, and I wonder how excited LaVonne will be to join me.

I was eating when LaVonne called. "Hey, Jack, what do you think?"

"I think you'll drive me to Sioux Falls this afternoon. I have an idea where she may be."

"Jack, are you kidding me? Is this an undercover tactic to get me to sleep with you in some Best Western in Sioux Falls?"

Chuckling, I replied, "Now that you mention it, that does have some appeal, but that's not my plan. Pack an overnight bag and pick me up. It's only a four-hour drive. Do you remember where I live?"

"Real funny, Jack. This better be worth it for me to leave my office today, and who knows for how long."

"LaVonne, how would a letter of recommendation look with a federal judge's signature on the bottom? That could be the step you need for a federal judgeship. Your dream job."

"I'll pick you up in an hour." And the line went dead.

*****

Right on time, LaVonne pulled up in front of my house in a four-door black Mercedes. I admired the car when I got up from my chair on the porch and walked down the driveway. As I opened the passenger door, I asked, "Don't suppose this is a county fleet vehicle?" Slamming the door behind me, I buckled the seat belt.

"No, Jack," LaVonne answered with a pained condescending tone. "It is all mine, every beautiful inch of her. So relax and enjoy the ride. After that Jeep of yours, you will think you are floating."

"Don't diss the Jeep. We have a connection." Chuckling to myself, I added, "I don't necessarily want to give you directions, but if you take I-35 South to I-90, we can be in Sioux Falls in less than four hours. You can drive eighty on I-90 in South Dakota."

"What makes you think Josie is in Sioux Falls?"

"The girls were drinking with two cowboys before Josie's friend was picked up by her sister, and they didn't take the time to look for her. She was abandoned. There was a team roping championship at the county fairgrounds, and I found out the cowboys were in Sioux Falls for the next roping competition. I've contacted the Minnehaha County Sheriff's Office to make them aware we would be conducting an interview at the fairgrounds. We would call them if we needed any assistance. I have the number there to call if we need to."

"Least possible information, Jack, do you know your audacity often finds you in violation of professional conduct taking such bold risks? Always cut through the red tape."

"Yes, I have. Anything I can do to minimize the bureaucracy and comfort a family, I'm all for it."

"So we drive four hours, locate the fairgrounds and a band of cowboys. How many interrogations before we find Josie?"

"We have a possible name from your statement—Troy, who is probably missing his right thumb."

"And if we don't find her?"

"We're going to a speakeasy I have heard about and going to check into the most expensive hotel in Sioux Falls."

"Recline your seat, Sherlock, and get some rest. Jack, how do you know so much about cowboys? Avocation?"

Putting the seat back into a comfortable position, I replied, "After my parents passed, I lived with my aunt and uncle for about five years in Arizona."

"I heard you lived in Arizona for a while as a young man. I was thinking Phoenix."

"The San Rafael Valley. It's near Patagonia. We lived on a working cattle ranch, The Lazy J. My aunt and uncle cared for me until he was killed in a plane crash at the ranch. I came back to Minnesota and was placed in a foster home."

"Did you like the ranch?"

"I loved the Lazy J. There was always something fun to do— moving cattle, riding horses. I still remember my horse, Blue. He was a large blue roan, and I was just a little guy. He took good care of me.

He was very gentle. I missed the ranch and Blue like crazy when I returned to Minnesota. Those are good memories."

For the remainder of the ride, we talked shop, current cases, and past ones that we had in common. LaVonne also mentioned the serial rapist continued to be at large, and the task force increased in size.

Four hours later, almost to the minute, we passed the "Welcome to Sioux Falls" sign. We began looking for the regional airport, which was supposed to be near the county fairgrounds.

My preparation for this missing-person case was basic—gun, speed loader, handcuffs, identification, and instinct.

"Jack, I hope you don't intend to arrest this cowboy if we locate him. The last time you arrested a perp out of state, it was determined to be illegal. In Wisconsin, if my memory serves me correctly."

"LaVonne, yes, it was in Wisconsin. I thought a citizen's arrest for a person suspected of stabbing a Stillwater woman twenty-three times was necessary to keep him from fleeing justice. Who would have known being a resident of Wisconsin was a critical element of a citizen's arrest? I have no intention of arresting anyone in South Dakota."

Driving into the fairground's empty parking lot, we decided to take the concession road, as we could see the agriculture and animal barns ahead. Since the fairgrounds were closed at the moment, it was easy to know where the trailers, trucks, and tractors were parked. Carnies. Okay, Jack, you know anything can happen here. I had a little history dealing with people who worked the carnival circuit. It was not a good history. With some apprehension, I asked LaVonne to park near the white horse trailer as I pointed to its location.

As I exited the Mercedes, I said, "Stay in the car unless I'm on the ground and losing." I started walking around the white horse trailer covered in mud. Some adjacent trailers had interior lights, not the horse trailer with hand-painted letters *Show Horses*.

I walked to the trailer door and knocked hard several times. I could sense movement and sounds from inside. Finally the door opened, and a very tall Caucasian cowboy-looking man stepped outside and, down one step, turned and locked the door.

His right thumb was missing. I saw the curtains open at the fifth-wheel horse trailer's small upper front window. Someone was looking out, but I couldn't see very clearly.

The cowboy wore crusty brown boots, blue jeans that had seen better days, and a red-white-and-blue Wrangler shirt. He had lots of facial hair. I asked him if his name was Troy.

He replied jeeringly, "Who wants to know?"

"I'm Detective Sergeant Jack Janssen, friend from Minnesota. We are here to pick up Josie."

"Never heard of a Josie. Guess you'll have to look elsewhere." And he began walking away.

I took hold of his thumbless hand and twisted his arm behind him as I slammed him against his trailer beside the door. While holding him against the trailer, I said, "Don't make this any more difficult than it needs to be, friend. Here are your options—you can open this door and let me check for Josie, or I will call the Minnehaha Sheriff's Office for assistance. Your choice. The easy way or the hard way. What's your pleasure?"

Looking over his shoulder past me, with a gasping breath, he said, "Hey, easy, man. Lighten up. Who's in the black Mercedes?"

I responded, "That is Josie's mother, and she is not a happy camper, friend." While I slowly released my hold on Troy, who now had a bloody nose, the cowboy reluctantly turned and unlocked the door before bolting toward the barns like a dust storm, leaving the keys dangling in the lock.

LaVonne was exiting the Mercedes. I signaled with my hand to stop while opening the door. A tearful girl with a black eye, a bloody swollen lip, wearing jean shorts and red cowgirl boots, looked at me with frightened and suspicious bloodshot blue eyes.

I smiled, saying, "Josie, we are here to take you home."

I motioned for LaVonne to come to the trailer. I asked LaVonne to help Josie gather her belongings and walked a short distance away to make a couple of phone calls. While LaVonne and Josie talked briefly, I contacted Sanford Hospital Emergency Department to brief the hospital that we were bringing a victim of sexual assault to the emergency room.

With her arm around Josie, LaVonne came out of the trailer and slowly walked to the car. I asked Lavonne to take the back seat with Josie and said we were driving to the Sanford Emergency Room for an exam. I made it clear that this wasn't an option and that whatever happened wasn't her fault.

While Josie was in the exam room, LaVonne called Josie's parents. LaVonne reported back that Judge Magnuson was very grateful to both of us.

"I'll get us coffee. This exam may take some time."

Stopping me before I moved, LaVonne asked, "Where should we report this, Jack? Which agency should get the evidence?"

"LaVonne, I think Josie needs to be back home with her parents tonight, not giving a statement to Minnehaha County Sheriff's Office for the next two to three hours. Don't you?" At her nod, I continued, "When the doctor has completed the exam, they can send the reports, billing, and evidence to Washington County. You and Minnehaha can figure out the rest.

"The FBI has a unit called the Violent Criminal Apprehension Program, VICAP, responsible for tracking certain sex crimes. Feds may want the collar for interstate charges. Troy may have left a trail of victims in multiple states that follow the horse-roping competition circuit. Let's give Josie's father, Judge Magnuson, an opinion of our cowboy with a missing appendage after a preliminary investigation initiated by Minnesota law enforcement."

It was a long dark subdued ride back to Stillwater. Josie and LaVonne were both sound asleep in the back seat, and my stomach was growling for breakfast at Omar's.

I woke LaVonne up as we approached Stillwater and daybreak on Highway 36, heading to my home in Bayport. Josie was still asleep. Pulling into my driveway, LaVonne came to the driver's door and said, "You are a lifesaver. Thank you so much, Jack."

Always the flirtatious LaVonne, she gave me a wet kiss and a prolonged hug. Looking toward the house as LaVonne was hugging me, I saw Ms. Adeline peeking out the window with a big smile and her little wave.

CHAPTER 9

Hilltop is a small city surrounded by Columbia Heights, with a population of 744 and the location of Scott's storage unit. I had no business in that part of the Twin Cities other than doing a favor for a friend.

As I drove, I recalled many good times with Scott—social gatherings and fishing trips and, after work, decompressing at Club 36. The closer I got to my destination, the more depressing my thoughts became. I was doing a favor for a friend who was dying. I would do anything for him. If only I could change the end of Scott's story. Our time together is short, I know.

I once had the honor of meeting a Columbia Heights officer killed in the line of duty shortly before his retirement. I was only starting my career then. I know Scott would have preferred to go out in the line of duty rather than this slowly progressing disease that was stealing his life, piece by piece.

Scott had put in all those years of service, and it had come down to a shadow box and one brown duffel bag containing a uniform. Funeral attire for someone I had been proud to serve with and who I love like a father. I would go much farther than the other side of the Twin Cities to do a favor for him.

It wasn't challenging to locate Hilltop Storage, with only three-by-two-square city blocks making up the city of Hilltop. I stopped in the office. A young man handed me Scott's brown duffel after I gave him my name and identification. It turned out he was the owner's son. Scott had worked the streets of Minneapolis with his father.

Opening the back of the Jeep, I stowed the duffel bag in the rear and checked the contents. A Washington County Sheriff's

Office brown uniform carefully folded and packed in plastic. A cigar box contained badges, ribbons, misc lapel pins, and Scott's walnut-trimmed Minneapolis Police shadow box. I could not find his Washington County shadow box that I was sure he had but may have given to his granddaughter, Erin.

Heading north on I-35 was an easy drive to Superior Shores Care Center. I was looking forward to a visit with Scott. I had some news for him for a change. Although I would be arriving after lunch, I planned to pick up a large cup of coffee for Scott. He always enjoyed the coffee from Grandpa's Snack Cart in Canal Park.

About ten miles from Duluth, I saw one voice mail from LaVonne and listened to the message. I-35 had numerous areas of no cell coverage. LaVonne's recording was, "*Hey, Jack. I have good news and bad news. The good news is that Judge Magnuson thanked you and said if you ever run for sheriff, give him a call. Now the bad news. Commander Jacobson called me and was upset that you didn't check in with him regarding Josie Magnuson. Call me.*"

When I visit Commander Jacobson's office, I may have a checklist of topics and concerns.

After stopping at Grandpa's snack wagon for Scott's coffee, I proceeded up the hill to Superior Shores Care Center. The city of Duluth has many hills that can be challenging, particularly in the winter months. Not today.

As I pulled into the parking lot, I could see several residents outside near the Lake Superior Viewing Area. It was a perfect day to look out over the lake. The view was breathtaking. Scott was far from the others and comfortable sitting in his wheelchair. One of the Superior Shores staff had thoughtfully tucked a blanket over Scott's lap to ward off the chill in the air. It is a rare day when the breeze off the lake doesn't have a cooling effect. The light breeze blew patchy clouds across the sky, allowing only a few sunrays to appear. It made beams of light appear, capturing the attention of the onlookers at the care center, including Scott, who never saw me pull into the parking lot.

The beautiful scenery enthralled the residents. The waters of Lake Superior looked ocean blue, reflecting the sky and creating an inspirational moment for the aging folks to focus on their questions about the hereafter. Their faith, hope, and beliefs that will come to fruition at their passing—some sooner than others. Scott had a satisfied smile as he took in the view.

As I walked up to Scott, carrying this duffel bag of funeral attire, I was tentative. What do I say to Scott? Here is your funeral suit. Will I get choked up? I am confident that Scott will give me a hard time, designed to help me through this awkward moment as he had many other times.

While I handed Scott his coffee, he said, "Hey, kiddo, this is what I'm talking about, the view, the ships, and aqua-blue water. Marvelous!"

Holding back tears, I said, "This must be the best view of the harbor."

"Son, look at that rusty tub approaching the canal. That is one of the thousand-footers. She is enormous." The Ariel Bridge was now fully elevated, providing 180 feet of vertical clearance, and the ship was passing under the bridge. As we were both intently watching, I could hear a scratchy voice from a distance away and muffled by static, indiscernible to my ears.

Scott filled in the commentary for me, "*James R. Barker*, a thousand-foot vessel from the Great Lakes Fleet, a coal hauler."

"You could understand what they were announcing?" I asked incredulously.

With a chuckle, Scott held up his phone and said, "Jack, I have an app on my phone with ship arrivals and departures. My hearing isn't that good."

The conversation paused while we focused on the ship passing at a snail's pace. Still focused on the vessel, Scott said, "Well, have you made a date with Wanda? I think she likes you, son."

"Scott, you never cease to amaze me. I'm holding a duffel bag with your burial clothes, and you're talking about women."

"Jack, I've already accepted my passing. Son, you are the project I am working on now."

"Scott, be assured that I will have a drink with Wanda. I promise. Do you want me to bring your duffel bag to your room?"

"Not right now. I'm enjoying my time watching the ships and drifting clouds. Besides, a salty is arriving soon—*The Federal Weser*, a newer cargo ship from the Marshall Islands. I want to see it."

Grabbing a chair and bringing it beside him, I sat down to watch with him. "Have you been given a firm date on your surgery?" I asked.

Scott replied absently, busy watching the action in the port, "The nursing staff is on top of all that stuff. I will give you a call when the date is firm."

"Make sure you do, or have the staff give me a call with the date. I want to be there."

"I will have Wanda give you a call. You can take care of a date for that drink while you are at it," he said with a wink of his eye.

"Did I hear my name mentioned? Are you boys talking about me?" Wanda had approached without either of us noticing her. "Are you planning to spend the night? It is Jack?" I nodded and then realized she probably thought I meant I was going to spend the night.

Feeling foolish and awkward, I corrected myself, "I mean, yes, my name is Jack. The duffel bag is Mr. McCloud's. He asked me to bring it up for him." I never get like this with Vivian. With her, I am confident and feel almost relaxed. I sounded tongue-tied and shy with other women, which was embarrassing.

Never taking his eyes off the lake, Scott responded, "Jack and I are taking a trip up the North Shore to Grand Marais. Would you like to come with us? In a couple of weeks, the autumn colors will be glorious."

"Mr. McCloud, that is the best offer I have had in a long time." Chuckling, she playfully nudged his shoulder as she turned to seek safety from Scott's teasing.

"God, Scott, you embarrassed her!"

"Jack, didn't you hear her, son? She likes you and is waiting for you to call. She is a great girl. You could do a lot worse, trust me." He slapped his thigh with his hand, as if Scott had firmed up the plan. His action focused my attention on his vanishing legs with sadness.

Maybe if I tell him about Vivian, he will relax about my love life or lack thereof. Not quite yet, I thought.

"Scott, I appreciate your matchmaking, and you are pretty good at it. I will be sure to call her very soon. Really," I said as he looked up at me with some doubt.

I was having a wonderful time with Scott, watching the activity down in Canal Park. It was great seeing Scott enjoying himself. I broke the silence between us by saying, "Scott, I've been invited to attend a fundraiser for Breast Cancer Awareness Month on the St. Croix River."

"What the hell for?" he asked, clearly puzzled why I would want to attend this event. "Don't you get enough time on the river?" Still watching the scene below near the lift bridge, he continued, "How much are those tickets?"

With an enormous smile, I paused until he looked over and saw it on my face. I replied, "I don't care. Judge Lord bought them, and she is my date."

That got his attention. His head jerked back in surprise and focused on me and our conversation instead of the lake. "When did this happen? From friendly colleague to girlfriend? I am happy for you. She would be a perfect match for you." He started ticking off Vivian's good qualities that would make her perfect for me. "She is patient, compassionate, smart as a whip, and a good looker! When does this event occur, and what have I missed getting to this point?"

I was getting a little red in the face. Scott had us walking down the aisle instead of on a simple date. "It is on October 1. The beginning of Breast Cancer Awareness month. The only bad thing about the event is Vivian says I have to wear a tux." There was a grimace on my face when I said the last words.

"Well, I'll be damned, son. You found the perfect woman, and I didn't even have to point you in the right direction." He reached over and gave me a playful punch in the arm. "You keep me posted. October could be pretty chilly on the water. That might work in your favor too. And don't whine about the tux. It's a small price to pay for a date with a woman like the Honorable Judge Lord. Have a bourbon for me. I'll be thinking about you that night for sure.

"Oh, and by the way, Jack, I gave my granddaughter, Erin, your phone number. She is the executor of my estate. She is working days in Minneapolis at Precinct One, internal affairs. That job could be even more difficult than your child abuse investigations. I'm real proud of her."

I nodded that I understood and then raised my eyebrow when he began determining the level of difficulty of police work. I had done almost every assignment at the Sheriff's Office except for internal affairs. Once assigned to the rat squad, your coworkers suddenly keep an arm's length from you. It's an isolated assignment.

Changing the subject, I decided to ask about the duffel bag. "Why did you suddenly want me to bring it? Erin could have picked up your belongings."

"I just wanted to reminisce with you, and I need to decide on the burial uniform. You know, blue versus brown, that's all. Erin is searching out a Minneapolis uniform before I make a final decision. Frankly, Jack, I have always liked the blue uniform more than the brown. It looks better on me, kiddo," he said the last with a wink.

As we awaited the arrival of the *Federal Weser* ship, a salty ocean vessel visiting the Great Lakes, I advised Scott of my plans to meet with Commander Jacobson.

I explained to Scott that LaVonne Williams had contacted me regarding a missing female juvenile from Washington County, who we subsequently found in South Dakota. Together we had brought her back to Stillwater. Our actions pissed off the commander for not giving him a heads-up regarding our involvement.

"And if that isn't going to make him mad enough, I have poked my nose into a serial rapist case. So far, the task force has kept it pretty quiet. It hasn't made the papers yet. I think that Jacobson is worried at this point about the public's reaction. Why weren't we told? You know how it goes."

"So what is the MO?" Scott asked, falling right back into the job.

"Do you remember Sandy Pittman?" At Scott's nod, I continued, "It is remarkably similar. Lower bedroom windows or doors are the entry point. He is gloved since they have found no matching prints. He wears a mask. He tapes the victim's mouth, restrains their hands, and blinds them with light. He enters the apartments between 3:00 and 3:30 a.m."

"And Pittman is still in the clink?" Scott asked. I smiled at the word *clink*—good old Irish cop.

"Yes. Pittman is still locked up, but, Scott, the similarities are uncanny. The evidence is piling up. The task force has DNA from the crime scenes, but no matches in the system."

Scott was staring out at the canal, but I knew he was thinking about the case. He had his cop face engaged. It was good to see it.

"Jack, it sounds like a ballsy youngster with no criminal history and also very lucky he hasn't entered to find a shotgun pointed at his head."

"Scott, this guy is doing his homework. Just like Pittman. He has watched these women. The perp has targeted the homes and victims, and not by accident. Just like Pittman. Only a solitary woman in residence. It is as though Pittman had written a how-to book for a successful rape."

Scott continued to stare, thinking, not looking. "I could understand Pittman bragging to his fellow inmates, but they would have a record to be found. What about family? Have you checked his visitor log?"

"He has only had two visitors. A girlfriend, Crystal Boutwell, from Somerset, and his lawyer, Earl Greystone."

Scott chuckled. "Earl the Pearl, huh? Why is it that he represents all these lowlife sex offenders?"

"Probably because he is so damn good at it. I was always a little nervous about him as defense counsel. He never messed me up, but I always figured my luck would run out someday."

"Jack, has someone from Washington County attended the tri-county meetings and issued bulletins?"

"Yes, some of the meetings take place in the War Room. According to Lavonne, they hold weekly meetings with a team of county detectives. Scott, they have a pin map that is filling up with locations of rapes, and they have very few leads so far."

He heaved a sigh. He said, "Son, you're retired and need to spend more time dating and attending parties. I want to see a picture of you and the judge on the river. You two will be a beautiful couple. Ah, here she comes."

He pointed to the lake; sure enough, a big ship was coming into view, headed for the canal.

We enjoyed more time quietly watching the ship move toward its destination. I finally asked, "Should I bring your duffel to your room?"

Scott replied, "No need. Someone will be out soon to bring me in for meds. We will take it in then."

I waited until the big ship had cleared the bridge and was in the harbor, then said, "I'll be heading back to the cities now." It seemed like a good time to go before they came out to wheel him back in. We could pretend things were like they used to be. I stood up and leaned over to hug Scott. We were both slightly uncomfortable with the action, but I needed it.

With a wink, Scott thanked me for the visit and the duffel and said, "Remember to call Wanda for that drink. Having one in the wings is a good strategy.

"And, Jack, don't put Jacobson in a corner. He has always felt threatened by you. He would arrest you in a minute. These aren't your cases anymore, son."

"You're right, Scott. See you soon."

Heading south on I-35 was a journey I had taken many times. It gave me time to think. A visit to the Sheriff's Office was in order. Since retirement, I hadn't stepped foot into the law enforcement center, not even for a visit with coworkers. Now seemed like a good time to stop by and renew old acquaintances.

I knew that Commander Jacobson wanted to talk to me, but I didn't want to cede control of that conversation to him, so a causal stop seemed like just the thing for tomorrow. I knew what I wanted to say, but he wouldn't have time to get his ducks in a row. He was a stickler for professional etiquette and wouldn't be happy about my breach of protocol. I didn't care. My action would be crystal clear to Commander Jacobson, who knows why.

Commander Jacobson had delayed an assignment of a child abuse report for three days until I returned to work after a brief vacation.

My caseload was child abuse involving neglect and physical or sexual abuse, mostly sexual abuse. Most suspects were family members or people in authority over a child—for example, a daycare worker, schoolteacher, church pastor, attorney, or police officer. I have made arrests in each category. The alleged perpetrator could be wealthy or poor but more apt to be in the middle class of society—the largest demographic.

The ages of suspects can vary. I had petitioned many juveniles—suspects under eighteen—into court for physical or sexual abuse of a family member. I have arrested older men as well. My oldest arrestee was a man named Bert Bailey for the sexual abuse of multiple young girls. Bert had the distinction of being the most senior man incarcerated at Stillwater Prison at "the sexy young age of eighty-two," as reported by the prison newspaper, the *Prison Mirror*. The paper claims to be the country's longest continuously published prison newspaper.

So let's say I've seen and investigated hundreds of child abuse cases from all walks of life and all professions. But there is always one case that haunts you. Mine is the delayed response to an abuse report of a mother violently shaking her newborn baby. This type of case is my greatest fear, as it should be for every child protection worker and law enforcement officer.

This action can result in a condition known as Shaken Baby Syndrome. The victims are relatively young babies. Infants have weak neck muscles and a large heavy head. When forcefully shaken, an infant's or toddler's fragile brain bounces back and forth inside the skull, which can lead to subdural hemorrhage or bleeding in the brain. The results can be permanent, resulting in severe brain damage or death. The victims of Shaken Baby Syndrome are nonverbal. These victims are helpless and at the mercy of their caregivers.

When a caregiver is out of control, there is no telling what could happen. A delay caused by a family member's hesitancy to report or any cause for delay is always dangerous for the helpless child. Hesitation in this circumstance could be fatal.

Whenever a responsible agency receives a report of this type of abuse, it should flash big emergency lights in their minds. This report is an emergency! A delay could have been the difference between life and death for this infant. In my mind, the delayed response contributed to little Mary's death. Also in my early retirement and continued sleepless nights.

Commander Jacobson, my former supervisor, without personal knowledge of the situation, decided it could wait because Mary's mother was a registered nurse. He ignored the flashing lights in his mind—if there were any—and in my opinion, he shouldn't be in a command position. I was looking forward to this meeting tomorrow.

CHAPTER 10

Driving to the Sheriff's Office, I looked forward to seeing some of my old coworkers. I had many good times and made some good friends in the years I spent in law enforcement. Overall, law enforcement is a satisfying and noble career and draws the best of humanity. But like all professions, some bad apples get through. I was going to meet one of them.

Looking through the window in the security door, I pressed the button requesting entrance. The administrative staff immediately greeted me with handshakes and hugs. Joanne handed me a cup of black coffee. I took a sip and told her I was there to see Commander Jacobson. She thought he was in the War Room, the nickname for the large conference room used when a task force team is investigating a current major crime. I followed Joanne to the War Room, gained entry with her pass card, and walked into the room.

An investigation was underway, though the space was currently unoccupied. Looking at the whiteboards, numerous tables with computers, clipboards, photos with names, and mug shots piled on them. I determined that LaVonne was accurate. A serial rapist was on the loose without public knowledge or warning.

Large maps with multiple colored stickpins marked places where a rape had occurred, from Oakdale to Forest Lake and scattered locations around Washington County. One stickpin was particularly troubling. It was the pin on Arcola Trail, north of Vivian's home.

Before I could take a closer look at the stickpin on Arcola Trail, the security lock clicked, and in walked Commander Jacobson, already looking upset with me. "Jack, what are you doing in the War Room? It looks like you are snooping."

"Joanne thought you were in here, and she let me in. I got word that you wanted to see me." Leaning my hip casually against one of the tables and folding my arms over my chest, I said, "Well, here I am. What can I do for you?"

Commander Jacobson is not a handsome man. His face is acne-scarred, His brown eyes are too close together, and he keeps his blond hair cut military short. He is slender, like a cyclist, but not muscular. His usual sternness is absent. In its place is anger.

Jacobson moved up the ranks because of his college education. However, his germ phobia and weak stomach made it almost impossible for him to supervise bloody crime scenes. Particularly the gory scenes. Commander Jacobson would issue his orders from a distance, not only to the location of the crime, displaying weakness, but from his fellow officers, displaying his imagined superiority.

Jacobson has a master's degree in public administration. With honors, as I have been told numerous times. In my opinion, he is self-absorbed, sometimes arrogant, often misguided in criminal investigations, and has an intelligent failure.

He is wearing plain clothes today. With a blue sport coat and gray trousers.

Jacobson was trying hard to intimidate me with his practiced steely eyed stare. I don't intimidate. I continued to wait for his response, still leaning against the table.

Finally he broke the silent standoff with, "Let's go to my office. The War Room is off-limits to civilians."

Deciding that some things were more important than the animosity between us, I said, "Richard, I think I can help with this serial rapist investigation. It sounds like the MO is similar to an inmate at Stillwater Prison, Sandy Pittman. I want to help out."

"Where are you getting your information? The Sheriff's Office is not prepared to release any details. I am not interested in your two cents, but thanks."

I don't often employ psychological manipulation to intimidate, but Jacobson will fall into the trap every time. "Dick, I think I'll stay here. Now do you want to talk about Judge Magnuson's daughter? That is what you wanted to talk about. The sheriff may want to hear about my new friend, Judge Magnuson. I am expecting a dinner invite soon."

"Don't call me Dick! And from now on, make an appointment!"

Stepping closer to the pin map, I said, "Isn't this red-flag stick-pin close to Judge Lord's estate? I would be interested in that case," I said, totally ignoring his little snit.

The pompous and shamefully arrogant Jacobson was now visually pissed and starting to sweat but hadn't begun stammering yet. *I must be losing my touch*, I thought to myself. Maybe it would be a good time to leave before he gets upset. "Let the sheriff know I would be happy to help out Dick. I am available. I'll let myself out. I know the way."

Leaving, I dropped the guest coffee cup off with Joanne, and she asked, "Is everything all right, Jack? Commander Jacobson texted court security and requested two bailiffs to report to the War Room. Wasn't he in there with you? Did you pop him?"

"He was in the War Room with me, and no, I did not pop him. Rainbow lives for another day and another screwup."

Rainbow was the nickname the patrol used for Jacobson behind his back because he always showed up after the storm. While he was on patrol, you knew that you were on your own if he was your backup.

"Keep in touch, Joanne. You're the best."

Heading down the hall, I passed the two court security deputies walking toward the Sheriff's Office at a fast clip. I gave them a nod and left the building.

While heading toward Geister's for a sandwich, I received a call from Vivian.

"Jack, I am leaving Ramsey Hospital with Mary. Can you meet me at my house? I should be there in a half-hour. Her boyfriend assaulted Amanda, and I'm bringing Mary to my home."

"How is Amanda?"

"Amanda should be all right. They are just keeping her for observation."

"I'm closer. I'll be there when you arrive."

I heard the relief in her voice when she said, "Thanks, Jack," before disconnecting.

As expected, I arrived before Vivian and Mary, so I walked down to the water. Walking along the shoreline, I paused and thought about beefing up security with cameras or sound-sensing alarms. It could be as easy as a wildlife camera, which might be interesting to check for activity periodically. One suggestion for Vivian's property was to alarm the beach house since the power ran into that building. In addition, we could also have sensors on the door and windows. Easy fix. I need to call Anne and include that recommendation in the report. I walked back to the house and around the front to wait for Vivian.

As Vivian pulled through the gate and approached the garages, I was standing with arms crossed and a troubled expression on my face. I'm not too fond of the thought of anyone—friend or family—being a victim of crime. It always makes me feel helpless, which pisses me off.

Vivian got out of the car and walked toward me. I put my arms out, and she walked into them and wrapped her arms around me. "Don't frown at me. I need you to comfort me, not be mad."

"Sorry," I said as I rubbed her back. "I didn't know I was frowning. Should we get Mary?"

"She fell asleep in the car."

"I'll carry her up to her room and turn on the monitor. Why don't you get us a glass of that great tea, and we can talk." I gave her a quick kiss on the forehead as I passed with the little girl in my arms.

Mary had a bedroom at Auntie Vivian's house. It was a little princess's room with a coloring corner, a dollhouse, a giant bin of Magna-Tiles, stuffed animals, and the requisite pink canopy bed.

Bending down with my knees so I didn't disturb Mary, I threw the bedspread, covered in fairies and unicorns, back and recoiled as Tabby jumped up on the bed and walked up near the pillow, looked up at me as if to say, *Put her right here*. It's shift change. I'll watch over her from here. I gently placed Mary in the middle of the bed. I wrapped her arms around the doll I had grabbed when I got her out of the car. As I pulled the sheet up over her, I thought, *You may have drawn the short straw in the Mommy department, but at least you have an aunt who is a fairy godmother.* Tabby immediately curled into Mary's side, laid her head on the doll's leg that dangled loose, and closed her eyes. I looked at the pair for a minute, thinking how incredible animals were. Then, turning, I snapped on the monitor as I left the room, gently closing the door and headed back down the hall.

I walked into the kitchen just as Vivian put the tea glasses on the kitchen table. "She didn't even budge when I laid her down. Tabby almost gave me a heart attack jumping up on the bed. I hadn't even seen her before she jumped up. She must have radar. Mary sure is lucky to have you as an aunt. Let's sit, and you can tell me what happened."

"Well, I don't have too many details. Amanda called me and asked me to come. I rushed down there, not knowing what was going on. When I got there, I saw Mary curled up in the corner of a cubicle in the ER on a hard chair, clinging to her doll. Amanda was lying down. She had a bloody lip and some dried blood from her ear. I guess that is why they want to keep her overnight."

Taking a sip of her tea, she began, "Jack, I know I have told you a little about Amanda and Mary, but not all of it. Amanda has issues. She's had them as long as I can remember. But as a kid, you don't overthink it. I feel bad I wasn't more help for my folks. I didn't know the half of it. They kept it to themselves. First, Amanda has never held a job for longer than two weeks. She quits and now has a criminal history. Primarily for driving offenses, but she does have possession of drug charges, which are supposed to be deferred if she completes treatment.

"Amanda and Mary were passengers in the boyfriend's car, and they were driving to a restaurant on West Seventh in St. Paul, when a domestic erupted. The boyfriend hit Amanda on the upper jaw and pulled over. She grabbed Mary and jumped out. Amanda gave me the boyfriend's name, but I don't believe her. Arghaa!"

She leaned back with her hands on either side of her head and began to take her hair down. It fell into beautiful auburn waves to her shoulders. I was mesmerized.

Then dragging me back to reality, Vivian began, "Let's talk about what is important. That is Mary." Vivian was playing with the hairpins on the table when she continued, "I don't want to talk about this incident in Mary's presence. She understands more than you think."

I could tell she was angry, upset, and sad all at the same time. She was also clearly frustrated with her sister. "I tell you what. It is beautiful outside. Let's take the tea and the monitor out on the terrace, let the water work its magic, and help us calm down."

Vivian looked at me in some disbelief but stood up anyway. I grabbed the glasses, motioned for her to take the monitor, and moved out to the terrace. Sitting next to each other, facing the water, we sat silently for several minutes. I was thinking about five-year-old Mary, and had serious concerns about her health. With minimal knowledge, admittedly, I thought Mary looked like she could be a child of failure to thrive syndrome. I have investigated only a few cases since they are typically classified as neglect. In those cases, all the children were younger than Mary, about one year of age. Still, her appearance, being so much smaller than a typical five-year-old, and her poor verbal skills and demeanor appear similar to those investigations that I had conducted. I broke the silence with a question, "Vivian, has Mary ever had a comprehensive physical examination by a pediatrician? I have some connections in that regard."

"Amanda has taken Mary to the doctor for exams but usually for a cold or ear infection. Why?"

"I think we need to have Mary examined at Midwest Children's Center, MCC in St. Paul, I have a doctor friend, and she can talk with her and conduct a complete exam."

Changing the subject, she asked, "Jack, could you spend the night here? I am free for the rest of today, but I must be in court early tomorrow morning. Madel doesn't usually arrive until just before eleven."

"Sure, I can do that. I'll just run home, grab a change of clothes, and be back. What is Mary's favorite food? Can I pick up dinner for her? Pizza, or I could get a happy meal if she likes them?"

Vivian leaned over and put her head on my shoulder. "You are so sweet, Jack. She loves cheese pizza. No toppings, just cheese. She would love that."

"Then that's what I will bring back. I'm bringing a pepperoni and mushroom for us," I said as I put my arm around her and squeezed her.

We just sat like that for a while, letting the water smooth out the rough edges of our moods. A pontoon went by as we watched. It had a young family on it, and the kids played with squirt guns. Their dad was driving the boat. Poor guy, he was getting the worst of it. It brought a smile to both of our faces.

My arm had stayed where I had put it while comforting her. I continued to stroke her arm. She seemed to like it. I was enjoying the contact as well, maybe too much. Given the circumstances, I thought it was time to get up and head out. I heard Mary on the monitor just before I was ready to move. So did Vivian. She jumped up to comfort Mary.

I said, "I am heading out. I will be back within two hours." It wasn't a long drive, but the afternoon traffic around Stillwater is terrible in the summer.

"Thank you so much, Jack." She smiled at me as she rushed to Mary.

*****

I was right. Traffic was miserable. By the time I reached my house, I had gone through almost an hour of my time. I threw a change of underwear, socks, and a fresh T-shirt into my gym bag and headed back out. I wore a button-down shirt for my meeting at the Sheriff's Office today, but I usually wear a T-shirt.

Ms. Adeline was on her front porch when I came back out.

"You're working out late today, aren't you, Jackie?"

89

"Hi, Ms. Adeline. I am spending the night at Judge Lord's house to help with her niece in the morning till her housekeeper comes. I promised to bring dinner back, and traffic is a bear, so I have to run."

"That's nice of you, Jackie," she said with a twinkle in her eye. "You have fun."

"You have my number if anything comes up. See you tomorrow," I said as I threw my bag into the back of the Jeep.

On the way back, I called Carlo's Pizza on the north end of town and placed an order. I took the long way around town on the western side. It was usually a longer route, but I figured I could save about twenty minutes during rush hour. I pulled through the gate with two minutes to spare, with dinner on the seat beside me. As I turned into the driveway, I saw Vivian, Mary, and the cat walking along the pathway toward the backyard. I walked around the house with the pizzas balancing on my left arm and the salad in my right hand. I called out as I came around the corner, "Anyone for pizza?"

Mary looked up with a big smile, then saw me, and jumped up to hide behind Vivian, with Tabby on her heels. Vivian smiled at me and turned to coax Mary around to her lap. Gathering her in her arms, she struggled to stand up and began walking toward me. Tabby walked right beside her, looking up at Mary all the way. Mary was hiding her face in Vivian's neck.

"Mary, Jack brought you your very own cheese pizza for dinner. Shall we eat on the terrace?" She spoke while walking toward the steps to the terrace, just off the kitchen, so I turned to meet her halfway there.

As we arrived at the terrace, I said, "I will put these down and go into the kitchen to get plates and silverware." Mary put her head up.

Vivian said, "Setting the table is something she enjoys doing. Why don't I get the things from the kitchen with Mary? You sit and relax. What would you like to drink?"

"I would love a beer if you have one. And bring bowls too. I brought an antipasto salad too."

"Perfect! Thanks," she said as she carried Mary into the kitchen. I stood beside the door to open it as they came back out so I could watch them in the kitchen. The first thing Vivian did was fill a bowl with cat food and hand it to Mary. Mary walked over to the cat's water dish and set the bowl down right next to the water. Mary gave Tabby a long pat before moving back to Vivian. As long as I was on the other side of the door, Mary was fine being down. It seemed she didn't remember our last time together, or her experience of this afternoon had put her off men. I wasn't sure.

Mary began to set the table. She was very intent on her chore. She opened the drawer and got out forks and spoons. I guess she isn't allowed to get the knives. I didn't know what we would do with the spoons, but watching her was entertaining. I could tell she was watching Vivian grab plates and bowls. Maybe so she would know how many of each she needed. She even put one fork and spoon back in the drawer. *Smart*, I thought.

Vivian had the plates and the napkins, Mary had the utensils, and they were heading back to the door. I opened it, and Vivian came out first. When Mary paused, Vivian said, "Come on, Mary, we have to set the table." Mary rushed through the door to her aunt and helped to set the table outside. She placed one fork and one spoon on the napkin as Vivian put the napkin down. "Jack, could you grab the beverages? They are right there on the counter."

Nodding, I went in and got two beers and what looked like one glass of water. Tabby was at the door, waiting to go out, shaking my head at this supernatural bond between cat and kid. I have never seen it before. As I set the beverages on the table, staying on the opposite side from Vivian and Mary, I whispered in Vivian's ear, "She only gets water?"

"She likes water, don't you, Mary?" Nodding yes, Mary took her glass and almost emptied the entire glass.

Dinner was delightful. Vivian was right. Mary loves cheese pizza. She ate almost the entire small pizza on her own. After dinner, we played ball out in the yard for a while, and it appeared that since I wasn't that close to her, Mary was fine having me around. She even thought it was funny to throw the ball a long way from me so I would have to run to save it from going into the river. She laughed right out loud. Tabby sat on the sidelines watching over Mary.

Eventually Mary was tired of the ball game and lay down on the grass, where Tabby immediately pounced on her, and they began to roll around playing with each other. Pretty soon, though, it was time to call it a night, and Aunt Vivian took Mary upstairs to take a bath and read a book before bed.

After I heard Vivian going back into Mary's room, I gave them a few minutes to get Mary into her pajamas, then I tiptoed down the hall and stood in the doorway. Mary had climbed into bed with a book in her little hand, her trusty guardian cat by her side. She was ready to hand the book to Vivian when she noticed me in the doorway. She sat there and looked at me. So did Vivian. Neither of us moved while we waited for Mary's next move. Then suddenly, I could see on her little face that she had made a decision. She stretched both arms out, holding the book between them.

"Do you want me to read your book to you, Mary?" I asked in surprise.

She nodded her little head in a very affirmative manner. I walked forward slowly and said, "Can Aunt Vivian stay, too, to hear the book?" Again she nodded her head, so I read the *Good Night Moon* book to her, and I felt like I had passed the most important test of my life. Mary snuggled under her covers as we finished the book, and Vivian leaned down to kiss her. After Vivian's kiss, Mary looked at me and pointed to her cheek.

"Can I give you a kiss good night, too?" I asked quietly. Once again, Mary gave me the go-ahead with a nod. I leaned down to kiss her cheek, thinking that that was one of the most consequential kisses I had ever given.

As we left the room, Vivian turned on Mary's night-light, flipped the switch off the overhead light, and turned on her monitor. I turned back to look at Mary. She already had her eyes closed, and I think she may have been asleep.

I followed Vivian down the hall and around the corner to the family room adjacent to the kitchen. Vivian had walked past the furniture, which looked pretty darn comfortable with its deep seats and rolled arms, to stand looking out over the water. She raised her arms to fold them across her body. At that moment, I felt like an intruder.

Rather than walk up behind her, I chose to sit on the sofa. I was right. It was very comfortable. I raised my arms to the back of the sofa, and while Vivian watched the water, I watched her.

I'm in big trouble. How did I get in so deep, so fast? And what am I going to do about it? It was like my own real-life version of *Lady and the Tramp*. I chuckled a little, and that drew her eye to me.

Turning to face me, but without lowering her arms, she asked me why I was chuckling.

"Wouldn't you like to know," I said. I lowered my right arm and patted the seat beside me. "If you come to sit with me, I may be willing to share my private joke with you."

Lowering her chin to her chest and giving a shy yet provocative smile, she came and sat beside me, and I returned my arm to the back of the couch. Vivian immediately rested her head back on my arm.

God, she is beautiful. I couldn't help myself. I leaned over and kissed the side of her neck. She made a noise—a little like a purr—and I kissed her again. Then I placed the fingers of my left hand against her cheek and turned her head gently my way. She kept her eyes closed. I just left my hand against her cheek, not moving, until she opened her eyes and looked at me.

Very quietly, for her ears alone, I said, "I am going to kiss you, Vivian. Now is the time to say no if you don't want that."

In answer to me, she raised her head so she could lower her lips to mine. Her lips were soft, and so was the kiss, but I couldn't leave it there. It was beyond me to stop what I wanted to happen so badly. I hadn't been with a woman in a long time. I had never been with a woman who made me feel the things that Vivian made me feel. We shifted positions without separating our lips, and lay her on the couch. I lay beside her and deepened the kiss. She opened her mouth, and her tongue dueled with mine.

My hands were in her hair, and hers were on the back of my jeans, holding me tightly. My hands ran down the entire length of her hair till my hands ran out of hair and continued down her back. Still, the kiss continued. I didn't want to ever stop. I have never been this turned on, I thought. With a simple kiss. What am I doing? Finally I lifted my lips from hers and just looked down at her. Her eyes had closed again, and there was a pleased smile on her lips that looked very well kissed.

"Jack, why did you stop?" Lifting her hands, she tried to pull my head back to hers.

"Vivian, I don't want to stop kissing you ever. God, I didn't mean to say that exactly," I said when her eyebrows lifted. "Hell, Vivian, I am a fifty-one-year-old man who feels like I am making out with the best thing that has ever happened to me. And by the way, this is one fine make-out sofa. But I need to know that we are on the same page." Lifting myself up and allowing her to get out from under me but not sit up, I looked at her and took a leap of faith.

"Vivian, remember you wanted to know what I was laughing at?" At her nod, I continued, "Okay, here is why I was laughing. I thought I was in the middle of my version of *The Lady and the Tramp*. I mean, look at you. Look at me. The beautiful widow. A professional success. Well respected in legal circles and a member of the elite society of the St. Croix Valley. And to top it off, wealthy as hell.

"Now we come to the tramp—me. A burned-out cop, probably struggling with PTSD, lives in a duplex with an older lady as a neighbor. She is the closest thing I have to family besides Scott McCloud. They are about the only people I have talked to in the last two months. I don't even travel in cop circles anymore, let alone high society. Don't you think everyone would be looking at you and wondering if you have lost your mind or thinking I am taking advantage of you?"

"Jack, I could care less what people think of me. If you think I could be taken advantage of, you don't know me. I have been widowed for three years since I was forty-four years old. I haven't been interested in a man since my husband died. We were a power couple. That is what we both wanted when we married. We had a plan for our life, and it was coming together. Then he died. I went numb.

"I don't know what I would have done if it hadn't been for Amanda and Mary. They gave me a focus. I haven't missed having a man in my life. I'm not sure I thought it would ever happen again. I don't know," she said, rubbing her hand over her forehead and pushing her hair back from her face. "But, Jack, when trouble came, and

I started feeling afraid in my own house, you were the only person I thought to call. I knew I could count on you. I knew you would be there for me. I don't know what that means. I never gave it a thought beyond 'Jack will help.' And, of course, you are. Maybe I knew this would happen all along, I don't know. But I do know that you are not washed up. You're strong and confident, you're compassionate, and you're not afraid to take control when needed or step back when it isn't. I think that is the definition of a hot, sexy man, and I am so glad that we have found each other. I am excited to see where this is going. Are you?"

"Vivian, you have made me want someone in my life. I don't think I have ever wanted that before. Not since my parents died. I suddenly have all these feelings for you and that little girl upstairs. I am like a kid looking through the window at a treat just out of reach."

"So reach for it, Jack. Take a chance." She reached up and pulled my head toward her for another kiss.

CHAPTER 11

"Good morning, Jack," Vivian greeted me as I came out of the hall from the guest room. She was ready for the day, in a black suit with the skirt just skimming her knees. *Man, Vivian has nice legs*, I thought to myself. She hadn't put her shoes on yet, so I had the chance to enjoy her bare feet and painted toenails too. Her hair was in her usual twist at the back of her head. She put the cup in her hand down and gave me a hug and a kiss that hinted at the promise of last night. "Can I make you a coffee?"

"Yes, please," I said with a grumble. "I don't think I can figure out that espresso machine. What is wrong with a Mr. Coffee?"

"Oh, you will see. Once you taste the magic this machine can do, you will never go back to Mr. Coffee. You like your coffee strong, without additives, right?"

"Right, black works for me."

Fiddling with her knobs and switches on the machine, I heard coffee filling a cup. She handed me a mug of coffee that smelled like heaven. I groaned after the first sip. She was right. Mr. Coffee and I would be splitting up soon.

Vivian smiled at my reaction to the coffee and said, "Jack, can I show you what is important in my life?" I raised my eyebrow in question as I took another sip of coffee. She motioned me to follow her, and we quickly walked down the hall to Mary's bedroom. We stopped outside the door, Vivian raised her forefinger to her lips to ensure I would be quiet, and she slowly opened the door. With my arm around Vivian's waist, I peered into the room. Vivian pointed and whispered, "Mary is the little girl I never had. I love her like she is my own." We watched her sleeping with Tabby snuggling alongside her. Mary's small delicate hand dangled over Tabby's orange back, which I imagined they both enjoyed. Clearly Mary and Tabby were best friends.

Quietly closing the door, we walked back to the breakfast room and enjoyed the light conversation and plans for the day.

During my second cup of coffee with a butter cookie, I heard little footsteps just before Mary came into view, followed closely by Tabby. The smile on her face disappeared when she saw me at the table with Vivian. Vivian put her arms out for the little girl and said, "Honey, you remember playing ball with Jack yesterday? Good morning to you." Lifting the little girl into her lap, she gave her a hug and a butter cookie. Tabby walked by the table and leaped effortlessly to her bird's-eye perch on a custom-fit cushion on the windowsill.

"Mary," I said, leaning toward her across the table, "you have a very pretty orange kitty." Mary looked toward the window and Tabby and went back to her cookie.

Suddenly a couple of hours with this little girl sounded terrifying. I looked up from Mary to Vivian's face. She was giving me a wide-eyed look. So knowing that Mary liked to feed the fish from the dock, I said, "Mary, Auntie Vivian has to go to work soon." Her little head snapped back, and she looked up at Vivian. Before she could respond, I continued, "Aunt Vivian says you like to feed fish from the dock." *Good*, I thought, *I have her attention again*. "I was wondering if you could take me to the dock while we wait for Madel and show me how to feed the fish. I have never done that before."

She just looked at me for a long time. Then she looked up at Vivian. "Would you like to show Jack how to feed the fish, honey?" Vivian asked.

Mary had to think about that for a bit. Then she nodded yes.

"Oh good," Vivian said. "Let's go get some clothes on. Then you can share some Lucky Charms with Jack, then go down and feed the fish."

Mary scrambled down off Vivian's lap and headed for her room, with Tabby right behind her.

"Are you sure that Tabby isn't part golden retriever? She sure acts like one. I've never seen a cat like that before."

"She is amazing, isn't she? She was my cat before Mary came along. Now when Mary is around, I am invisible. Here is the Lucky Charms." She smiled at the face I made. "It is Mary's favorite. The bowls are in that cupboard," she said over her shoulder as she headed down the hall after Mary.

When they returned, Mary was in a cute little plaything. I don't know what it is called, but she looked adorable, her hair pulled back in a ponytail. Mary scrambled up to the table. I reached over and poured a little milk into her cereal, then mine. Just as I sat down, Vivian came into the room, hopping on one foot as she put on her other shoe. Sedate-looking black heels. "Well, you two, I have to get going. Judges can't be late for work. Madel will be here around eleven. Mary, you take good care of Jack, okay, honey?" She leaned down for a milky kiss. Mary looked at me and nodded. Vivian came around the table and kissed me too. "You be good now, Jack. Mary is in charge," she said with a little twinkle in her eye just for me.

"Oh, don't I know it. Have a good day. We will talk later." She gave us both a wave and headed for the door. Minutes later, I heard the gate beep as it opened.

Mary was an excellent eater. First, the pizza last night, and she had two bowls of cereal this morning. I could barely finish one. When she finished eating, she took her bowl over to the counter by the sink and lifted it onto the counter. She came back for mine. She looked at what was left in the bowl. She gave me a little frown, but she took it anyway and put it beside her own.

Then she moved to the cupboard nearest the sliding glass door and pointed to the overhead cabinet. I got up from the table and opened the cupboard. There, right inside the door, was a big ziplock bag full of bread pieces.

"Is this what we feed the fish?" I asked the little girl. She nodded at me when I took it down. Then she went over to Tabby's bowl, picked it up, returned, and handed it to me. "Honey, I don't know where Aunt Vivian keeps Tabby's food." Silently she went to another cupboard and took out a small can of cat food. She brought it back and handed it to me. *Boy, she really says a lot without ever saying a word*, I thought to myself. Peeling back the top of the cat food, I scraped it into the bowl and handed it back to Mary.

She walked over to the cat and showed her the bowl. The cat jumped down and followed Mary back to the water dish, and Mary put her food down and stood watching Tabby eat.

"Mary, you are very grown-up. You have lots of jobs around the house, don't you?"

Mary beamed at me from across the room. She looked quite proud of herself as she nodded.

When the food was all gone, and Tabby began to wash, Mary went to the table where she had left the bread bag and went to the door. She turned back and looked at me.

"Is it time to go feed the fish?" I asked her. At her nod, I opened the door, let Mary and Tabby out, then closed the door. I was shocked when Mary took my hand and began walking down the steps toward the dock. I guess she remembered she had accepted me last night after she had woken up a bit.

We walked down toward the dock, stopping at the beach house. Mary opened the door and went inside. I went as far as the door to see what she was doing. Beside the door were some hooks. She took a little pink PFD off the hook and put it on. She even zipped the zipper herself. She turned back and looked at me, then went further down and picked out a blue PFD. Wouldn't you know, she picked the right size, too? Retaking my hand, we left the boat house, closed the door behind us, and walked down to the swim platform at the end of the dock. Mary got down on her tummy. I couldn't help laughing out loud as the cat mimicked her position. She set her bread bag down on the dock, unzipped the top, took out her first piece of bread, and held it out just into the water. She looked up at me, and I sat down on the opposite side that the cat was on and held the bread bag.

"Okay, let's see some fish."

It was one of the most enjoyable mornings I could remember. I didn't realize how much pleasure an adult could have just watching a child enjoy themselves. The cat was a hoot too. As a fish would come up to nibble on Mary's piece of bread, the cat would lean down as far as she could without getting wet to look at the fish.

The funny thing was she didn't scare the fish away! The fish must have been used to the cat. I was starting to get a little concerned as we were coming to the end of the bread. What was I going to do with Mary then? There is a god of helpless men, though. I heard Madel calling from the house with one piece of bread left.

Mary jumped up, ran to the terrace stairs, and threw herself into Madel's arms. Clearly these two have a bond. When I caught up with her, I greeted Madel, then leaned down to Mary and said, "I am going to get going now, Mary. I will bring your PFD back down to the beach house with mine. Okay? Can I come back and draw some pictures together or play with those Magna-Tiles and build something? Would that be okay?"

Mary gave me an enthusiastic nod and a big hug. Then she took her PFD off, handed it to me, ran into the house, and disappeared.

"Mr. Jack, little Mary likes you. That is good. She doesn't like men. Ms. Vivian, she calls to ask me to come early to help you."

"It was touch and go last night, but I may have won her over. I don't know the plans, but I will be back soon. I'm trying to win them both over, and I don't want to let them forget what a nice guy I am," I said, chuckling. Madel laughed as well.

"I will grab my bag out of the guest room and head out. See you later, Madel." Running down to the guest room, I grabbed my bag and headed for my Jeep. I had a tuxedo to pick up, and after last night, this gala thing didn't sound as bad as it had before.

CHAPTER 12

Brushing aside my frustration with Commander Jacobson and that waste of a meeting, I deliberately started to look toward the evening with Vivian. I can't remember ever looking forward to a date quite so much. I have never been to such an elegant event, and I am worried I will do something stupid and look like a fool. But even that concern doesn't dampen my enthusiasm.

With the help of LaVonne, I think I've done everything possible to clean up this retired cop's chassis for the Twin Cities' social event of the month—the Breast Cancer Awareness Gala.

LaVonne said that she would not be in attendance; although the county attorney has plans to attend himself. My conversation with LaVonne was interesting, as her suspicions about my developing relationship with Vivian were confirmed. We are the number 1 topic on the county gossip line. I think she is suspicious that it may be becoming rather serious.

After work, LaVonne had even commented that she had never seen me wear anything but George Strait jeans and deck shoes. She continued that she was a little jealous that she wouldn't see me in my tux. She said she could picture it and thought I would look fantastic.

I had reminded her that she was the one that had put an end to our dating relationship. She had said that she had no plans for marriage and thought I was looking for more permanence in our relationship than she was. At that comment, she asked how serious I was about Vivian. I blew the question off and continued to ask her about protocol at a fancy gala. She filled me in, and I told her I had decided on the black jacket instead of the summer white. The truth is, I was afraid I would spill something on myself. Telling her that I would send her a picture, I headed home.

Proudly driving my freshly detailed Jeep and heading to Vivian's, I admit I was a little fired up. On the other hand, there was a fluttering in my stomach that I knew was nerves. I sure don't want to embarrass Vivian, or myself, with some dumb off-the-cuff comment. But I must say, my Jeep has never looked so sharp.

Arriving at the gate to Vivian's, I paused at the entrance. I looked at our accomplishments, which made Vivian's home comfortable and safe, except for the riverfront access. CSO Reed is continuing to explore more options for that specific property area.

I also did a quick inventory of my appearance. I hope that Vivian will approve of the black tuxedo and white shirt with all the details of pink. Including my tie, the pocket square, and even my socks. I thought that was a nice touch.

As the gate opened and while proceeding to the garage area, I noticed Vivian's black Bimmer was parked in the circle by the front door. I wondered, *What's that about?*

Getting out of the car and glancing at the Bimmer, I heard the front door open, and I was stunned, frozen in place. Suddenly I thought, *Was I supposed to have a corsage?* I felt like an eighteen-year-old going to his first prom.

"You look beautiful," I said, still standing on the step. Vivian smiled at me and held up the keys to the BMW. I lifted my eyebrow at her in the way of a question.

"How about you drive my car tonight?" she suggested in a slightly pleading tone.

"What? My Jeep isn't elegant enough for a judge's arrival? Is there going to be a red carpet or something?"

Vivian just shrugged and continued to hold the keys out with a pleading look in her eyes.

I held my hand out, and she dropped the keys into my palm, but rather than taking her hand and leading her to the car, I put both hands—one holding the keys—on her shoulders, which were temptingly bare. "I think I need a little compensation for my dissed car." Drawing her forward, I placed my lips gently on hers. I intended the kiss to be a little playful, but instead, sparks flew, and I was surprised at how quickly it heated up.

Vivian reached forward to put her hands on either side of my waist and tilted her head just a little to increase the depth of the kiss. "Wow!" I whispered as I raised my head.

"Yeah, wow," she repeated as she rested her forehead briefly on my chest. I made small circles on her shoulders and began to move lower down her arms, when suddenly she jumped back, flustered, and said in a breathy, unsteady voice, "I think we better go. We wouldn't want to miss the boat."

I looked at her face for just a moment. I didn't just imagine her reaction to that kiss, did I? I know I didn't, but she wouldn't look at me. She busied herself, locking the door. So, deciding to keep it light, I said, "No, sure wouldn't want to miss the boat. Your upgraded wheels await, Your Honor." And with a slight bow and a sweep of my arm, I pointed toward the black Bimmer sparkling in the evening sun.

Pulling slowly away from Vivian's home had a different view from the driver's seat of a Bimmer. It felt surreal, a real beauty-and-the-police moment. I have to admit that I was thoroughly enjoying myself. During the short drive to the St. Croix Boats in Stillwater, I occasionally glanced toward Vivian. She is gorgeous, this evening in particular. Her silky pink or rose gown would be closer to the color. The material fell from just below her shoulders and continued in a straight column down to her ankles, clinging in all the right places. She wore a beautiful pounded gold necklace that looked a little primitive yet somehow made the perfect statement with the gown.

I glanced down at her feet as Vivian crossed her legs and sat in her car's passenger seat. Her pink-painted nails matched her dress's color and peeked out of her gold sandals. I said a silent thank you that her heels were only a couple of inches high. Raising my eyes to her profile the next time I took my eyes off the road, I saw the curve of her neck, with her earrings echoing the feel of the necklace. The way she had her hair in some kind of a twist at the back of her head made her neck look beautiful. She looked regal. Pulling my eyes back to the road, I was surprised how affected I was by her beauty. *She is always beautiful*, I thought to myself. *What is different tonight?*

I suddenly noticed how preoccupied she was, and it roused my curiosity. "Everything all right, Vivian?"

Glancing over at me with a smile, she replied, "Jack, it is very much all right. I am just giving some thought to this evening's program. I am the keynote speaker."

"I'm looking forward to it, but I have never known you to be at a loss for words. You will do great."

"Thanks, Jack. It's not only the keynote speech, it's somewhat more complicated, and I hope you understand."

Thinking she thought I wouldn't understand her speech, I replied, "You can count on me, Vivian. If I don't understand it, I will make sure I look like I do. I'll clap in all the right places."

"Jack," she said with a chuckle but was unable to complete her thought as we had arrived at the boat and were approaching the front of the valet line. I surmised she was thinking about this evening putting any doubt of our relationship to an end, and she didn't know if she was ready for that. I thought, *No time like the present.*

Walking around the car and opening her door, I took her hand as we walked toward the dock. Stepping carefully onto the pier, up the boarding gangway and through the entrance of the boat, both of us had smiles on our faces. All eyes turned to us as we walked deeper into the room, and the crowd grew with each second that passed.

I leaned down and whispered in her ear, "Have I told you how beautiful you look?"

Turning toward me, she smiled and replied, "Yes, several times, Jack, with one *striking* thrown in there."

The crowd began to move toward her, and at the last minute I had alone with her, I whispered in her ear, "Please don't let me embarrass you tonight." She smiled up at me, and the crowds arrived.

"Welcome aboard, Judge Lord," an older somewhat-portly man in a pink tuxedo said as he handed us a flute of pink champagne.

We were escorted to our table on the *Majestic Lady*, on the second-level dining deck. The *Majestic Lady* is a yacht beyond all expectations. She has four levels: the sundeck, dining level, piano lounge, and entertainment deck. The piano lounge deck sounded like my favorite spot, and I hoped we could spend some time on it. I couldn't stop smiling. I kept thinking of that kiss and hoping there would be more of the same later in the evening. "Patience, Jack, old boy, patience," I said to myself.

There were a lot of pink gowns. I thought Vivian's was the best, hands down. I also noted several pink tuxedos. God, how did men let their wives talk them into that? One guy was tall and had a long neck, and I was glad I didn't recognize him. I would always think of him in that pink tux if I knew him. Always. God, he looked like a flamingo. No cause was worth humiliating yourself like that. I had even questioned the pink tie and pocket square, but LaVonne said they were a must, so I also threw in the pink socks. You couldn't see them yet, but I bet I was the only one with them. I am glad that I got the tie and pocket square. I would have looked really out of place without them.

I was feeling pretty good about the evening now. I even spotted a few people that I knew from the county. I would have no trouble finding conversation. The pink champagne was flowing, and almost everyone was carrying a glass. We began to make our way around the room. It seemed like Vivian knew virtually everyone here, and I recognized only a handful.

The *Majestic Lady* was an elegant vessel, a unique location for a first public date with Vivian.

We separated while talking with friends, and I managed to be working on my third glass of pink champagne. From a distance, I could see her talking with the County Attorney and admired her elegance and grace. These were my fanciful thoughts, but I swear she almost cast a glow in the room. I knew right then I was in love with her.

As though she could read my thoughts from across the room, she turned her head in my direction and gave me a wink. That moment—just that one moment of silent communication—made me relax in this room full of influential and powerful people. Or maybe it was the champagne that made me feel ten feet tall. I knew then that Vivian was in love with me too.

My thoughts of Vivian were interrupted by an announcement instructing guests to be seated for dinner, and I joined Vivian at our table. I pulled the chair out for her, and smiling at me, she was seated. After I had sat beside her, she leaned toward me slightly and said, "Have I told you how handsome you look? I love the delicious pink trimmings. The socks are an excellent touch." She responded to my questioning look, "I saw them peeking out when you were driving."

Let the dinner begin, I thought. The waitstaff delivered the first course: salad, and a choice of different types of bread, accompanied by a wine that complimented the salad, followed by the main entrée. We had both chosen a garlic-crusted chicken breast, some fancy potatoes, and some delicious-looking green beans. The waitstaff brought wine, which was paired with the various dinner entrées.

I was enjoying the evening. It surprised me. I thought I would feel like a fish out of water, but spending a beautiful evening on my favorite body of water with this fantastic woman, well, some things are worth waiting for, I guess. I felt that life going forward would only get better for us.

After the carrot cake and coffee, the Master of Ceremonies was at the podium, and the program began. First order of business— detailing contribution sources during the past year and where the breast cancer funds collected would be donated. Then some awards were presented to special guests of the evening. Frankly it wasn't very interesting. Good thing the carrot cake and coffee were good. Finally I heard the Honorable Judge Vivian Lord's introduction. I squeezed her hand under the table just before she rose.

As she walked to the podium, I thought to myself, *Jack, that is one beautiful girlfriend you have.*

Vivian was a beautiful articulate speaker. A talent honed in law school. However, she did appear to display some uneasiness a few minutes into her speech. At the end of one sentence, thanking the board and the honored guests, she took a deep breath as she began the body of her remarks.

She announced that she was a survivor of breast cancer and was just over one year cancer-free. After that big announcement and after the crowd's murmurs had died down, she continued and looked more confident. But I felt like the floor had opened up under me. Did she say she had breast cancer? She survived breast cancer?

I just kept repeating those phrases in my head. I was looking at her, but I couldn't see her through the tears I struggled to keep from falling down my face. I absently took out my pocket square to palm in my hand and dab at the corners of my eyes. I found out a pocket square is not intended to be functional. The first clue is the plastic you tuck into your pocket, but it was easy to conceal in my hand. I was desperate. I felt like every eye in the place was focused on me rather than Vivian. Jack, sit up straight and look at her like she didn't just drop a bomb onto your lap. Look at her like she is the best thing in your life, and you love her.

Vivian's speech had moved into the closing comments as my ears began to work again. I had missed most of the speech.

As people stood for a supportive standing ovation, I couldn't have been more proud of Vivian. Walking back to our table, I held her chair as she sat down. She leaned over toward me and whispered in my ear, "You did better than I thought you would. I'm sorry I didn't tell you sooner. I didn't know how."

I responded, also in a whisper, "I love you. I will always love you. I hope you know that."

The MC announced where the activities would be occurring for the evening. All of the decks would be open for the guest's pleasure. The upper deck provided a beautiful view of the scenic river valley. You will find it is a bit chilly. The entertainment deck would provide an opportunity for dancing with a full band. The piano lounge was also available for conversation.

"The cruise will take us south on the river toward Afton, then return to Stillwater. On behalf of our host, the Andersen family, please enjoy yourselves on the *Majestic Lady*."

I suggested we go to the upper deck. I needed some fresh air. As we exited the banquet room, I noticed the elevator. This boat had everything.

By mutual agreement, we chose a secluded location next to the handrail at the stern. It seems as though most people had gone to the third level for dancing. Having my arm around Vivian, we enjoyed the ambiance of the evening, with the stars just coming out and the lights from the stately homes along the river. I struggled to pull together something supportive to say, as we stood side by side, watching the river.

Vivian said, "Is it going to make a difference, Jack, my cancer? I wanted to tell you. I just never felt the time was right, and then it was today. I didn't mean to blindside you."

Taking her by the shoulders, I turned her to face me. I tilted her face to mine and said, "Vivian, I have never been so grateful for anything in my life that you could stand up there tonight as a survivor."

I gently touched her lips with mine, and resting my forehead on hers for a moment, I said, "Tonight is a night for dancing. Will you dance with me?" She gave me a thousand-watt smile. I took her hand, and we walked toward the music.

We danced to fast dances, slow dances, and even polkas as time flew by. I could see the cruise was concluding as the aerial lift bridge was now in view. It looked like the cruise would be disembarking soon. It would take some time. The people were slowly making their way down to the lower decks. I suggested that we go down and check out the piano lounge.

We found the lounge empty, and I asked Vivian to sit on the white bench in front of the large white Steinway grand piano. Without sheet music, I began to play some of my favorite music. Vivian looked surprised and said, "What other talents do you have that I don't know about, Detective?"

"That question sounds probative, Your Honor. Why don't you face the music and enjoy it?"

Music had always been a safe harbor for me. An outlet for emotions that I kept to myself. A way to unwind from the tensions and frustrations of a workday. I had always enjoyed playing. I think my playing without sheet music might be affected by alcohol—and not in a good way—but sharing it with Vivian was beyond exceptional, and we were enjoying ourselves.

Vivian would ask me to play a song, and I would give it a try, and in between the songs, we laughed, hugged, and enjoyed an occasional wet kiss, then we would laugh again.

We didn't notice that the background noise had disappeared some time ago until Vivian elbowed me with a disarming smile and said, "I think we may be in trouble, Jack." Vivian giggled. I turned to see a man entering the lounge, which brought more laughter, this time mine. I thought she saw a past shared defendant of ours because she suddenly looked so serious.

The man walked up to the piano and said, "You kids look cozy. Having fun?"

"Mr. Andersen! This is—"

Mr. Andersen interrupted me and said, "Jack, I know who Judge Lord is." He offered his hand to both of us. "Jack, the cleaning crew will be here in an hour. You kids enjoy and help yourself to a nightcap. My treat." With a backward wave, he continued walking toward the door and final inspection of his yacht.

That only brought more laughter and kissing. We felt like kids who got caught necking under the gymnasium bleachers after a basketball game. It was the most memorable event of my life. I played one more song, then turned to give Vivian a long delicious kiss. We didn't need any more music. This kiss was between two people who had fallen in love. Our hearts were beating in tandem. I could feel both of them as I held her against me. Life was perfect.

Right here on the bench of a Steinway piano, on the yacht, The *Majestic Lady*.

CHAPTER 13

A single ray of sun snuck through the blinds and pierced my eye-lids as the sun appeared over the horizon. I began to roll over, but my left arm was held down. I opened my eyes a crack, and last night flooded back into my mind, and I didn't want to roll over anymore.

Vivian. She was beautiful even in her sleep. All the gorgeous hair was falling over her shoulder, partially hiding her face from me. I wanted to reach out, run my fingers through it, and move it out of her face, but I didn't want to wake her up, so I rolled back toward her and soaked her in.

My magic, my miracle. How does someone get to be my age without feeling this incredible connection with another person? The total joy I felt just looking at her was the perfect way to start the day. I had seen love between two people before. I could recognize the connection. I just never knew what it felt like before.

Her eyelids twitched a little, a slow smile came to her lips, and her eyes opened. It was like watching a beautiful sunrise. She just looked at me with that smile on her face. I just stared back. Vivian was the one to break the silence finally.

"Jack, do you think having two great loves in one life is possible?"

I smiled then and said, "For my sake, I sure hope so."

Continuing to smile, she reached over and caressed my face. "It was different from what I feel for you. When we met and fell in love, Charles and I were young and eager. We had a common goal, and we worked hard to get there. I think that was the bond between us. What I feel for you is different. It makes me feel young, alive, complete, and so darn happy I can hardly stand it."

"I was thinking almost the same thing before you woke up. I have gone my whole life not knowing what love felt like. I've dated, but believe me, not much more than you," I said with a chuckle. "I enjoyed some female company, but what I feel for you is a miracle. You're my miracle."

She smiled at me and then rolled over on her back, scooping her hair away, raising her arms over her head, and stretching. "I feel like coffee. Do you feel like coffee?"

"I thought you would never ask."

"Jack, I don't even have a robe down here."

"Doesn't seem like a problem to me." Smiling at her. "But if you must, you can use my shirt. Please don't lose it. I have to return it by tomorrow." Reaching the floor, I snagged the shirt I had worn last night and handed it to her. She took it from my hand, leaned over, and kissed me quickly.

"I'll meet you in the kitchen." And she fled the room.

Going into the bathroom, I took care of the basics and pulled on my tuxedo pants. I didn't have any clothes here at all. At least Vivian could run up and get her robe. I should buy this tux. It sure brought me luck.

It was still early, so we had plenty of time to talk over coffee and toast. We talked about magic from the night before, her speech, and the impromptu piano recital. We refilled our coffee cups and talked more. She reached out and wiped a crumb from my lip. I placed a stray piece of hair behind her ear. Time passed. We didn't care until Vivian happened to look at the clock.

"Oh my god, I will be late if I don't leave in the next half-hour. I'm sorry, Jack. I love you."

"No worries. Get going. I'll see you tonight."

*****

I pulled into my driveway, getting out of the Jeep; I saw Ms. Adeline rocking on the porch and gave her a wave. As I climbed the steps, she greeted me with, "I assume that the evening was a success, based on the big smile on your face and the fact it looks like you slept in that tuxedo." My smile got even broader as I walked up to her, bent over, and kissed her.

"It was great, but a gentleman doesn't kiss and tell." Going over the rail to my side of the duplex, I let myself in and could still hear Ms. Adeline laughing.

I showered and shaved, then chose what I would wear with a little more thought than I usually spared on my clothes. Had I ever done that for anyone else? I couldn't remember. I laughed as I put a few things in a gym bag. Things I would need if I stayed overnight again. I wasn't going to take anything for granted. I just wanted to be prepared. I would leave the bag in the car. Smiling, I headed through the kitchen, grabbed some snacks, made a thermos of coffee, then continued to the car. Backing down the driveway, I headed south to visit the parents.

The cemetery, located on Point Douglas Drive South in Denmark Township, was a few miles from home before my parents' passing. Point Douglas Cemetery buried its first resident in 1861. It is on a hill that overlooks the Hastings Bridge with a partial view of the Mississippi River, where my dad introduced me to fishing as a kid.

Point Douglas Cemetery is very small, so it doesn't take long to reach the grave site. The gentleman who cared for the cemetery grounds was meticulous in its maintenance. The lawn was always watered and beautiful. He also watered the plants on the graves. Sadly many of the graves were unadorned.

Some people think it is weird that I sit beside them and tell them about my life. I find it comforting.

During more stressful times in child abuse investigations, I would have coworkers suggest daily meditation or gardening. I placed a planter with flowers every spring at their grave, so my parents' final resting place is my reflection/meditation garden. It usually did the job too.

I grabbed the thermos and the cheese and sausage I had thrown in a bag and headed down the path to my parents' grave.

I had begun these trips to their grave as soon as I had wheels and could come alone. Over the years, these visits have become very important to me. I often came just to share my life with them. Talking things through here, where I felt close to them, always brought me peace. But today, I could hardly wait to share what I hope will be my new life.

I had an old tattered boat cushion that I always brought to sit on. Placing it neatly beside the stone, I began. Although I'm not Catholic, I always made the sign of the cross and said a short prayer before sitting down for my one-way conversation.

My excitement overflowed for the new love that Vivian and I were discovering. I told my mom everything about her. I told her about her beauty, her intelligence, and how she took such loving care of her niece. "I wish you could meet her mom. I think she loves me. Dad, she has a beautiful big yacht, but there is even room for my fishing boat at her dock. Did I tell you Vivian is a judge in Washington County? I have testified many times in her court. I always admired her, and we were friendly, but I never saw this coming.

"She has a beautiful home just before you get to the high bridge. I took her niece, Mary, down on the dock to feed the fish. Vivian has a cat, and the cat follows Mary everywhere. Mary lay down on her belly to feed the fish, and the cat lay down on her belly right beside her. It made me laugh. Mary is almost five, but she doesn't talk. At least I have never heard her. It is not hard to tell what she wants. I can tell she is perceptive. She is patient, too, for her age."

My phone vibrated in my pocket. I looked and saw it was Vivian. "Hi, gorgeous. How is your day going?"

"I think people here think that I have lost my mind. I can't stop smiling. Clearly that is not very judge-like."

"I know what you mean. I kissed Ms. Adeline when she asked if I enjoyed myself last night. Good thing I didn't give her a heart attack.

Laughing, Vivian told me to be serious for a minute.

"Why? Is something wrong?"

"No, nothing is wrong, but Mary is staying with me tonight. I want you to come over, but I wanted to tell you we would not be alone if you wanted to stay home."

"Are you kidding? I think that little girl is almost as wonderful as you. I am looking forward to seeing her. We can play outside again."

"Jack, we can't sleep together tonight. Sometimes Mary comes into my room and climbs in with me in the middle of the night.

I paused, just for effect, and then replied, "You better be back in your bed by then, I guess."

"Oh, Jack." She chuckled, then said, "Yes, I'll be right there. Jack, I have to go." Lowering her voice, she whispered, "I love you."

"Ditto," I said, and she hung up. I shook my head and looked back at the grave.

"I had forgotten all about that until just now, Mom. Every time you would tell Dad you loved him, he would say, 'Ditto.' I remember you asked him why he couldn't just say it, and he said, 'Those are private words, just for when we are alone.' Were the words coming from him more special that way?"

I sat there remembering good times when I was young. They must have been excellent parents to a little boy for the man I would become to still feel the love for them that I do. My uncle had done his best with me, but his wife was never into the parenting thing, and when he died, she could hardly wait to ship me back to Stillwater and put me in the care of the county.

My foster homes weren't the horror story you hear about, but it was a business for them; there wasn't the affection I craved. I guess I knew what it felt like and have been looking for it since my folks died. "Mom and Dad, I think I have finally found what I have been looking for my whole life."

I sat there a little longer, eating my cheese and sausage and letting my thoughts go where they would. I spent a little of that time thinking about that serial rapist case. I wish I could work on that one, I thought. Yeah, Jacobson will let me have a piece of that. *Not!*

Not even Jacobson could spoil my mood today. Picking up my trash and thermos in one hand and my boat cushion in the other, I said my goodbyes to my parents and headed back to the car.

Thinking I would drop off my tux on the way up to Vivian's, I stopped by my place to pick it up. Ms. Adeline was weeding and watering the flower boxes. "They look great, Ms. Adeline. I like that long green and white stuff that hangs down."

"Vinca vine. I like that too. It softens the look of the box. What are you doing this evening? I know you will be doing something. You have been coming and going more in the last couple of weeks than you have the whole time I have lived here."

"Aw, Ms. Adeline, I think you miss me."

"Well, there is some truth there, but I am happy that you seem to have broken what has held you here, feeling guilty about something you had no responsibility for."

It hit me right then. I hadn't had a dream last night. "Well, I guess Vivian is good medicine. I am going back up to Judge Lord's house. I may not be home tonight, so don't worry if I'm not here."

"Good for you, Jackie. You have a good time."

"I will grab my tux to return it, then head up to Vivian's. See you later, Ms. A."

I ran in and grabbed the tuxedo bag and the shoes, and headed right back out. I caught Ms. Adeline just heading inside. She waved as I walked down the steps and headed to my car.

Dropping the tux off, I headed toward Arcola Trail. Vivian wouldn't be home yet, so I wanted to look around the neighborhood for a bit. That red peg on the board of the serial rapist case in the task force room was nagging at me.

I parked a distance from Vivian's house and went into the woods. There were many animal trails, most likely paths to the river, but as I walked a little deeper into the woods, I did find what looked like a four-wheeler path, with branches from the trail to the back of several properties. I made a note to myself.

Walking back to the car, I got back in and drove the rest of the way to Vivian's gate, pausing to buzz in rather than surprise Madel when I arrived.

"Yes?" Madel asked.

"It's me, Jack. Can you open the gate for me, Madel?"

"Oh yes, Mr. Jack."

The gate opened, and I drove up the drive, parking in my usual spot. Rather than going through the garage, I walked around the back and up onto the deck. I saw Mary coloring while Madel was busy at the stove. I knocked on the window. I looked at Mary and motioned for her to open the door. She looked at Madel for permission and let me in. She smiled and brought me to look at her drawings.

She was a pretty good artist, and my imagination was excellent, but I looked at the drawing carefully. Pointing at what I thought was a little girl, I asked if that was her. She gave me a million-watt smile as she nodded in the affirmative.

I felt like I had scored points with Mary. She was such a cutie. I wanted her to grow to like me. So I continued to look at her picture. There was a lot of green grass with an orange object on the green and a brown and white object beside it. Just then, Tabby rubbed against my leg to welcome me. I bent down to pet her.

Then I asked Mary, "Is this one Tabby?" As I pointed at the orange object in her drawing. She got so excited, and her little head bobbed so fast that I was afraid she would break her neck.

Okay, one down, one to go, I thought. "So, Mary, is this a friend of Tabby's?" She nodded and threw her arms around my legs. I felt like I had won a gold medal. I bent down to unwind her from my legs and picked her up. "Let's play outside until your aunt gets home, shall we?" Again with a nod, she struggled to get down. I put her down, and she ran out of the room. I looked at Madel, questioning Mary's behavior.

"It's all right, Mr. Jack. She goes to get her baby and goes to the bathroom. That is a rule—potty before going out."

A good rule, I thought.

"Mr. Jack, I am finishing up for today. Since you are here, maybe I will finish and leave early, yes?"

"That's fine with me, Madel. Will you come out and say good-bye to Mary before you leave? If she is okay with it, I am too."

"Yes, Mr. Jack."

Mary, Tabby, and the baby walked back into the room. She walked to the door without a pause, pushed it open, and then looked over at me. I went out the door before her. As I walked out into the yard, I picked up a twig that had fallen from the tree and held it as we walked around the yard, stopping now and then so Mary could examine something that caught her attention—a bug, a bloom, a rock in one of the garden beds. She was a curious little girl.

I finally moved back into the yard and lay down in the grass. Mary came and lay beside me, and Tabby lay between us.

Madel came out to say goodbye to Mary, who got up to hug her and then lay back beside me. Madel gave me a wave, and I gave her a thumbs-up. Mary played with her doll, and the cat and I watched them. At one point, Mary took the stick from my hand and began to tease the cat with it. She dangled it in front of Tabby, then ran around me with Tabby chasing her. She ran round and round until finally, she tipped over half on top of me and half off. The stick was on my other side, so Tabby jumped over me to get it. That made Mary laugh out loud.

It was the first sound I had heard her make. Laughing with her, I caught a movement out of the corner of my eye. Looking up, there she was—my miracle. She was looking at us with such tenderness and love. I smiled back at her and whispered to Mary, "Look who's here."

Mary looked up and saw Vivian. She jumped up and rushed to her. Flinging herself at Vivian with such force, Vivian had to take a couple of steps back to keep from falling. Life felt full right at that moment.

The ordinary evening that every family with small kids enjoyed—dinner, play, bath, book, and bed—was new to me. Each part was remarkable. We left the room and closed the door on a sleeping little girl. We both sighed. We were laughing at the shared sigh.

"Who knew how satisfying putting a little girl to bed could be," I commented.

"You are a natural. I often have a real struggle on my hands when I am doing this alone."

I leaned down to brush a kiss on her neck. We moved together toward the other end of the house. When we reached the steps to the guest bedroom, Vivian continued to move toward the kitchen, and I turned to go down the steps.

"Jack?" Vivian said in a warning tone.

"I promise I will escort you back to your room. You have the monitor. Come on, Vivian." My tone made it clear I was coaxing her. I pulled her toward me and nibbled on her lower lip, watching as her eyes closed. Vivian slowly allowed me to talk her into spending some time with me downstairs. She wrapped her arms around me, kissing my neck and moving toward my mouth.

Her lips detoured to my ear, and she whispered, "Why are we still standing here?"

ive, *love*, and *laugh* are words often seen together. I understand them better lately. I'm going to commit to blending these words in my daily activities, in addition to faith.

I felt invigorated driving to Red Wing, Minnesota, to have lunch with my foster brother, Doug Pratt. Doug and I often joked about being brothers because we were both placed in an emergency foster home in Stillwater. Doug was the closest person that I could relate to as a brother.

It occurred to me that though I often thought of myself as having no family, I had created one for myself. A small but loyal family, with Scott as a father figure, Adeline as a nurturing mother, and Doug, a friend I thought of as a brother. They were all there whenever I needed them. I hope that they felt the same.

The St. Croix River joined the Mississippi in Prescott, Wisconsin, thirty miles north of Red Wing.

The two river towns—Red Wing on the Mississippi and Stillwater on the St. Croix—have a similar history. Stillwater is smaller, with a population of 16,459. Red Wing, a slightly larger population of 17,084, is on the shores of the Mississippi River. The similarities didn't end at the river. The historic buildings in both cities are carefully maintained. They are both tourist attractions with an abundance of antique shops and restaurants. They are both surrounded by large farming communities, making it an appealing drive to both.

Red Wing lays on the banks of the muddy Mississippi, while Stillwater overlooks the blue waters of the National Scenic Waterway, the pristine St. Croix River.

I met Doug at our favorite restaurant, the Red Wing Diner. It was the go-to spot for the locals. Doug was younger than me and slightly taller, but we had both started with blue eyes and blonde hair. Mine was considerably grayer than Doug's, but I felt he would catch up in a few years. No one would have given it a thought if we had introduced the other as a brother.

And except for blood, we indeed had a family history. Fate had brought us together in a Stillwater foster home. Doug arrived first and volunteered to show me the ropes around Stillwater. We became instant best friends.

Arriving on time, at eleven thirty, for lunch was important. Ten minutes late, and I would be picking up the tab. Additionally bringing a cell phone to lunch would be a violation that would have the bill handed to you. Today I was within the parameters of our agreement.

I was waiting as Doug approached the table. We usually connected monthly for lunch to catch up on our activities. After a handshake and quick hug, we sat across from each other. Our waitress had already placed the pot of coffee on the table. I poured us each a cup as Doug started the conversation by asking how retirement was going.

"Funny you should ask." I began to tell him all about Vivian. We had eaten our lunch, and our waitress had cleared the table before I ran out of things to say to him about the last month.

"Jack, it sounds like you struck gold. I can't wait to meet her, but I may lose my job if I don't get back to work soon."

Like me, Doug was a deputy sheriff. Only he held that position in Goodhue County. He had investigated child abuse for a time. We usually talked shop over lunch, but Vivian was the topic of today's lunch.

"Doug, I'm sorry I monopolized the entire conversation."

"Hey, are you kidding? I have never heard you so excited about a woman before. I'm happy for you, brother. Now don't screw it up. Okay?"

I picked up the tab and told him it was the least I could do, and we walked to the cars together. Doug parked his unmarked white Dodge Charger next to the Jeep. We hugged each other.

Doug said, "See you next month. I will look forward to hearing more about your hot romance."

Climbing into the Jeep, I started back toward Stillwater, taking my time and enjoying the scenery. Just as I picked up speed after leaving the city proper, I received a text from Anne Reed. I was passing Bay Point Park, so I turned into the parking lot to read the text.

I saw then that I had multiple texts. Anne's text read: *Mary is missing from Judge Lord's home. WCSO notified. Judge Lord needs a call.*

I was an hour away from Vivian's. What the hell was going on?

As I called Vivian, I accelerated out of the parking lot. "Thank God, Jack," Vivian answered. I could hear the panic in her voice that she was trying so hard to control. "I canceled court and came back home. Madel put an emergency call into my chambers. She said Mary's backpack was found in the yard by the river, but there was no sign of her. Amanda wasn't supposed to drop her off until eleven. She must have dropped her off early, and no one was home." She lost it after that and began sobbing.

"Vivian, I am on my way. I'm in Red Wing, but I will be there as fast as possible."

"Jack, what if—"

I interrupted her before she could continue with that train of thought. "Vivian, don't go there. I am on my way, honey. You have to hang on for me a little longer. Panicking won't help."

"God, Jack, hurry, I need you."

I could still hear the tears in her voice, but she wasn't reaching for that panic button. "I'll be there. Just hang in there a little longer."

I was driving as fast as I could, flexing my fingers around the steering wheel and running what-ifs through my head, ignoring the advice I had just given Vivian.

Damn if that silent funny little girl hadn't wiggled her way into my heart. Chill, Jack, Vivian, and Mary need your help. Panicking won't help anybody. It's your cop brain you need to channel, not your newfound family side.

Breathing deeply, I began to run possible scenarios through my mind. More often than not, children were located walking away from home or hiding in a basement closet, sound asleep. They will find her before I get there. I'll get a call any minute.

However, the cop brain fighting my panic was listening to my gut and sensing trouble.

I called Anne and indicated I was en route from Red Wing. Anne reported the Sheriff's Office deployed all resources in the search. "We have three deputies on the scene with a K-9 deputy coming from his home. The state patrol helicopter will be in the air overhead within the hour. The Stillwater Rescue Team is searching the shoreline, and many volunteers are walking the woods."

As I continued driving toward Vivian's, breaking the speed limit whenever traffic allowed, I was slightly comforted by the missing person operations now on high alert, with every expectation of locating Mary. There was no guarantee that they would find her alive.

"Anne, what are your thoughts?" I paused, and she took a while to answer my question.

"Jack, this appears to be water related. However, Mary's mother and her associates are one direction to look. Maybe a boyfriend or the bio dad could have taken her. There are too many unanswered questions. Jack, Mary's mother hasn't been located yet, which slows the process of issuing an Amber Alert."

"Anne, I'll be there in thirty minutes or less. Priority 1, we need to get that Amber Alert issued somehow. Push it. Lead with difficult circumstances. Tell them this is a special-needs child, then find Amanda. See you soon."

An Amber Alert requires the child's age to be less than seventeen years, a detailed description of the child, law enforcement believes an abduction has occurred, and the child is in danger. The National Crime Information Center receives specific information regarding the missing child. An Amber Alert would then be issued.

However, until Mary's mother, Amanda, has been located by the Sheriff's Office to confirm that Mary is missing, the Amber Alert will be delayed. I knew that, but god, I hated red tape. I dismiss red tape whenever possible.

On the positive side, the missing person report worked this time, unlike my recent experience with Judge Magnuson's daughter.

The 911 call triggered law enforcement's multitude of actions. All possible resources for assistance were contacted. It wasn't easing my mind at all. In my years on the job, I had seen too much to believe that all searches had happy endings.

Is there a family member that would have taken her? Who is the biological father? We know that Amanda's boyfriend has been abusive in the past, and a perpetrator's most accurate prediction of future criminal behavior is a criminal history pattern.

Data supports that the suspect is known to the family in 90 percent of abduction cases. Furthermore, strangers abduct less than 1 percent of children. Could she have walked into the adjacent wooded area or, worse yet, the strong currents of the St. Croix River?

I was focusing on something more concrete, frustrated with the red tape delaying the Amber Alert. The damn bureaucratic delays may be a missed opportunity in locating Mary.

Suddenly my thought process and decision-making skills kicked in. I called Anne.

"This is what needs to happen. Call the shift commander and advise that five-year-old Mary is a nonverbal special-needs child. Satisfactory descriptions with photographs are available. The location of the abduction is where Madel found Mary's backpack. Because of the absence of a vehicle or suspect, have dispatch enter Amanda's car and name her as a possible victim in Mary's disappearance. We may be able to locate Amanda sooner rather than waiting to hear from her and avoid a critical delay in the issuance of the Amber Alert. Have the shift commander call me if there are any remaining questions."

Within five minutes, Anne texted: Amber Alert issued, Jack!

Finally, pulling into Vivian's driveway, the property appeared to be a serious crime scene. Four Washington County marked squads, including one K-9, flanked Vivian's driveway; volunteers were parked and walking along Arcola Trail in yellow reflective vests, and a Stillwater Fire Rescue truck was parked near the garages.

As I entered the circle entrance near the front door, Vivian came running toward me with a look of fear and panic.

"Jack, I can't stand it! What if something has happened to her?"

I squeezed Vivian, rubbing her shoulders gently, and said, "Let's go find Madel, and let me find out what this is all about." I put my arm over her shoulders and turned her to walk inside.

Madel was sitting in the solarium next to a tissue box, weeping. "Oh, Mr. Jack, I am so glad to see you. I don't know what to do. Where is my little *chica*? I have been calling, and she no answers me."

Vivian sat next to Madel, and taking her hand, she took the Kleenex from it and dried Madel's eyes. Vivian said, "We still haven't heard from Amanda."

Trying to remain calm, I fell into a familiar investigation mode and asked Madel to explain what had happened when she arrived.

"I told the deputy I was changing sheets on Ms. Vivian's bed and collecting towels for the wash. I walked to the laundry room and then to kitchen to make my chica a snack. She was supposed to be dropped off at eleven. She always likes a snack first thing when she gets here."

She said all this with tears running down her face. I told Madel she was doing a good job, and she continued, "Well, as I say, I was making the snack, and I glanced out the window toward the river and saw something on the grass. I no seen it earlier, so I thought, what it is? I went out to see what it was, and it was Ms. Mary's backpack, but Ms. Mary, she no there. I look around and see no one. I went inside and called for Ms. Mary, but no answer. I call judge's office and said *la emergencia*, and I need to speak to Judge Vivian."

Madel began to sob in earnest. "Ms. Mandy, she always comes at eleven or after. She never early. I don't understand. Where is my little chica?" At that, she lay her head on Vivian's shoulder and sobbed.

"Thank you, Madel. We will find her." I caught Vivian's eye and indicated that I would step outside. I walked away, leaving Vivian and Madel alone to comfort each other.

I needed some space. Think, Jack! What the hell are we dealing with? Is Amanda at home? What about her vehicle? Could she be in danger? Questions whirled through my head with no answers. I watched the activity around the riverfront yard for a few minutes, then went back inside.

I spoke quietly with Vivian. She told me that Amanda had a landline at her house, and she hasn't answered there or on her cell phone. Okay, that question was answered. I began making a few suggestions. I thought Madel should go home for the rest of the day. I also suggested she pack an overnight bag and go to her sister's house in Bloomington. I thought being with Amanda when she learned Mary was missing would be a big help and comfort to Amanda. Being a comfort to each other was all they could do at this point.

She gently told Madel she could go home. Assuring her we would let her know when we found Mary.

Having something to do besides standing around brought out Vivian's more take-charge attitude. She agreed that being with Amanda, away from this alarming scene, made a lot of sense but only agreed if I remained and became an indispensable part of the effort to find Mary. She didn't want to leave the house unattended while she was away. Madel and Buster were around during the day, and she was always home at night, and still, frightening things had been happening. Now this! I promised her I would be there at night until she came home.

Vivian said she would let Anne follow her to Amanda's house and check out the town house. After the details that she could think of had been taken care of, Vivian said, "I need fifteen minutes to pack a bag. I will meet Anne at my car."

Anne conversed with two volunteer search-party members near the entrance gate as I walked toward her. Drawing her aside, I asked if she would be available to accompany Vivian to Bloomington to check for Mary's mother, Amanda.

"It should only take an hour or so."

"Sure, Jack, I can do that."

"Thanks, Anne, I appreciate it. Anne, if there is anything suspicious, anything at all, or if something makes either of you uncomfortable, you call the Bloomington Police right away."

"Of course I will, Jack."

I thanked her and asked her to let me know what or who they find at Amanda's house.

"I will let you know right away, Jack," Ann replied.

125

I nodded and explained that Vivian would be ready in about fifteen minutes, as soon as she had a bag packed.

"Okay, Jack, I will meet Judge Lord at her car."

I walked Vivian to the car and shared a kiss and a long hug.

Anne came into the garage and told Vivian her car was on the road and that she would follow her. Vivian got in the car, and with one last quick kiss, I closed the door, and she backed out of the garage.

I watched as she drove down the driveway and out of view, wondering what our world would be like when we saw each other again. Alone with no fear of saying what I was thinking aloud, I speculated on what kind of a mother would leave their child alone without a handoff to transfer the care and responsibility for the child's welfare.

Could this be a troubling sign at some level? Or could something more nefarious have occurred? Would the search expand to include Mary's mother?

I received a text from Anne about forty-five minutes after Vivian had pulled out of her driveway. It simply said, *All okay at town house. Amanda not present. Vivian will call you as soon as she hears from Amanda.* Indicating that I had received the text with a thumbs-up, I went around the house and stood on the downstairs patio, out of the way of the search crew, and paced while observing the activity in the yard.

The sun was starting to set when the patrol sergeant in charge of the search walked toward me. I stopped my pacing and waited for him to reach me.

I recognized him and extended my hand as I simply said, "Jim."

Shaking my hand, he said, "Jack, we haven't found anything. Nothing around the dock or the yard that would indicate someone has taken the little girl." He hesitated, knowing the next words would be hard for me to hear. "Jack, you know the next step is to call in the dive team."

It was a gut punch. Even though I had known it was the next step, I could hardly bear to hear the words. *How could I tell Vivian if I couldn't stand to hear it myself?* I thought.

Thanking him for all of his efforts, I shook his hand again, and he walked away.

I stood in the driveway watching the last of the squads leave and head down Arcola Trail. I pushed the button inside the garage to close the gate and walked down the drive to make sure the gate was secured. I knew I was stalling, but I couldn't bring myself to call Vivian.

Going inside and making sure everything was secure upstairs, I walked down the steps to the guest suite. I made myself a drink and sat down in the recliner, staring out the window. I couldn't put it off any longer. I knew waiting to hear from me, all alone, must be a torture as well. Picking up my cell phone, I hit 1. I had already programmed her number into my speed-dial list. She was the first and only person I had ever put on speed dial.

Vivian answered on the first ring. "Jack," she said breathlessly, "have they found her?"

How I wished that was the news I was calling to tell her. From that hope to what my actual news would be was a long drop.

"No, honey," I said quietly. Setting my drink down, I leaned back and closed my eyes, hoping and praying for some divine guidance. "They didn't find her."

I heard her expel the breath she had been holding on a sob. "Oh god, Jack, what do we do now?"

It was killing me. "Don't give up, Vivian. We are going to find her, but the next step is going to be hard to hear. Vivian, the dive team will be here at first light tomorrow to search the river."

Vivian broke down and sobbed. I didn't know women could cry that hard. "Vivian, honey. Come on, honey, don't give up on me or Mary. I don't think she is in the river, but the Sheriff's Office has to rule that possibility out before going any further. So far, they are doing everything right. The Amber Alert has been issued, and they conducted an exhaustive search of the area. Everything is being done. This is the next step.

"Aw, honey, come on. You have to get a grip. You're killing me here. I can't stand to hear you crying. Have you given up?"

I listened for several minutes as she tried to calm herself. Finally she was able to answer; though I could tell she was still crying.

"No, I haven't given up." And a little more firmly, "I will never give up. I just can't stand the thought of her being in that water."

"Then don't think of it. I know the sergeant of the dive team personally, and he has my complete trust. They just don't come any better as both a law officer or a diver. If you trust me, you can trust him."

"You know I trust you." She sounded better. "I need something to do. This waiting is driving me crazy. I still haven't heard from Amanda. I've called work, and she didn't come in. I don't know her friends or even if she has any. If she does, they probably aren't the kind of friends I would want for her. Oh, Jack…" she just trailed off and stopped talking.

"I wish I could be there waiting with you, but I don't dare leave. What if she found her way back, and no one was here? I can't leave."

"Oh, Jack, what a hopeful thought. You still believe we will find her? We will find her alive?"

"Yes, Vivian. I won't ever stop believing that. Not until someone finds her body. I won't ever stop believing she is alive." I put as much confidence in my voice as I possibly could, praying it would give her hope as well. We talked for a long time, until finally, there was nothing left to say about the situation. Neither of us could think of anything else to talk about. So I began the good byes.

"I am going to take walks around the yard periodically tonight, just in case she finds her way home. I will call you the second I hear anything."

Thank you, Jack. I will call you as soon as I hear from Amanda."

"Good. Don't give up, Vivian, Don't give up."

"I won't. Thanks again, Jack. Bye."

I got up with drink in hand and walked out the sliding door. I had left every light I could find on upstairs, lighting Mary's way home if she was still out there. It illuminated most of the yard, too, so I could see quite well as I roamed looking into the gloom just beyond, hoping to see Mary walking toward me. I continued to take a walk around the yard every half-hour, taking different routes each time, seeing the space from a different view.

My phone rang just before midnight. It was Vivian. Grabbing the phone, I answered, "Vivian?"

"Yes, it's me. Amanda just got home a few minutes ago. She is right here. She knows you're my friend. Do you want to talk to her?"

"Has she told you anything?"

"Nothing much more than we already knew. She said that she had dropped Mary off early because she was late for her court-ordered appointment with her probation office. She has lost her cell phone, so she couldn't call ahead. That is all the information I have been able to get so far. She is understandably upset. She is sobbing and pretty much unable to talk much right now anyway."

"Well, that is the important information that we were missing. She did drop her off, so she went missing from here. It's not much, but we did need that confirmed. Try to get some sleep, Vivian. I will talk to you in the morning."

"You too, Jack. Thank you so much for everything. Bye."

CHAPTER 15

Rain gear would be the day's uniform on this cloud-covered and misty early morning. The search and possible recovery of a five-year-old child from the turbid waters of the St. Croix River will be challenging and emotional.

Years past, the water recovery team utilized a grid search pattern and dragging hooks to locate and recover bodies in the water. This old-fashioned tedious method was often successful, however, gruesome for the family members and the water recovery team.

Frequently there is confusion between the Sheriff's Office dive team and water recovery Unit. Rescue Dive Teams in some cities are available for rapid deployment for rescue operations for a person in the water or possibly going underwater. Time is of the essence.

The water recovery team is for the water recovery of vehicles, evidence, and, quite often, bodies.

Television network team reporters had erected large satellite antennas and broadband links from the field and set up covered platform terraces for the inclement weather.

The gallery of reporters was competing for that incredible video footage of a child-size body bag removed from the St. Croix River and the bereaved family who have received the most devastating news imaginable. It won't happen on my watch.

The media, law enforcement, water recovery members, gawkers, walkers, and divers had now infiltrated Vivian's property. It was appalling to me. The decision to have Vivian remain at her sister's home in Bloomington was spot on.

I stood on the downstairs patio, out of view of the crowd, as Bubbles approached. "Morning, Brad."

"Hey, Jack. My apologies to Judge Lord. We made some tire grooves into the lawn. It was a pretty tight turn for the trailer."

"Brad, that's the last thing on her mind today. Besides, she's in Bloomington with her sister, Mary's mother."

"It's a beautiful estate that Lord has. I've always admired it from the river. Her housekeeper is amazing. She set the search team up with coffee and fresh donuts in the beach house."

"Madel is like family. She takes good care of the judge and her niece."

There was a pause in the conversation. Small talk dried up pretty quickly under these grim circumstances. Brad was the first to break the silence, moving into professional mode.

"So, Jack, this is the situation we have for recovery. I've already been in the water and determined visibility, current, water temp, depth, and bottom for debris, like trees or old docks. My biggest fear is having a diver get entangled in fishing lines or branches. Good news, Jack, we have a bottom that is relatively clean of debris. We find this typical along some areas of the St. Croix with wealthy residents who pay for beach cleaning and dredging the site without a permit from the National Park Service, and not condoned. The bad news is the visibility, Jack. We've got zero visibility. It is like chocolate pudding. Divers call it Braille diving—by touch only."

"How long do you anticipate the dive will take you, Brad?"

"We will be at it for the better part of the day. Right now, we are waiting for the water patrol boats to shut down boat traffic on the west side of the river to prevent gawkers from stirring up the water with waves. We will also have the inflatable using a side sonar to offer the divers a possible target to check. I have instructed the divers to remove any foreign material for our first dive, followed by a second dive, usually shorter in duration. Jack, we have a couple of newbies, but overall, our water recovery team is the best in the Midwest. If Mary is in the river, we will bring her to the loving arms of her mother and the judge."

I was having trouble controlling my emotions and struggling with words of appreciation. Hagen could sense it. He has had to deal with emotional families waiting for comment, but he hasn't dealt with a friend in this position.

He pulled me into a brief hug, then patted me on the back. Moving away, he was back in search mode. "Those boats are too close to shore. Move them out to the middle of the river!"

Going back inside, I went upstairs to talk with Madel.

"Oh, Detective Jack, how is Ms. Vivian doing?"

"Under the circumstances, Madel, good as can be expected. I came inside to call her now. I will be in the guest suite if you need me."

Handing me a cup of coffee, she said, "Of course."

Accepting the cup, I raised it and said thank you before heading down the steps.

The guest suite has a remarkable view of the marina and beach house. Sipping coffee, I watched the synchronized movements of the water recovery team. I wanted to calm my nerves with something more substantial than coffee before I called Vivian. But I knew I was her crutch, and it wouldn't help her if her crutch was less than 100 percent. My focus was supporting her and finding Mary. I needed to be effective in that endeavor.

She answered the phone before the first ring had stopped. "Jack, any news?" Her tone was urgent and breathy. Her nerves stretched to breaking.

"No, honey. The dive team just got started. I spoke to Sergeant Brad Hagen, in charge of the team. Vivian, he is the best. He said they would be at it most of the day."

"Jack, I can barely stand the thought of seeing Mary's little body brought up from the water." She broke into a sob. I felt so helpless.

"How is Amanda doing?"

"Oh, Jack, she is a mess. I thought being together would help her and me. But that isn't the case. She finally took a sleeping aid early this morning. She has been asleep for a while now."

"So essentially, you are alone with your thoughts and haven't slept. I hate that." She quickly assured me that knowing I was here comforted her.

"Jack, I couldn't take it, being there, watching and waiting. I am so glad you are there. I know how hard this is for you."

We both were silent, suffering in place, each where we needed to be but wanting to give the other some physical comfort.

I finally broke the silence and said, "Vivian, you should know that Hagen said if Mary is in the river, they will find her. I believe that. I trust Hagen completely."

Her end of the call was silent. There were no words to answer that stark statement. "Vivian, I want you to go lie down. Close your eyes, and try to get some sleep. I will call the minute I have any news. I promise."

Her voice was quieter when she finally answered and resigned to the worst.

"Okay, Jack, I will try. I love you."

There wasn't anything else to say. "I love you, too, Vivian." And I hit the end button. I felt helpless and hopeless. My fierce determination to find words or prayers offered some comfort. *Please help me find her, help me find her*, kept repeating in one part of my brain. I did not plan on the recovery dive team finding Mary because, in my heart, I knew she was alive. This search was just a way to eliminate the worst possible outcome. At least for today.

It was turning out to be a long exhausting day. I watched boats, divers, and the river's water. There was an accumulation of items on the dock found by the water recovery team, possibly for evidentiary purposes, with maybe a minor cleanup thrown in. Blue mesh bags were stacked with smaller items on the shore and dock.

Madel came downstairs with a fresh pot of coffee, a selection of fruit, and cookies. I could use a Madel in my life.

I asked, "Madel, could I ask you a question?"

"Yes, Detective Jack, please."

"I overheard conversations about a white VW Jetta seen in the area of Vivian's driveway before Mary was taken."

"Yes, yes, Detective Jack. I see white VW Jetta pulling out of the driveway. I only know it is a Jetta, because Buster had one."

"Could you see the driver, Madel? Could you tell if it was a male or female?"

"No, Detective Jack, I'm sorry. That would be important, yes?"

She looked so anxious to be helpful, and the worry about Mary was causing her so much stress. I could see it on her face, yet she was waiting on me.

"Thanks, Madel. It's just another piece of the puzzle I'm trying to put together. But thank you for taking such good care of me. I know you are worried too."

Tears filled her eyes, and she lifted her apron to wipe them. "Detective Jack, I love that little niña. I don't believe she is in that river. I feel her here in my heart, you know?" She put her hand over her heart before continuing, "I love that little niña. I would know this. You have to find her, Detective Jack."

Madel profoundly believed that Mary was alive and that boosted my feelings. I didn't share that information with her, though. I said, "Madel, you do not have to call me Detective. Just Jack will be fine."

"*Si*, Mr. Jack. You will tell me if you hear anything, yes?"

"I absolutely will, Madel. Keep the faith," I said as she turned to go back up the stairs.

I was speculating on the worst-case scenario as I watched the activity on the dock. What if Mary's body is found? What would my response be? I need a strategic plan to prepare Vivian and myself for a tragic outcome.

A typical protocol would be requesting a death notification from Bloomington Police to contact the victim's mother at her residence. However, with the media swarming in numbers right outside the gate of Vivian's home, any reporter could easily be breaking news from any network.

I could hear it: A body was recovered from a private estate on the St. Croix River by the Washington County Sheriff's Office today. The name is to be released pending family notification.

Vivian would know immediately who the victim was. Her niece—five-year-old Mary Hastings.

Pushing closer to lunch, I saw a group of divers walking toward the staging area. That didn't look good. Going outside from the sliding patio door in the guest suite, I met Hagen, who looked dismayed.

"Jack, this is what we have. Our newest diver was assigned the dock area, east of *Courtship*, in deeper water, and believed he found the remains of Mary. While quickly surfacing, he hit his head on *Courtship*'s prop and has a large cut that is going to need stitching. When he surfaced, he was spitting blood and gasping for air. He panicked. It happens. We are going to transport him to Ramsey."

My face must have been awash in emotion because Hagen put his hand on my shoulder and said, "Jack, don't overreact. Give me thirty minutes. I will go down myself and check it out. I first need to get this diver tucked into the ambulance."

I turned to go back inside to hide my reaction. I didn't have my emotions as under control as I had thought. As Hagen spoke, I could feel the panic rising from my stomach. I felt like I was going to throw up. Inside, I could hide my intense emotions. I stood with my back to the door as the tears flowed. I was in shock. I hadn't believed that they would find her in the river.

The first aid treatment for shock is to lay the person down and elevate the legs. So let's take a pause. Jack, lie down.

A knock on the door, and Madel appeared and said very excitedly, "Mr. Jack, the ambulance left in a hurry with flashing lights. What is happening?"

With no words to comfort Madel, I put my feeling aside and just went over to her and hugged her. "It is going to be Okay, Madel. A diver cut himself. They are transporting him to the hospital for stitches."

"Oh, Mr. Jack, I don't know what I was thinking. I am so sorry. I have been—what is the word—*wrecked*? Since our niña has gone missing."

"Madel, we are all stressed for sure. The Sheriff's Office will probably be here until this evening. I'm sure Ms. Vivian wouldn't mind if you left early. I'll spend the next few days here if anything is needed."

"Thank you, Mr. Jack. I will call Ms. Vivian."

"Oh, and by the way, have you fed Tabby? Or should I feed her?" I asked.

"Mr. Jack, I no seen Tabby since our Mary goes missing. She is with our Mary, I know. She never leave Mary, never. This I know. This is good?"

The cat—I never thought of the cat! I said to Madel, "I hope you are right. You call Vivian. I'll stay here and keep an eye on the house."

"Thank you, Mr. Jack."

Stranger things have never crossed my mind with any other case I have investigated. You miss a few puzzle pieces, but the process is usually linear. This case is all over the place. Now I suddenly have a missing cat. A cat that never leaves Mary's side. We just never thought of her. But this is good, I thought. If we believe that Tabby never leaves Mary—and apparently, that is absolutely true—Mary isn't in the river. I took a deep breath for the first time since Brad filled me in.

Confidence overwhelmed me. Mary was alive. I just had to find her cat, Tabby.

How can a five-year-old child disappear from a gated estate without a trace of evidence or witnesses? Now Madel is also reporting that Tabby the cat vanished simultaneously. The thought of an alternate universe enters my mind while checking out the window to see if Hagen has surfaced with any results.

All day, light misty rain has increased the darkness and made the scene at the river unnaturally eerie, and there is a light chop on the water.

A very haunting dark object emerged beyond Courtship. I presumed it was Hagen slowly drifting to shore. Donned in a full-face AGA communications mask with multiple black-hose attachments, red buoyancy control inflator and dry suit, black rubber gloves, an orange weight belt, and a single air tank.

Reaching a depth where he could stand, Hagen slowly walked toward the shore. He was holding a blonde-haired child-size doll under his left arm with his fins in his right hand.

The rookie diver had felt the body of a doll. *Thank God*, I thought, going limp with relief, while I leaned on the doorframe. The doll was large, wearing a plaid dress, and could have been the size of Mary. Hagen placed the doll, dripping with water, on a blue folding chair with the name *Courtship* embroidered on the back. Hagen could see me looking out the sliding door, turned the chair toward me, and pointed at the doll.

It was cop humor that only an officer would understand. I opened the sliding door and gave Hagen the first hand signal that divers learn. Joining the thumb and index fingers to form a loop and extend the third, fourth, and fifth fingers—*okay!* We both felt good, and together, we felt relieved. It must be difficult for Hagen or any diver to recover a human body from the water, especially that of a child.

My first instinct was to call Vivian, but knowing that would be a long conversation, and there were still things I had to do, I texted her the good news right away and explained that as soon as I finished up here, I would call her.

I also texted Madel with the news. Then I moved over to sit in the recliner and let myself relax and enjoy a moment of relief. Only a moment, though, because my cell phone immediately began to vibrate.

It was LaVonne. *What next?* I thought to myself. Answering, "Janssen."

"Jack, It's LaVonne. Are you at Lord's? I was watching a local news alert that an ambulance with emergency lights left the judge's estate, apparently heading to Ramsey. What's going on?"

"A diver was cut under Lord's boat and needs stitches. Other than recovering a doll, it's quiet here, LaVonne."

LaVonne seemed deflated when she responded, "Oh. You will let me know if the water recovery team finds Mary, won't you?"

"Yes, LaVonne, I will let you know, but they won't find her. I believe she is alive and with her cat, Tabby."

"A cat? Well, I hope you're right." And she continued to the next subject.

"So a new twist in the serial rapist case. The local news in Hudson, Wisconsin, is reporting that interviews of three victims of the rapist will be on their program and will be answering questions, more importantly, asking questions about a law enforcement cover-up of the cases."

"Well, it's about time. Are the tricounty team of detectives any closer to identifying a suspect?"

"No, the task force has hundreds of fingerprints and DNA evidence, but there have been no matches in the system. It has to be a clever youngster with no adult record."

"So that's it?" I asked. "We wait until one early morning when our rapist finds himself looking down the barrel of a twelve-gauge shotgun?"

In a weak attempt at humor, Lavonne replied, "Maybe. Hope it is sooner than later."

"Lavonne, it's uncanny how this serial rapist's MO is similar to Sandy Pittman's. He is an inmate at Stillwater Prison. It is almost like he was a student of Pittman's."

LaVonne interrupted, "Oh, wait, a new twist in the serial rapist case to tell you—the serial rapist has mailed letters to the victims after the rapes. I've not seen the letters, but it sounds like the victims are being revictimized. The letters are postmarked from Hammond, Wisconsin, in large brown envelopes."

"Letters? Is this guy asking to be caught? That would be contrary to Pittman. He never wrote any letters, to my knowledge. Hey, Lavonne, I am going to talk to the dive team. Let me know if any developments surface. Whoever this rapist is, he may be our only lead to finding Mary. There is no connection, but my mind keeps tying the cases together."

I decided to take a walk around Vivian's property. I could see only one television network remaining with equipment. Maybe the rest are heading to Hudson about the breaking news of the rape victim's disclosures.

The water recovery team was packing empty air tanks and drying themselves off.

As I walked up and around Lord's vineyard, I noticed a path at the northeast corner going into the woods. Walking to the trail, it appeared to continue down to the river. Interesting, I thought. Turning around, I saw a tree stump with several cigarette butts pushed into an opening. These were of interest to me—no filter, hand-rolled. I think I'll have Anne stop by and bag them for me.

As time passed, I saw Hagen walking toward me. His crew had loaded up their gear and was almost prepared to leave.

"Well, Jack, we're finished here. I am 100 percent confident that Mary is not in our target search area. Do you think Judge Lord wants any of the items we found in the river? Nothing looks of an evidentiary value, except the cell phone."

"How about we put everything in the back of my Jeep. I'll let Vivian make that decision."

"Sounds good."

I gave Hagen a firm handshake and said, "Thanks, Brad, thanks a lot. Vivian will be glad to get this news. We still don't have Mary, but we know she is not in the river."

A very exhausting day that was not over yet. I needed to contact Anne Reed to bag the cigarette butts from the path near the vineyard. Someone was smoking out of sight on Vivian's property. It could be important or not, but it needs to be determined either way.

While checking the assorted items recovered by the dive team in the back of my Jeep, I realized most was litter—beer and soda cans, a San Sebastián Cabernet wine bottle, and broken red plastic cups.

Items of interest to Vivian may be the cell phone, three pairs of sunglasses, a crescent wrench, a telescoping boat hook, a large key ring with several keys, and a blue teakwood-armed folding boat chair with the name *Courtship* embroidered on the back. Finally the size-able blond-hair blue-eyed doll looks very sad and a little creepy at the same time.

While organizing the items in my Jeep, I found the paper on which I had written the license plate number of the white VW Jetta that I had seen at the Arcola High Bridge the night I responded to Vivian's alarm—Wisconsin dealer plate, WI7900SF. I need to have Anne run the license.

I think my agenda is a cocktail, a hot shower, and an early bed. My clothes had been damp since morning, but I decided to wait till Anne left. She said she would stop by shortly to bag the discarded cigarettes and bring the registration for the VW Jetta.

The occasional showers today made the grass soggy, which made the grass vulnerable to vehicle tires, and Vivian's grass sustained quite a bit of damage.

Upon Anne's arrival, she provided me with the printout of the Wisconsin dealer plate and a stolen report. "Jack, the dealer plate was stolen from Hammond, Wisconsin, three weeks ago, a dead end. Sorry."

We walked to the vineyard area, where I pointed out the discarded cigarettes pushed into a woodpecker hole in a stump. Anne promptly bagged the five partially smoked cigarettes. As we walked back to her car, I told Anne about the day's events and showed her the back of my Jeep.

"Hagen and the dive team recovered all these items."

"So this is the doll that the diver found and panicked?" Anne asked.

"A doll that large could have been mistaken for a child underwater in poor visibility," I replied. "Sure has made a mess of my Jeep." And I handed her the recovered cell phone. "So now that I have you here, do you know that the alarm code for the gate and the Lord residence are the same? Both have the code 8-222-9 numbers that correspond to *Tabby*. I will be talking to Vivian about the security passcode. She probably used the same code for convenience."

"I agree, Jack, it should be changed. Someone who gains access through the gate would easily access Lord's residence. Delivery people, service people, vineyard workers, and others don't need access to the residence."

"I'll walk you to your car. I should get the mail as long as I'm out here. Thanks for picking up the cigarettes. There are no filters on the butts, maybe hand-rolled."

As Anne was pulling out of the driveway, I gathered Vivian's mail, which contained a large brown envelope, handwritten and addressed to Judge Vivian Lord.

Just as LaVonne had described the letters that the rape victims had gotten. Was it a coincidence that the Jetta's stolen plate was also from Wisconsin? I don't believe in coincidences. I quickly called Anne and asked her to come back.

When she pulled alongside the mailbox, I handed her the brown envelope and said, "Have this carefully processed under the task force case number. It may contain additional evidence or a threatening letter from the suspect. I talked with LaVonne, from the County Attorney's Office and the victims are receiving thank-you cards from their rapist."

"Jack, you look worn out. You should be in bed. Don't worry. I will have this envelope processed, the cigarette butts, along with the cell phone. Take care. I will get back to you."

"Thanks, Anne." I stood watching her drive away before heading back to the house.

Anne will make a great deputy.

CHAPTER 16

Adjusting to Vivian's guest suite was easy and very comfortable. I only wish that we were sharing it. I hated thinking of her sleeping at night, trying to fight her fears and anxiety all alone. Even knowing how strong-willed she is, I have gotten to my breaking point in life myself. I know how fast it can sneak up on you. I want to hold her, comfort her, and ease her pain. Mary's abduction could break Vivian's spirit, and I don't want that to happen to her.

Pouring myself a strong Bullet Bourbon over ice, I sat down in the recliner, popped up the footrest, leaned back, and took a swig. Finally I could try to unwind. Usually a glass of Bullet would help me to unload the baggage of the day and move into something close to feeling relaxed. I took a second sip and closed my eyes. Wow, my brain was on overdrive. All the thoughts I had been having were swirling around in my brain, which wasn't helping. If I couldn't relax, maybe I could put it all in some order so it would make sense.

I reached for my pocket tablet on the nightstand next to my gun and speed loader. If a glass of Bullet wouldn't do it, making notes usually did. Hopefully, it would give me a sense of who we were dealing with. My current psychological profile on the rapist is one that Scott concurs with. Mary's kidnapping is a crime of opportunity. However, is there a connection with the serial rapist on the loose in Washington County?

The serial rapist appears to be a young athletic man that has been off the grid with no DNA or fingerprints on file. Additionally he seems to have a well-thought-out plan. Until the tricounty task force can locate a suspect for comparison purposes, the perpetrator remains free, with the victim count increasing.

According to my brief visit to the War Room and my intel from LaVonne, three counties have triggered the investigation to help solve this major crime. Washington County, Minnesota, St. Croix County and Pierce County—both in Wisconsin—have had a rash of recent sexual assaults within their borders with similar MOs.

The perp needs to be stopped before he can add another victim to the list. Only one vehicle under suspicion was driving on Arcola Trail during the early morning hours of an attempted break-in was observed. It is a white VW Jetta with no known license plate.

According to LaVonne, the masked suspect was scared off and never found. The red flag pin location, identified on the War Room map, was identifying an attempted break-in.

Also on tomorrow's list is to have a conversation with Vivian regarding changing alarm codes.

I had been using the remote control to open the gate and garage when coming to Vivian's. Before that, I had used the keypad at the gate to gain entrance, so I knew the code.

Now that I am the house's sole resident, I'm also turning on the silent alarm that notifies the alarm company of an unauthorized entry. An alarm keypad is also located inside the garage to access the residence. I also have a garage remote.

However, I have discovered a weakness in Vivian's alarm system. The codes are the same. After discovering the duplications of those two codes, I tried the keypad for the garage door. It was a trifecta! All three were the same. That means if someone manages to get the code for the gate, they have uninterrupted access to the house.

It is one thing to trust Madel and Buster with the code to the house, but what about the delivery driver or the Somerset Winery employees? No telling how many people at those businesses have access to that code. The codes need to be changed immediately.

Splashing a little more Bullet in my glass was probably not a good idea. I am exhausted. I didn't even want to get out of the recliner; it seemed like it would take more energy than I had, so I reached over and grabbed a pillow off the bed, turned the TV to the news—which always put me to sleep—set the timer on the TV, and closed my eyes.

Just then, the local weather came on. I leaned my head against the pillow and could swear that I smelled Vivian. Turning my face more directly into the pillow, I could smell her fragrance. I smiled. She must have sprayed some of her perfume on it before she left for Amanda's. Did Vivian know that I thought about her even in my dreams? A welcome relief from the recent nightmares.

That was my last thought until I tried to turn rolled over. Not an easy move in a chair. Glancing at the illuminated clock on the microwave, I saw that it was three thirty-two. I briefly thought about diving into bed for the rest of the night, but it seemed like a lot of work.

Suddenly I heard a sound. Maybe from the garage? I briefly thought I was dreaming until the noise came again, definitely from the garage. I waited for the alert tone that would be calling the alarm company. Nothing. No sound to indicate help was on the way. Listening intently, I tried to determine if it was a man or an animal. It was a person.

I slipped on my deck shoes and jeans. In one swipe, I grabbed my revolver, speed loader, and cell phone off the nightstand. Slipping them all into my pockets, I headed for the stairs.

The steps creaked each time I shifted my weight to the next step. The upper door to the guest suite was closed but not locked. Reaching the top of the stairs, I slowly opened the door. Suddenly I was struck with a powerful blow to the temple and stumbled back, falling down the stairs.

I hardly felt the fall. The pain in my head was so intense. Upon landing at the bottom, I could hear someone running through the garage. An intruder? I thought, *This couldn't be happening.*

If this is a home invasion, it may be my chance to catch the serial rapist and find Mary. I stumbled to my feet, running my hand up to my temple. No blood. *You are not getting away from here, asshole. You picked the wrong house.*

The first few steps were a little slow, but I had picked up steam by the time I got to the top of the stairs. I ran down the hall and out to the garage. At the open door, I paused to check for any sound that would tell me the direction of travel. *North,* I thought, *I can still hear him.* He can't be too far ahead because I listened to him going through the vineyard.

I would be able to see him above the vines. From there, he would only have two options to escape on foot. The intruder would take the path along the river toward the Arcola Rail Road Bridge or the easement path to Buster Greeley's.

I ran toward the vineyard, crossed to Arcola Trail, and quietly walked on the pavement. I slowed my walk and attempted to hear the suspect in the woods.

The early morning hours were still, and the clear sky put a chill in the air. Checking my cell, I found no coverage. I continued walking north on Arcola Trail, reaching Buster's house and continuing to the easement path. I didn't hear any activity and started running to the Arcola Bridge, keeping to the paved road. I was almost at the small parking area for the bridge, so I paused and listened.

Now I have you, asshole. I could hear someone on the bridge, walking east toward Wisconsin. The bridge is old, and you can hear almost every step. As I ran, I noted that no one had parked their cars nearby.

The sound of footsteps on the bridge was unmistakable now. This bridge is supposed to be the most haunted bridge in the Midwest. I have also heard it is the world's most spectacular multis-pan steel-arch bridge. Right now, it may be the most dangerous.

Although I never crossed the bridge myself, I often ordered kids off it, threatening them with arrest for trespassing.

I attempted to call the Sheriff's Office unsuccessfully but still no coverage. I may get a text to go through. Anne was the only person I knew who may check a text at 4:00 a.m.

Quickly I texted her: *911 Arcola RR Bridge, officer down.* A radio call for an officer who needs help will give you immediate backup dispatched. A radio call for an officer down will bring squads from anywhere in the county. My gut instinct was telling me this wasn't going to end well.

Stopping at the edge of this 2,682-foot-long bridge, I felt like I could hear every step the intruder made over the bridge's rocks, rails, and ties. I had chased suspects in the dark, through alleys, with occasional shots fired. That didn't scare me as much as crossing this bridge did. There was nothing to prevent someone from falling 184 feet to the St. Croix River below, except for a single four-foot high pipe guardrail, with a lower two-foot rail for support, on the south side of the bridge. I presumed the railing was for railroad workers' safety and stretched from Minnesota to Wisconsin.

Carefully and with great hesitation, I began to make my way across the bridge. I could now see a small image of the suspect about twenty yards in front of me, and I decided to try a different strategy. Surprisingly I was not out of breath; though my throbbing head was making itself known. I could feel a little blood dripping from my left ear. I had placed my phone back in my pocket, so no light was visible to give away my position.

Hanging on the rail, I yelled, "Sheriff's Office, it's over. Give yourself up." The intruder stopped walking. The sudden silence was deafening. At this rate, it will be light before we get to the other side anyway. My first chance to arrest him, and I am twenty yards behind him. I hope he doesn't think of that.

Suddenly gunfire erupted as ten *pow-pow-pow-pow-pow-pow-pow-pow-pow-pow* bullets were hitting all around me. I dove face-first into the rocks, taking cover in a prone position. The only option for me was lying flat. I could feel my right leg heating up in pain.

The distance of the suspect was probably more than fifty yards, now that I could judge the muzzle flashes of his gun. Additionally since I could hear the shots, I determined that the suspect was probably carrying a 9 mm semiautomatic weapon with a maximum capacity magazine of ten rounds. Why else would he have stopped at ten? Training had me counting the shots fired. I surmised he must have had night sights on the gun, that glow in the dark.

The smell of the creosote from the treated railroad ties was almost overpowering this close to them. I calculated that the suspect was young, inexperienced, and afraid since he had discharged all of his ammo in one stream of shots in an attempt to take me out. The suspect had wanted me to know that he had a firearm and had recklessly demonstrated his fear of his current situation by shooting randomly. I believed he had another magazine of ten rounds and had probably already reloaded.

My inventory was a fully loaded Smith and Wesson revolver with night sights, and a speed loader, which amounts to twelve rounds. If I make it out of this, I'm trading this old revolver in for an automatic. I should have listened to the guys at the range. They always teased me about my antique gun and said it belonged in a shadow box. Maybe they were right.

I faced a critical dilemma on the Arcola Railroad High Bridge. The only suspect in Mary's disappearance wanted me *dead*, and I needed him *alive*.

My tactical gambit shifted to offensive, with discretion. The only sound I could hear from my suspect was becoming more distant. Standing upright in combat position, with both hands on my weapon, I aimed where I believed the suspect was now.

Bluffing, I hollered, "Give it up, pal, the Sheriff's Office is coming from the Wisconsin side."

I positioned my night sights in alignment with the sounds of my target—the suspect. I was starting to squeeze the trigger slowly. I pulled my weapon slightly to the left and released two rounds near the suspect but not to kill him. *Kaboom-kaboom.* The sound echoed and amplified off the water and sounded like cannon fire repeating off the banks of the St. Croix, shattering the peaceful tranquility of the river bluffs like nothing I could ever have imagined.

My ears instantly began ringing, and the muzzle flash from my two shots of .357 Magnum cartridges in the dead of night caused me momentary blindness. Did I not learn of preserving your night vision by closing one eye before discharging your weapon at night? Rookie move, Jack. "Shit," I whispered.

My advantage over the suspect had diminished for several minutes until my eyes adjusted. The ringing in my ears would continue longer. I could no longer see or hear the suspect. However, I was confident he wouldn't run in either direction on this rickety and dangerous bridge.

My suspect had received two forceful messages: I am armed, and my weapon is more powerful. Thinking of my position, I concluded it could only improve as dawn approached. However, that may be a couple of hours from now.

Feeling somewhat weaker, as my eyes adjusted, I thought I could see a single white light approaching from the bluffs on the Wisconsin side of the river. Well, Jack, old boy, that is either a train, or you're dying. Neither seems like a good choice. I believed the suspect may now be halfway to Wisconsin, which is still four football fields away.

I concluded the single white light was an approaching train. However, the railcars do not travel quickly crossing the Arcola High Bridge. I'm aware of their slow cautious speeds on the bridge.

I had coffee once with the railway police, or Bulls as they call themselves, and learned that the Arcola Railroad Bridge has sensor alarms to alert their division when trespassers are on the bridge.

The suspect had now reversed course and was slowly moving toward my position, an armed fleeing felon that an officer should never underestimate under any circumstances. I began to move west and back toward the Minnesota shore slowly. Completely aware of my soon-to-be predictable problem, I wanted the suspect to hear my final orders before a gunfight erupted.

Returning to a painful prone position, now about fifty yards from the Minnesota shore, I could feel the wetness of blood from my injured right leg. With only four rounds left in my gun, I placed my speed loader on the ground on my left side. I intended to hunker down and remain focused.

With both hands on my revolver, I screamed my final words to the suspect, "Sheriff's Office, friend, give it up and drop your gun before that train runs us both over."

The approaching train was far too close, and I was puzzled as to why I couldn't hear or feel the enormous weight of this looming danger. As the suspect got closer, I saw his profile walking toward me while holding tightly to the guardrail with his left hand and carrying his weapon in his right.

In my prone tactical shooting position, with night sights lined properly on my human target, I repeatedly recalled shooting from this same distance in training. The train's bright circular light produced a human silhouette, similar to a qualification target, and with the squeeze of the trigger, I could place a bullet in the kill zone.

The force of my powerful hollow point .357 bullet would take him off this bridge in seconds, and he would plunge into the river below. However, if I shoot, he would take any knowledge of Mary's whereabouts with him, and she may never be located.

Watching the suspect was becoming increasingly difficult. He was moving closer but fading in and out. My head was throbbing, and my right thigh was feeling frigid. I thought, *If I kill him, Mary will die. If I don't shoot, he will shoot me. Dear Lord, let me die, but let Mary live. Please, bring her home.*

I could now see flashing red and blue lights approaching from the Minnesota side of the river. I surmised that my text to Anne had been successful. My pain level had escalated to almost ten. Which, they tell me, is the maximum pain level a person can tolerate before passing out.

I tightly gripped my weapon with both hands, index finger resting on the trigger, and pointed directly at my suspect's chest center. Unless my suspect wore a Kevlar vest, he would be my first kill in my twenty-seven years in law enforcement.

The last thing I remember hearing was a strong commanding voice saying, "Stop, Railway Police, put down your gun!" I witnessed my suspect launch himself over the railing.

CHAPTER 17

It was like floating. I thought, *Why am I floating? I need to find Mary.*

Again, I thought I was floating, but I could hear Vivian's voice. I tried to talk to her, to reach out, but I drifted away again.

The next time I neared consciousness, I could feel the pain in my leg and a headache. I could hear voices; I thought one was Vivian's. Her voice alone was enough to force me through the fog and back to reality, even though avoiding the pain in oblivion was a pleasant alternative.

Suddenly Mary's face appeared in my mind. Mary's face was what brought me back. I opened my eyes to reality, confusion, and pain.

What the hell? Why is Anne in my room?

"Anne? Where am I?"

"Ramsey Hospital, Jack, you just missed Vivian."

Shock rippled through me, followed by the adrenaline surge, delivered by reality, slamming me back into full consciousness. "How long have I been out?"

"Just over two days. How are you feeling?"

"I have a little headache and sore leg, but I need to be out of here. I need to find Mary." I began sitting up and pulling off the covers, only to stop short when I realized all I had on was a hospital gown raised too high.

"Damn it," I muttered as I pulled the covers back.

"Jack, the sheriff said I should remain with you at the hospital to help any way I can. So let's chill for a minute and devise a plan."

I didn't take more than a minute. We've already wasted too much time. "So number 1, your priority is getting me discharged

150

from Ramsey today." I thought, *My god, I sound like Scott, making a list of demands.*

"How about the suspect doing a high dive on the Arcola Bridge? Did he escape?"

"No, unfortunately, and, Jack, the death is being investigated by the Bureau of Criminal Apprehension. The sheriff believes the state should take over the case, with multiple jurisdictions being involved in the sexual assaults by the suspect. Plus, the media is very aggressive. They are setting up camp in front of the courthouse."

"So the suspect didn't live?"

Shaking her head, Anne continued, "Kenneth Clayton came to a sudden stop on the concrete bridge foundation and missed splashing into the river by two feet. It was an ugly crime scene, Jack."

"Do we know anything about him?"

"Not much. Nineteen-year-old from Somerset, driving his mother's white VW Jetta, was found on the Wisconsin side of the bridge. Railway Police received an alarm from the high bridge and dispatched a railcar. The suspect has no criminal record, but our office has already confirmed his fingerprints match several of the rapes in our county. With the DNA pending, we will know more after the medical examiner does the postmortem on Clayton."

"What do we know about the VW Jetta? It seems like a VW Jetta had been seen in the area before Mary disappeared."

Anne had checked her notes and said, "The Jetta, registered to a Crystal Boutwell of Somerset, Wisconsin. She is supposed to be the owner of Somerset Winery in St. Croix County. The Sheriff's Office delivered the death notification yesterday. Jack, what's wrong? It looks like you're in pain. Should I call for a nurse?"

"No, I'm okay. Anne, Somerset Winery contracts with Vivian for her vineyard. Boutwell probably has the alarm code, which means her son, Clayton, had access to it as well, damn it. Boutwell's prison boyfriend is Sandy Pittman, a serial rapist I put away a couple of years ago. Damn it, anyways! I had a one-on-one discussion with Pittman at the Stillwater Prison. We think he was the author of the threatening letters to Vivian.

"Clayton would have been our prime suspect in Mary's disappearance, and now he is dead!

"Number 2 on our list is to determine if Clayton could have taken Mary on the day of her abduction. We have to eliminate him from the kidnapping. Contact the BCA and make them aware of Clayton being a person of interest in Mary's disappearance. I know a lot of the investigators over there. Maybe my name will help. I used to teach a statewide course on child abuse investigation for the BCA."

"So, Jack, as I said, Clayton was found on the bridge concrete footing, sitting upright, wearing a stocking mask and backpack. The backpack had burglary tools—zip ties, duct tape, handcuffs, and of particular interest, a wooden twenty-two-inch training bat, which probably has your blood on it. They haven't found his gun but believe it to be a 9 mm because of the casings found. It's not determined if you hit Clayton with the two bullets fired from your .357 until the ME has completed the autopsy. The detectives have taken possession of your gun."

"Nice," I said, wincing more from frustration than pain. "Third on your list is find me a gun. What do you carry?"

"Jack, I'm not authorized by the Sheriff's Office to carry on duty."

"Well, that needs to be changed in your job description. What gun do you own?"

"I don't own a gun."

"How can you go into law enforcement and not own a gun?"

Sounding a bit put out by my response, Anne replied, "I will work on buying a gun with your help."

Changing the topic, she said, "I've been meaning to tell you that I did get your 911 Arcola Railroad Bridge text that you sent, and I called dispatch with an officer down on Arcola High Bridge. The Railway Police were on the scene before Washington County. Jack, they drive a marked black and white. It looks like a squad, lights and all, only it has rail capabilities in addition to roadways."

Ann picked up the cup of water on the bedside table and handed it to me before continuing.

"Jack, I think the sheriff referred the investigation to the BCA because of the strong possibility that you shot Clayton with your two bullets."

Taking a long pull of water from the straw and handing it back to her, I assured her, "Anne, the ME won't find any bullets unless the Railway Police shot him. Where is my cell phone?"

"Jack, your belongings, including your clothes and cell, have been taken as evidence in the death investigation."

"Just perfect," I said in disgust. "No gun, cell phone, pants, with only a blue hospital gown to escape. It looks like we're going to be partners for a while. I appreciate your help. As soon as the doctor makes their regular rounds, you're going to grab a wheelchair and take me outside for fresh air. Then we will make a break for it like Bonnie and Clyde."

"Well, Bonnie did break Clyde out of jail once. That's where the similarity ends. Bonnie was a tiny white chick. I have at least a foot on her and not a blonde," she joked. She got a chuckle out of me, but that immediately made my head hurt.

A knock sounded on the door just before a female doctor entered the room, and the fun ended. I looked at Anne with a wink, asked her to contact the BCA regarding our conversation, and excused the doctor and me for a few minutes.

The physician approached my bedside and introduced herself to me as Dr. Denise Mishow. She had a cap of short brown hair, a medium build, and pretty features, with her lips being the most prominent.

She paused to review my chart, then caught me completely off guard when she said, "Detective, do you have any pain that needs to be taken care of?"

How did this doctor, on doctor rounds, know that I was a detective? A doctor that I don't know how to pronounce her name. It said Michaud on her name tag, but I know it sounded French when she said it. I asked her, "Did I get registered as Detective Janssen, or do you know me personally?"

"Detective Janssen, we shared a private moment here at Ramsey." She smiled at me and giggled just a little, enjoying my discomfort.

"You even took the liberty of placing your arm around my waist. What! You forgot our hospital room moment so fast?"

I responded in kind, teasing her back a little, "Really, Doctor, if I had my arm around you, it would have also involved a long passionate kiss and dim lights. You must be mistaken."

Sobering, Dr. Michaud replied, "Detective Janssen, it involved a two-month-old baby who had been shaken to death by her mother. You had your arm around me as we talked, cried, and asked ourselves why?"

Our dialogue quickly shifted to talk about that terrible morning and the subsequent memories that plagued our hearts, minds, and souls. The most difficult for me is nights.

"Doctor, please forgive me. I do remember you. You had longer hair then, and I was in quite an emotional state, having just taken a confession from the mother. I'm sorry. That case did a number on me. Have you had any trouble handling your emotions since?"

"Detective—"

I interrupted her to say, "Please call me Jack."

"Okay, Jack. Yes, I have nightmares almost every night after treating a child abuse patient. I have gotten used to them and expect them for a while after each battered child."

"Do the nightmares ever stop?" I asked.

"For me, yes, they stop. Then they start again when another victim of child abuse comes under my care. Then my dreams have a new child with a new name and terrible story. Jack, I don't know how long I can continue treating the abuse cases. I am seriously considering private practice. One where I don't have to deal with child abuse. At least not as often. I remember each one—all of those children were damaged somehow. I haven't forgotten one. I will never forget those baby-blue eyes, wide open, and you reach over and gently close them. You made a sign of the cross on her little forehead. I just remembered that."

Dr. Michaud bent down, placed her arms on my shoulders and her head next to mine, kissed my brow, and said, "We can't give up, Jack. We are responsible for the effort to help the many abused children that come our way for help. I apologize for bringing that up during our second hospital encounter. After all, you are now the patient."

"Doctor, can I ask a huge professional favor from you?" My eyes never left her face, so she couldn't hide the need to wipe at her sad eyes with a tissue.

"Of course you may, Jack."

"I am desperately trying to find a Washington County judge's five-year-old niece that has disappeared. I can't waste time lying in a hospital bed. I need to continue my search. Can you give me discharge papers, so I don't go AWOL?"

The sad eyes took on a more militant look, and she paused a moment, thinking before she said, "Yes, I can do that, Jack, but with certain conditions. I am concerned about the concussion and the residual bleeding from the ricocheted bullet to your right leg. There is only minor muscle damage. However, there could be additional bleeding. My conditions are one, no driving for forty-eight hours. Two, no drinking. Both of those conditions are due to your concussion, and the last condition is that you return in forty-eight hours to be checked personally by me."

I quickly accepted those conditions. That meant no sneaking out. "Who should I ask for when I return?"

"Dr. Denise."

CHAPTER 18

A brisk moonless night has brought me out aimlessly driving my Jeep around the Arcola Trail area, in violation of Dr. Denise's orders. Twenty-three hundred hours, 11:00 p.m. It reminded me of a night-shift patrol. I loved the job of patrolling. It was like riding a roller coaster. Fast-paced, challenging at times, or quiet, with only the stars and your private thoughts for company.

Tonight I was driving, letting my mind wander through the facts and information we have regarding Mary's disappearance. I felt that if I could just put all the pieces together, clarity would come. Police investigations are like putting a jigsaw puzzle together with no picture. Collect all the parts, put them in a pile, and still don't know what the picture looks like. Suddenly the last piece falls into place, and you have clarity.

A patrol officer is the heartbeat of the motto Protect and Serve. They are the face of the police presence in a community. A good patrol officer must have the gift of common sense. Contrary to the name, it isn't common. Most people don't have it. A good cop needs it. That is the first tool, and then you add the skills and equipment.

The northern patrol car in Washington County called their geographic area the *Corncob Jungle*. Patrolling north was a mixed blessing. Mostly quiet, but your backup was far away when things heated up. You were pretty much on your own.

In my early days with the Sheriff's Office, the smaller populated communities sometimes had their night-shift officers clock off duty, subject to call, during less-busy times. The Sheriff's Office would then respond to emergency calls for service. The dispatcher occasionally radios for the deputy to call communications for an important alert when they don't want sensitive information put over the air-waves. Finding a pay phone today would be difficult. Years ago, pay phones were commonplace. Patrol deputies knew where they were located. I would head to the nearest one, call 911, and talk with a dispatcher. Problem solved but time wasted. Today with cell phones, as long as you have a signal, it was no problem.

Still scanning the area as I drove, I remembered the biggest problem of the night-shift work was sleep. People think everything is fine once you get used to working nights and sleeping days. I can tell you the human body never gets used to it. If you have any doubts, ask someone who works the night shift to confirm my conclusion. I loved patrol, but I never got used to sleeping days.

It is a melancholy drive tonight with untapped emotions pushing their way into my mind and no one to consult with at this time of night. The only bright spot was the aurora borealis or northern lights. They were putting on quite a show.

I suppose the clairvoyant I will be meeting later today will tell me that they were a supernatural communication for me, trying to tell me what to do. Not a revelation, but I sure enjoyed the sky.

Reining in my wandering mind, I refocused on the one priority—my commitment to Vivian and Mary. I had to find her. The reality that Mary's chance of survival diminishes every day, every night that passes, is incredibly difficult for me to stomach.

The golden hour in medicine suggests that a sick or injured person must receive definitive treatment in the first hour after the injury or when symptoms first appear for optimum recovery. Police instructors for child abductions theorize a golden month. It is the first thirty days following a police report of a missing child that law enforcement has the best chance of a positive outcome for the child.

Less than 1 percent of missing children get taken by strangers. Of those found, most are within twelve miles of their home. Those two statistics kept going through my mind. At home, I constantly review notes, missing person reports, and pirated reports from the Sheriff's Office. My bedroom has transformed into a task force room for one. The lack of an aggressive investigation by the Sheriff's Office has me baffled and frustrated.

There is a missing five-year-old niece of a Washington County magistrate. The Sheriff's Office put the investigation on the back burner. Not on my back burner. I lived and breathed it.

I kept going over reports and what little data we had. I have ideas but no proof. It was driving me crazy. Sleepless nights are nothing new to me; constant thoughts of Mary have replaced my nightmares, and some nights are even worse.

It is Vivian's Mary on the table in my dreams. The thought of having that dream keeps me awake and searching for that one piece of information that will solve the puzzle.

My lack of direction or concrete evidence drives me around at night, hoping something will come to mind. My only partner in this task force is McCloud. He is only part-time since he is in Duluth and uses a wheelchair. Knowing that Scott stays up and watches late-night TV, I chanced it and called him.

"Hey, kiddo, you're up late, son."

"I am. I was driving and thinking. I called to see if your surgery date is scheduled. Hey, how did you know it was me?"

"You are the only person I know these days who would be up this late. Also, the only person who would call me this late. Anything breaking on the judge's niece?"

"Nothing, Scott, no leads. She just vanished, along with the judge's cat."

"Cats do wander off, Jack. Most likely, the cat will come back."

"Not this cat, Scott. She's a tabby orange. They are popular and smart. The judge even had a microchip implanted. She claims the cat never leaves the yard and always follows Mary."

"Okay, I don't suppose this chip has a location frequency so somebody can locate the cat?"

"No, the chip stores a unique identification number so that someone like a vet can use a scanner to locate the owner."

"Well, sounds like if you find Tabby, you'll find Mary. What about the divers? Was there any evidence recovered?"

"I still have everything the divers found in the back of my Jeep. I'm supposed to give it all to the judge if she wants it—three prescription Ray-Ban sunglasses, a cell phone, probably from Vivian's deceased husband, a crescent wrench, miscellaneous cans and bottles, a large ring of keys, a telescoping boat hook. A cloth doll that belonged to Mary.

"A rookie diver found the doll toward the end of the day. Pretty overcast to start with, making terrible visibility. All the diver saw was hair and eyes. He thought it was Mary and surfaced like he had run out of air and was spitting blood. Brad went down and recovered the doll. I was so relieved."

"Did Lord see that drama?"

"Thankfully no. Vivian is staying with her sister, Mary's mother, in Bloomington."

"Okay. Tell me more about the ring of keys. Doesn't sound like something that would belong to the Lords or their guests unless the keys are from a maintenance person."

"Let me grab the keys. They're covered in mud. I just threw them in the Jeep with everything else." Exiting the Jeep, I retrieved the ring of keys from the back of my Jeep, mixed in the box with the recovered evidence.

"Okay, got 'em." I climbed back into the driver's seat and closed the door. "There are five keys. Two of them are small keys. They look like they're for padlocks. One key looks like a house key, and two are heavy industrial keys with something written. I'll get them in the light for a minute and rub some of this mud off. It says 'Do Not Duplicate.' There is something written on it." I rubbed the keys on my jeans to get some more of the dried mud loose, then holding my flashlight closer, I could read, "The letters are M-C-F stamped onto both keys."

"Son, those are Minnesota Correctional Facility keys. If the Lords had the warden of the Stillwater Prison himself on their dock, I don't believe he would carry a ring of keys like those. Those keys came from a worker bee. Are there any other identifiers on them? Other letters or numbers? Maybe for an inventory of some kind?"

"No, that's it. Maybe someone at the prison could help."

"Maybe. Check that out in the morning. So, Jack, how is the judge holding up?"

"She is pale and frightened, but she has a spine of steel. It is beating her down, though, and every day, more and more. I can tell she is shakier than she was the last time I saw her. I haven't seen her for a few days, but we talk often. She goes into a different room from her sister and cries. I listen and try to give her something to hang on to.

"How about you, son?"

"Scott, I made a huge mistake when Mary went missing. I promised Vivian I would find her. Here I am, scratching for any leads. Also, Scott, I was at Ramsey for two days. I was asleep in Vivian's guest room and had someone break in, and I chased him to the Arcola Railroad High Bridge at about four in the morning. A few shots were fired, and the suspect jumped from the bridge."

"Jesus Christ, Jack, you buried the lead story here, son. Are you hurt? Did you kill him?"

"No on both counts. I fired a couple of shots to let him know I had a gun. I didn't want to hit him. He would have fallen off the bridge from the impact. In the end, that is just what he did. Scott, he may have been the only person who knows Mary's whereabouts. How ironic, I never took a bullet for twenty-seven years, and less than six months into retirement, I get shot."

With a lighthearted chuckle, Scott said, "Maybe you should go back to work at the Sheriff's Office. It pays better and sounds safer than retirement. Are you okay?"

"I did take a ricocheted bullet in the right leg, just muscle damage, not going to be a problem. The guy rang my bell pretty well with a baseball bat, but I only have a little headache remaining. I'm sorry, Scott, I should be spending more time with you."

Scott interrupted me, saying, "Listen to me, son, you're going to find that little girl and bring her to see those big ships coming into Canal Park one day. Count on it. My eyes are getting a little droopy now. I should let you go, son."

"Okay, talk to you soon, Scott." I paused and never said this to him before, but something compelled me to say it now. "I love you, Scott." And I disconnected. His eyes are droopy, and mine are tearing up—what a pair.

I realized that Scott hadn't said anything about his upcoming surgery. It was probably postponed again.

At Vivian's request, I stayed at her house for a few days, so I finally rode down Arcola Trail one last time and opened the gate with the code. Walking into the house felt weird. No one was there. Walking toward the steps, I passed the coffee maker and thought, *I hope that contraption works for me in the morning.*

CHAPTER 19

With very little sleep, I managed to get something that resembled coffee out of that miserable machine. It didn't taste like Vivian's coffee but had caffeine, an essential ingredient. I had two hours to spend alone. I can see why Vivian didn't like being here alone. It is beautiful and peaceful but so quiet it almost makes my ears hurt. They are straining for sound, and there is simply nothing to hear.

Taking my coffee down to my room, I organized my morning. Coffee, shower—in that order—then I was going to meet with a clairvoyant who had contacted Vivian. She had initially discounted the psychic's offer. However, after giving it some thought, she welcomed any assistance that may result in finding Mary.

Our only contact yesterday had been by phone. Vivian was with Amanda. She had told me about the psychic and asked me to escort Ariel LaVeaux, around her property—outside only, including the dock area and river shoreline.

Vivian told me that Madel had left a bag on the golf cart's seat in the garage with an article of Mary's clothing, indicating that the pink sundress was Mary's favorite.

Then she brought up the *Majestic Lady* evening. The dancing, the music, and our private piano time were very special to her. "I think of it often. Those memories are keeping me sane," she said. She even volunteered that she had kept my tuxedo's pink pocket square as a keepsake of the evening.

Then she told me that Amanda had requested that she continue to stay in Bloomington with her, and she had agreed. In addition to the appointment with the clairvoyant, she asked if I could continue to stay at the house. Madel and Buster may come and go, but she said she would feel better if someone was there.

"You don't have to stay all the time, but if someone came and went, I would feel better. I wish Amanda would agree to stay with me, but I couldn't talk her into it." She paused for a moment and then started again, "Jack, I know it's been on your mind why Amanda would have left Mary in the driveway instead of going into the house and handing her off in person to Madel."

I interrupted her, saying, "Honey, you don't need to explain that. My focus is on finding Mary. I am sure that Amanda wishes with her whole heart that she had done things differently. I'm sure she knows that single action or lack of action triggered this horrible situation with Mary. We will worry about how to handle future drop-offs after we find Mary."

"That is just it, Jack. I don't know if Amanda acknowledges that this is her fault! Nothing is ever her fault! This is what she told me happened.

"She had lost track of time and was late for a court-ordered meeting with her probation officer. She had lost her cell phone and was early to drop Mary off, hoping she could make up time by just dropping her in the drive and leaving.

"Jack, Amanda has lost her cell phone three times. This year! I pay for a landline at her town house to avoid situations like this! She blames people for putting all this pressure on her with meetings and time limits. She doesn't acknowledge her responsibility for anything, and she never has! I am so sorry that you are in the middle of all this, but I am so glad to have you there at the same time." She ended with a laugh that sounded more like a sob to me. I could hear the frustration in her voice, but more importantly, I could tell she was crying.

"Honey, you have nothing to be sorry for. I didn't realize you were dealing with problems with Amanda on top of Mary's disappearance, but it doesn't matter now. All that matters now is to get Mary back safely. We will get her back, Vivian. You have to keep believing that. I'll base out of your house until you get back. Don't worry about anything here. You take care of yourself and Amanda. Maybe she will think of something or someone she forgot to mention."

"Oh, Jack, I nearly forgot! Sunshine Marina will be picking up *Courtship* today for early storage. I didn't want you to think someone was stealing her."

"Got it, Vivian."

"Thank you so much, Jack." She paused, as if unsure what to say, then said, "I love you." And before I could respond, she hung up.

Should I call her back? After several minutes of weighing my options, I text her one word: *ditto*.

I conducted a cursory background on LaVeaux. I learned from her website that she specializes in missing children and pets. LaVeaux claims to have worked with several law enforcement agencies and has references available upon request. I remain a skeptic.

I had walked down toward the dock to gather my thoughts and enjoy the view when I heard the gate beep signaling that it was opening. I walked toward the drive in time to see a white Porsche parked in the circle in front of the house and a brown-complexioned woman stepping out the driver's door. She turned and reached back into her vehicle.

I reached for my holstered gun, forgetting the Sheriff's Office had taken possession of it. Ms. Ariel was going for a briefcase-type purse, and I relaxed my arm—twenty-seven years of training.

"Ya must be Mr. Jack Janssen. I am Ariel LaVeaux. I spoke with de Judge Lord about her missing niece."

Excellent, I thought. I'm not good with a Northeast Minneapolis accent, let alone a French or Creole-speaking psychic. I said, "Nice to meet you, Ariel," as I put my hand out to shake hers. "I am Jack. Who let you pass through the gate? Did you talk with someone on the speaker?"

Confronted with a language barrier, I seem to speak louder. I know it won't help, and I don't understand why it is my go-to solution to the problem, but I do it every time.

Now only a few feet away, I can see that she appears harmless, but I want an answer before I get too friendly.

Ariel had a cute snicker and said, "I just posh dah buttons, and dah gate opened."

For a moment, I thought, *This psychic is damn good. More likely, the gate is malfunctioning. I better check that out.*

Ariel stood five foot, ten inches in heels and had long black hair in a ponytail tied with a flower-patterned scarf. She had prominent lips, wore a beige pants suit, and carried a brown Coach purse. A purse that size must be expensive. I thanked Ariel for her interest in locating Mary and indicated that I would return with a golf cart for her tour, telling her that it would be much easier than walking around in her high heels.

According to my preparation for Ariel's tour, it should take only twenty or thirty minutes to give her Mary's pink sundress to hold and study or whatever they do to get their psychic skills lubricated. Then I can tell Vivian that the attractive psychic was an overpaid fraud.

Together we drove the estate property. I showed Ariel the vineyard, the shoreline, the dock area, and where Madel found Mary's backpack.

I parked near the beach house with a panoramic view of the St. Croix River Valley. We had completed the tour, and I thought she could give me her report while we enjoyed the tranquility of this paradise's flowing water and foliage.

During this pause, almost ten minutes or so, I became aware that Ariel had been watching me intently. "Ariel, I almost forgot—the pink sundress." I reached back, grabbed the paper bag, and gave it to her.

Ariel took the dress out, held it up, and said, "How cute," with a big smile. "I bet Mary looks very pretty in dis dress." Then she neatly folded the pink dress, put it back in the bag, and returned it to me.

I thought Ariel didn't spend much time with Mary's clothing and was quite disappointed. Ariel then asked, "Can I call you Jack?"

"Yes, you may."

"Jack, I see that you are mesmerized, almost hypnotized, by the currents of the St. Croix River. Did you know that dah water from des river joins the Mississippi River and continues south to dah Louisiana Mississippi Delta, where I was born and raised? My family started the Muddy Waters Blues band. I had taken a trip north along the muddy Mississippi and fell in love with dah Twin Cities. Here I am. So, Jack, being a medium is a gift I treasured my entire life."

I heard Ariel but could not take my eyes off the water. "Jack, you enjoy the water currents, yes?"

"Vivian's backyard always relieves my tensions and comforts me."

"Jack, sometimes people with dah gift get spiritual, almost supernatural phenomena that can benefit an investigation with certain directions or ideas. I cannot use my senses to track like a K-9 or a search dog," she said with a big smile on her face. "Psychics can provide spiritual guidance during difficult times as well. Jack, where do you work?"

"I'm a retired detective from Washington County and a friend of Judge Lord's."

"How nice of you to help, Jack. You are a man with solid convictions and difficult dreams. Jack, dah case you struggle with is not your fault. Dah dreams of dah baby girl crying, shaken to death by her mother's hands, are your subconscious. You are blaming yourself. You must stop. It is evident to me dat you had a demanding career with too much death and pain. Jack, sometimes people hold onto things they should let go for their health and survival."

How could she possibly know about the shaken baby case? "I can deal with my past investigations myself. Ariel, you are probably on target about my past, but today, I am more interested in finding Mary. As every day passes, the chances get less and less for her to be found alive. What can you tell me about her? You are here for that, and the race against time is on. The clock is ticking."

"Jack, you will find Mary and her kitten. I know you will. She is close to Stillwater—near water, but not this river. A reservoir or water source and a notable government building. It is your task to find them, Jack."

How did she know about Tabby? Did Vivian tell her?

"That is all I can read for you today, Jack. You can have Judge Lord call me if she wants, but I must leave for another appointment."

I should have tape-recorded Ariel's conversation with me. Very enlightening if true.

I transported Ariel back to her Porsche and walked to the car. As she got into the car and shut the door, she rolled down the window and said, "Jack, don't forget what I told you about your night dreams. They will destroy you."

She handed me her calling card. "Give me a call. My office is in the IDS Center in Minneapolis. We could do lunch or dinner sometime. So nice to meet you." She completed the circle in front of the house. As she drove toward the gate, she gave a backhanded wave out the driver's window, and the white Porsche disappeared. Like a dream.

During my visit with Ariel, I felt mesmerized. Almost hypnotized. Is it possible? I felt relaxed and could not stop watching the white Porsche driving away; although Ariel was gone for several minutes. I thought she was supposed to snap her fingers to pull me out of the intense mental focus and bring me back to the reality of my search for Mary. I thought about the brief time I had spent with Ariel and the ten minutes of enjoyment watching the tranquil waters of the St. Croix. How long does it take to be hypnotized?

Whatever the meaning of Ariel's words, I'm sure of one thing. Ariel said, specifically, her clear guidance was for me. It is my task to find Mary and Vivian's cat.

What did I have? Statistics say abducted children are found within twelve miles of the crime scene, only 1 percent taken by strangers, and—if Ariel is correct—near a water source, by a notable government building. No mention of a key ring.

I first have to decide if I want to use the clues Ariel gave me. She knew about my dreams and my shaken baby case. There is no way she could learn those things.

At least I would have some areas to follow up on. I also have the keys, which may or may not be relevant. I need my map. I need to go back to my place.

With a quick stop inside to grab my keys and make sure everything was locked up, I headed back to Bayport.

As I walked through the door, I saw the light on my answering machine blinking. A single message from Vivian.

"Jack, Sunshine Marina has Courtship *on bunks and is reporting a twelve-inch scratch in the bow. Could you please stop by Sunshine Marina tomorrow and check the damage?* Courtship *has not been off the dock all summer. We can talk about the Clairvoyant's guidance next time we talk, but I must admit having pessimistic expectations. Love you."*

CHAPTER 20

The sleepless nights were beginning to take their toll. Not sleeping nights when I was back in the patrol was one thing; I was a lot younger, but at least I slept during the day. I'm not that young cop anymore and have started to feel run-down. I have been getting very little sleep because of that damn dream. I could hardly focus. My mind kept shutting down on me, and I was hanging on by a thread.

I was pushing through by sheer force of will, trying desperately to locate Mary. Any missing child would have had my complete attention, but this was Mary. I had fallen for her in just minutes. I don't think anyone could resist Mary's appeal. The fact that she was Vivian's niece dug the spurs deeper. It wasn't only Mary's life hanging in the balance. Vivian's was too.

The woman who, on the surface, looked like she had everything had dealt with a lot these past few years. First, her husband's sudden death, followed by her breast cancer diagnosis. She held on, displaying an inner strength few people possessed. I feared it might break her forever if I didn't find Mary in time, which kept me up at night now. I finally found the love of my life, and if I don't locate Mary, I may lose them both.

Driving through the darkness and the streets of Washington County used to relax me, even when I needed to stay alert on patrol. It was a comfortable space. Oh, not on the interstate during holiday traffic, but on these country roads without traffic.

Tonight, like so many others in my past, I am gradually unwinding. The gunshot wound to my right leg was beginning to heal. I needed to drive through my target area in northern Washington County, the *Corncob Jungle.*

In possession of my road atlas, I had several areas to check, and my Jeep would come in handy on some of the rough back roads. I was looking for signs of recent traffic and tracks heading off the road that may look suspicious, near bodies of water.

While my eyes scanned the area illuminated by my high beams, I was praying. I prayed that I would find that little girl who had grabbed hold of my heart without saying a word.

Starting my tour on Arcola Trail near Vivian's home, I began my thought process with a careful review of what we knew. The serial rapist, Kenny Clayton, has been identified and confirmed as the perpetrator. Now he is deceased.

I suspected Buster Greeley may have knowledge of Mary's disappearance, making him complicit, or may have seen the assailant without being aware. That is a cop's gut feeling, but I had no proof.

Evidence includes the backpack and the backpack's location when found, near the river, at the shoreline. Vivian's fiberglass yacht has a twelve-inch slice in the starboard side of the bow with army-green transfer paint. That happened this summer, according to the Sunshine Marina. They assert it wasn't there this year when the boat was delivered and secured to the Lord's dock. Vivian confirmed that *Courtship* hadn't left the dock all season. In addition, Vivian reports two nautical-blue teak folding chairs, embroidered with *Courtship* on the back of the chairs, remain missing. One chair, recovered by the dive team, is currently in the back of the Jeep. One chair remains missing.

The ring of five keys found near Vivian's dock may be the best piece of inculpatory evidence we have in this case, now that my primary suspect is dead. The five keys. I keep coming back to the keys. Three of the keys appear to be standard household keys. The two large keys are marked with the initials MCF and labeled "Do Not Duplicate." These are the ones I keep coming back to, but they appear to be a dead end. The keys in my possession are of a type not utilized in the facility, and prison staff reports that no registry exists for them.

Then there are the psychic's premonitions. I hate to admit I am desperate enough to use them, but I am. So the first clue was a water source. Washington County is full of little out-of-the-way brooks, streams, and ponds. Some of the historic buildings on Main Street in Stillwater even have streams that run right through the basement of the buildings.

The underground streams were not corrected when built and flooded the basements. So the building owners dug out a pathway for the stream right through the cellars. Those streams still exist today. Could Mary be in one of these buildings? The businesses could be checked quickly, but no government buildings on Main Street existed. The downtown buildings are all occupied.

The notable government buildings Ariel referred to are numerous and exist within my twelve-mile radius. Historic Stillwater is, after all, the county seat. I kept coming back to the prison.

It was way too late to call Scott at Superior Shores, but it was never too early to have breakfast at Omar's. Some food and a lot of coffee would give me a lift, so I could drive around Bayport and check out some water sources around the prison until the Sunshine Marina opened.

I wanted to check out the damage on *Courtship* before it was shrink-wrapped. The employee I spoke to told me they routinely take pictures of the boats before moving them, so there was documentation of the condition of the boat before *Courtship* was splashed last spring.

Although the county crime scene technicians had searched *Courtship* at Vivian's dock, nothing of evidentiary value was found. However, they hadn't spun the boat around, so the techs would not have seen the damage on the starboard side or given it much thought.

I finished breakfast and started for Sunshine Marina, only a short distance from Omar's. *Courtship* was easy to spot, and I began inspecting the damage, aided by the dawning light. I had taken a few photos myself and was about to leave Sunshine when an employee approached me and introduced himself. The Sunshine employee repeated their account of the boat damage and was confident that it had occurred during the current boating season.

He unwittingly gave me another possible avenue to explore when he said, "It was probably the service pontoon operator out of

Bobber's Bait." He continued, "That operator has no clue of how important the direction of the wind is when piloting a boat or what *slow no wake* means."

He suspected the service boat's operator was responsible for many expensive watercraft damages along the St. Croix. "The operator never reports the damage he causes, so the boat owners must file an insurance claim."

My wandering thoughts were getting focused, and I now had a visual piece of the puzzle. I asked, "What do you know about the service boat operator?"

"This is off the record, right?" At my nod, he continued, "We believe most thefts from marinas on the river from Stillwater to Afton are his doing. He doesn't take anything big, just whatever is in plain view—cash, cigarettes, liquor, items that he can pocket and leave quietly. Most boat owners believe it's probably kids responsible, and they don't get reported. Some boat owners keep several hundred dollars onboard."

I asked if he knew the operator's name and where he lived.

"I think his name is Peter, and he lives in Bayport somewhere. I talked with him one time. Seems like he has some disabilities and operates some lawn service on the river for affluent folks."

I thanked the young man for the information and headed back to my Jeep. Wow, this was a whole new thread to pull. Hopefully it will be the one that unravels the entire ball.

My next stop is Bobber's Marina and Bait to look closely at the service pontoon. It was still early enough that the boat would be at the marina.

As I was pulling into the parking lot at Bobber's, I saw a lone white male pulling out of the marina. The pontoon boat was heading south. The operator was standing behind the wheel and holding the pontoon on course in the heavy wind. The pontoon boat was army green in color and displayed a diagonal white stripe along the side.

Damn, if I had only been a few minutes earlier. As long as I was here, I walked down the dock to check on *Coffee Can*. I hadn't been here in weeks. The Bobber's staff are good about keeping an eye on things, like running the bilge pump after heavy rain or tightening the mooring lines during windy days.

"Everything okay, Jack? I haven't seen you in a while."

"Hey, Bob, I'm fine, just spending time trying to find the missing little girl, Judge Lord's niece."

"Yeah, I heard about that. What a tragedy. You don't think she is in the river?"

"No, I pray not. The Sheriff's Office dive team did an exhaustive search. The dive team leader is confident she is not in the river, and I have a lot of confidence in Hagen. That's what keeps me going."

"I met Bubbles. Brad had a diver training class here on my beach and has an interesting job."

Switching topics, I asked what he could tell me about the man who operates the service boat that had just pulled out of the marina.

"Oh, Peter." He paused and seemed to think for a moment before he continued, "He's nice but a little slow. His uncle owns the pontoon and has a river service south of here. He helps with yard work—cutting brush, moving rocks, trash pickups, anything the residents request."

"Does he live in the area?" I asked.

"He lives in Bayport, near the prison, and usually rides a bike here. That's his bike over there." He pointed to a blue bicycle near the dock. Bob continued, "I think the bike is his only transportation. When it rains, he doesn't work. I can't remember the last time I saw him driving a car."

"Why does his service pontoon look like a National Park Service boat with a diagonal white stripe?" I asked.

"That is because it's a retired government boat. It's retired, just like you!"

I chuckled at his little joke as Bob continued, "The older boats that begin to break down, leak oil, or start looking shabby are sold at the Federal Surplus Auction. The owners are required to remove the markings. Peter doesn't have much ambition or imagination with his pontoon. The newer park service boats are white with green stripes. It was cheaper to order all white boats and add the green-stripe graphics."

"Do you have phone numbers or addresses for Peter or his uncle?"

"I can do better than that. I have the registration number and the owner's and operator's name in the office."

"Thanks, Bob. I'll be right there." As Bob headed for the office, I walked to Peter's blue bicycle. It looked newer and aluminum, which means it was an expensive bike. Shimano was the brand, and I wrote down the serial number.

Bob wrote down the owner's name, address, and phone number at the office and included registration numbers. Minnesota law requires that a boat display its numbers on both sides of the boat near the bow.

While Bob answered the phone with one hand, he handed me the information with the other. I waved my thanks and started heading for the door. I read the service pontoon owner information, and I stopped abruptly. I couldn't believe my eyes.

"Is everything okay, Jack?" Bob asked as he covered up the speaker on the receiver. "You let me know if I can do anything to help you and the judge find that little girl. I mean it, ask." And with a wave of my hand, he was back on his phone.

I walked out the door and had to reread the name, this time out loud, "Registered owner, Buster Greeley, operator Peter Manning."

Peter Manning. A pedophile and a registered sex offender.

Jumping into the Jeep, I spun around and headed out of the lot.

At Seventh St. North, near the driveway of Bobber's Marina and Bait, I pulled over. From here, I was in a good surveillance position to keep an eye on the marina and Manning's bike.

I wasn't tired anymore. I finally had a trail to follow, and I know it is the right one. I quickly called Anne Reed.

Anne Reed, Community Service Officer, has been instrumental in many successful programs throughout Washington County. She had her degree, but more important to me was her common sense, my favorite attribute in a cop.

Anne was hired under a state grant, reports directly to the sheriff, and makes her own schedule. She comes and goes as she pleases. Her key card allows her access to all the Sheriff's Office areas except the jail, evidence room, and the damn War Room. I need her help. Picking up Anne's cell phone, I called her work phone.

"Anne, I'm so glad to catch you. I have a question about Clayton. Did the task force clear Clayton from Mary's abduction? I'm focusing on a Bayport sex offender and must clear my mind regarding Clayton's whereabouts when Mary was abducted."

Anne replied, "I'm sorry, Jack, the task force has been overwhelmed with evidence and interviews of additional victims coming forward. However, I learned from his mother and confirmed by his credit report that Clayton had worked for a Hammond, Wisconsin, used auto dealership. I drove to the small dealership, and the management confirmed that Clayton was working from 7:30 a.m. to 3:30 p.m. when Mary was abducted. Clayton has been cleared."

"Copy that, Anne, thank you. I also have a huge favor to ask you."

Anne replied, "Is this favor going to get me fired or just in trouble?"

"Neither one, I hope. It may just get you a promotion. Can you meet me at Bobber's Bait in Lakeland in twenty minutes? I will be at the start of the driveway down to the river.

"I also want a stolen check for a bicycle. I will text you the serial number. Then obtain the full name and date of birth of Peter Manning. Get a criminal history report and mug photo. Find out his probation officer's name and cell phone. Let's make it thirty minutes, Anne."

"Good idea," she replied sarcastically. "I'll be there as fast as I can, Jack."

I sat in the car, tapping my foot and tapping my fingers on the steering wheel at the same time. At this point, waiting any amount of time is excruciating. Every minute counted. I thought about the police motto, To Serve and Protect. It dates back to 1955, long before it became personal to me. The public often sees it on law enforcement vehicle graphics. Officers take that motto very seriously, but when it is one of the families of law enforcement, which in this case includes Judge Lord, the entire criminal justice community moves into high gear.

It is everyone's case, and all eyes and ears are focused. It didn't matter if you were retired or not. You answered the call. It was my duty to find Mary, dead or alive. It was my promise to the woman I loved that I would locate Mary. I wouldn't fail either one.

I was praying that I would find her alive.

CHAPTER 21

Peter Manning is a blast from my past. Manning moved to Stillwater years ago and had family members in the area. Previously Manning had lived in a small town in southeastern Minnesota called Caledonia, the county seat of Houston County. Caledonia has a total population of 2,500. Manning had been charged and convicted of multiple counts of criminal sexual conduct in the first degree, which should have resulted in a prison sentence.

Manning had abused at least six boys. After some time in the Houston County Jail, Manning was released under the condition of probation and court-ordered counseling. The small county counseling services were not adequate for the seriousness of Manning's convictions. The court transferred his probation to Washington County, where his family lived, and intensive programs were available.

The files indicated that Manning was a victim of child abuse of a physical nature at a very young age, specifically Shaken Baby Syndrome. Manning's medical history revealed that he had the mental capacity of no more than a twelve or thirteen-year-old.

Once he relocated to Stillwater, it wasn't long before Manning found a position at a Lutheran Church as a weekend volunteer day care worker. Three months later, Manning had increased his victim count to thirteen, a baker's dozen.

One of the victims reported the abuse to his parents. The parents reported to law enforcement, and an investigation was initiated. Additional victims were identified during my interview process. It isn't uncommon to find other victims after the start of an inquiry. These children will never forget that their first sexual experience was with Peter Manning.

The courts stonewalled where Manning should have been sentenced and incarcerated due to his mental disabilities and vulnerabilities. Minnesota statutes were clear that the second conviction of a sex crime should result in a three-year prison sentence minimum.

Manning was too old to be sentenced to the correctional facility at St. Cloud, a prison for younger adults, and the County Attorney's Office was looking for other options for him to serve his sentence.

Eventually the County Attorney's Office and the court agreed with Manning's lawyer that St. Peter Security Hospital in St. Peter, Minnesota, was the appropriate place for Manning to serve his sentence. There he would be incarcerated and receive treatment.

Manning was sentenced to five years, two years longer than a sentence in the prison system. His civil commitment read, "Sexual psychopathic personality, a.k.a. sexually dangerous."

St. Peter Hospital and I had become familiar with each other before this case since several of my cases had resulted in a similar outcome, although typically for longer sentences. St. Peter Security Hospital was a safe, secure option for sex offenders who often didn't fare well in the prison system.

I attended a weeklong training class at the security hospital, where I learned the potential benefit of collaborating on two components: treatment and confinement for sex offenders. I also had the opportunity to speak with a person I had arrested and served his sentence at St. Peter during the time I was in class. He had been in law enforcement in Washington County. Sex offenders come in all shapes and sizes and professions.

As I continued to wait, I called dispatch to get the information for the Bayport officer on duty.

"Nine one one Washington County, what is your emergency?"

"Dispatch, this is retired Detective Janssen."

"Hello, Jack. How can I help?"

"Would you have the Bayport officer on duty call me at this number?"

"I can do that. It is Officer Dale McPherson. He is new. Don't think you would have met him yet, Jack. I will have him call right away."

I didn't know who Dale McPherson was, but I believe I had worked with his dad in the felony investigation unit. I hadn't met him yet, though.

He is quick, I thought as I answered my phone. "This is Jack Janssen."

"This is Bayport Officer McPherson. You wanted me to call you?"

"Yes, thank you. I am helping out with the search for the missing niece of Judge Lord and may need your help checking a residence in Bayport. Would you be available?"

"Any help I can be, you let me know, and by the way, you worked with my dad. He retired several years ago. He spoke highly of you."

"Your dad was a good cop. When I heard that Bayport had hired you, I knew that city was making a good decision. Can I call you at this number when I need your help?"

"Yes, that is my cell. I will be waiting to hear from you."

As I ended the call, I whispered aloud, "I'm coming for you, Mary."

I sat and waited for Anne. Thankfully I didn't have to wait long. A typical unmarked squad, a blue four-door Crown Victoria, pulled into the drive alongside me. Anne was driving. "You made good time, Anne, thanks."

"No worries," she replied. "What do you have going with this Peter Manning character? Does it involve Judge Lord's niece? And by the way, Jack, dispatch has a message from Judge Lord about a candlelight vigil reminder for tonight at a Bloomington Chapel with the address."

"Anne, everything is falling into place. I am hoping it will lead us to Mary."

"God, I hope so. So, Jack, I have Manning's criminal history report and mug shot. I have included his driver's license record. He's revoked. The serial number for the bike came back stolen. The report was taken by Bayport PD two months ago. I called court services to talk to Manning's probation officer. He wasn't in. I did leave a message for him to call me as soon as possible. Haven't heard back yet."

"Anne, remember when you checked for thefts along the river for Judge Lord's security survey? Most water-related petty thefts along the St. Croix were Peter Manning, a convicted sex offender. I was the last cop who arrested him. He had been arrested for the same crime in southern Minnesota before that."

Pointing behind me down the hill, I asked Anne if she saw the blue bicycle beside the end dock. "There is your stolen. Manning left it there. He will be returning on an old park service pontoon boat and should pull into the empty slip beside the bike. Call me when you see him. You have his mug and physical. Please keep all the paperwork on Manning. That is department property, and I am a civilian. I don't want to get you into a bad spot at work, at least not for that," I said with a smile.

"I'll be heading to Arcola Trail to check on a lead, Anne. Don't engage with Manning. He has never been a violent man, but never underestimate a felon. Just call me."

*****

I was driving at a fast pace, northbound toward Arcola Trail, to have a conversation with Buster Greeley, owner of the service pontoon boat. Buster Greeley was a fixture around the Arcola Trail neighborhood. He was the groundskeeper for the entire community. His home was originally the guest cottage of one of the wealthy homeowners on Arcola Trail. Although the charming cottage was small, the builder designed it at the time of the larger estate house to fit into the neighborhood. Buster had become close to the property's original owners and their families.

The owners had generously deeded the cottage to Buster as a lifetime occupancy estate deed until his passing. I hoped to catch him home. I didn't have time to waste trying to track him down in the neighborhood.

The whimsical Fieldstone cottage could have inspired a Thomas Kincaid painting. Flower gardens, stone walkways, and stained glass windows capped with a Fieldstone chimney looked charming. It sat across the road from the river but included an easement path to the St. Croix and is about a half-mile from Vivian's property.

Buster had been interviewed previously by the Sheriff's Office investigators. Buster's background and alibi were checked once by the Sheriff's Office. However, I wanted to talk to him armed with this new information. No one knows the area around Arcola Trail better than Buster. He knows the properties and all of the families probably better than the neighbors themselves.

I've seen Buster many times and became familiar with him while working patrol years ago. At that time, I was dispatched to a house on Arcola Trail for a medical. Buster had been cutting grass that abuts the bluffs of the St. Croix with a lawn tractor. The lawn ran right up to a cliff overlooking the river.

Buster had been dumping grass clippings over the thirty-five-foot cliff all day, which was part of his routine at that particular estate. He had been doing it for years. After dropping the clippings, Buster pulled away from the cliff. Or so he thought. He had neglected to put the tractor in forward gear, and when he accelerated, the tractor lurched backward.

Buster had been found at the bottom of the bluff next to his tractor. In a way, Buster himself had saved his own life. His long habit of dumping brush and grass over the edge had provided a relatively soft landing spot for his fall. Even so, he had sustained a fracture to his spine. To this day, Buster walks with a noticeable cockeyed gait.

I hoped I could catch Buster at home. Only seconds after knocking on the solid oak door to his cottage, Buster opened the door and said, "Detective Janssen, welcome. Come in please. Have a chair," while pointing to a leather recliner. "Can I bring you coffee or a beverage?"

"Sure, black coffee will be fine, thanks."

Buster was a tall lean man, somewhere in his midseventies. His years in the sun had made his skin leathery, with deep lines and wrinkles on his face. He usually looked like he has a fresh sunburn. His face was always red. In his later years, he had begun wearing wire-rimmed glasses. He had smoked a corn-cob pipe for as long as I have known him. He was rarely without one hanging from his mouth.

Buster's home was neat as a pin, with bookcases on every wall. *National Geographic* seemed to be his book of choice, but books on butterflies, fish, birds, and wildlife were scattered on the shelves and tables in his living room. What was of particular interest to me was a ceramic doll collection. Most of the dolls appear to be Japanese geisha. They all had colorful dresses: white, aqua, jade, and red.

Some had umbrellas, and all had shiny black hair pulled neatly into a bun. The dolls' skin was very white, and they had very red lips. There must have been twenty dolls—an interesting collection for a man. I asked him about his doll collection as he handed me a mug of steaming coffee.

"It was my wife's collection. She received them from the Bradfords. They had picked them up for her during their travels. They lived across the road, and they deeded this house to me after they passed away."

I didn't feel like making a lot of small talk. I knew I was close to a breakthrough in this case. I reminded myself to take it slow. Don't rush the process. "So, Buster, I have received some new information, and you may be helpful. Are you the pontoon boat owner that has it slipped at Bobber's Bait near Lakeland? I was aware of the pontoon boat on the St. Croix River north of Stillwater that Bobby Bell operates for you. Who is the driver of the South River Service pontoon?"

An expression of dismay came over Buster's face, making him look even older than before. He didn't answer at once. Several minutes passed before he responded. I had to keep reminding myself not to rush him. I have learned that firsthand during my interviews, interrogations, and from other detectives.

I just held my position comfortably and waited him out. Finally answering, Buster said, "I knew you would come. Peter Manning is the operator of my boat south of 94, and my nephew. But he never works any jobs north of the interstate." He went quiet again, and again, I waited him out. Finally after several minutes, he continued, "You don't suppose Peter was involved in the disappearance of Ms. Lord's niece? Peter has been clean for years and has not done anything wrong, according to his probation officer."

Buster looked frail, and I didn't want him to stop talking or breathing. I asked quietly, "Buster, do you know where Peter is working today? I know he is on the river. I also want to know where he lives?"

"He lives in a house between the Stillwater Prison and St. Michael's Cemetery. It's pretty secluded. You can hardly see it if you don't know it is there. I'm sorry I can't give you an address. It doesn't have one as far as I know, but I think it's owned by the Stillwater Prison and rented as a caretaker's quarters. Peter also helps out with landscaping duties locally. I can call him, but as you know, cell phone coverage is spotty on the St. Croix River."

"Buster, I want you to call Peter and find his location today, but whatever you do, don't tell him I'm looking for him, understand? I don't want to have you arrested." I couldn't help the sound of my voice at this point. I knew I was on the right track. My tolerance expired. Now minutes counted. I knew it. "Buster, do you understand?"

"Yes, sir, Detective Janssen, I understand."

In different circumstances, I would have felt sorry for the older man. A little younger, he would have been belted in the front seat of my Jeep. Buster wouldn't have been able to warn Peter Manning I was looking for him, and he could have taken me right to his nephew's house. But he looked beaten down, and there were tears in his eyes. I couldn't do it. Buster called Peter's cell phone number, which went to voice mail and said the mailbox was full.

I wrote my cell number for Buster, and Peter's cell number for myself. I stood up and motioned for him to remain seated. I gave him a comforting pat on his shoulder and some directions.

"If you hear from him, find out where he is and get any information on him you can. You will call me. Right, Buster?" At his nod, I continued, "Call me, and don't tell him I'm looking for him, do you understand?"

Buster looked up at me and nodded his head in the affirmative.

I was now heading back down Highway 95 toward Bayport. Being up all night is not one of those things that I miss about patrol; I don't have the energy I had during my uniform days.

I received a text from Anne, who reported dispatch received another message from Judge Lord regarding the candlelight vigil for Mary at a Bloomington Chapel with the address at seven o'clock tonight. Vivian had left numerous messages on my landline and cell phone unanswered. Probably because I hadn't checked my messages at home, and the Sheriff's Office confiscated my cell phone.

I wasn't thinking about the candlelight vigil, not yet. I had promised that I would find Mary, and I would. She would be alive. I believe that. I didn't want Vivian to give up on Mary or me. She said it was a prayer vigil so family and friends could pray together and offer support. It was essential to her that I would be there. There were several items on my checklist that I needed to do first.

I had five hours to find Mary. "I'm coming for you, Mary," I whispered, praying I was right and not too late.

CHAPTER 22

I was pulling up near the St. Michael's Cemetery entrance when Anne called. I could tell she was excited when she began, "Jack, I'm following Manning. I almost lost him when the owner stopped me and wanted to know who I was and what the hell I was doing on his docks. I had to show him my ID and tell him I was working with you before he let me leave. I almost lost him, but I have him now, though. He is heading toward Bayport. Also, I just sent you a picture."

"Copy that, Anne. Keep me posted."

My time would have been short if Manning was heading this way. Getting out of the Jeep, I started toward the cemetery, where Buster said I would find the house where Peter had been living.

A wooded area defined the back of the cemetery. The sun was casting rays through the branches providing some small amount of light to the dimness of the forested area. I kept walking as fast as my sore leg would allow until I spotted an old fence. The fence was made of woven wiring and topped with barbed wire.

The fence was rusted, with "No Trespassing" signs evenly spaced. The signs that I could see all had bullet holes in them. Peering past the fence, I could barely see a small one-story building made of the same medium brown bricks the prison had used in construction. Following the fence line, I came to a gate. There was an old path, barely discernible, that could have been a driveway. It looked like it may have ended at the house. From the entrance, I could see someone had closed all the interior window curtains on this side of the house. Could this small building be Manning's house?

Just then, my phone signaled an incoming text. It was a picture from Anne. It was of the pontoon that Manning operates. What do we have here? I thought as I enlarged the photo. The image was out of focus when enlarged, but there was a blue teak chair at the helm. It looked like the one I have in the back of my Jeep. The writing on the chair said *Courtship*. It was blurry, but I would stake my life on it. Peter had been at Vivian's dock!

I immediately called Anne as I stood beside the locked driveway gate. "Do you still have Manning in sight?"

"Jack, I'm sorry I lost him. He was near the Bayport City Park, the park by the river."

"Okay, Anne, I am going to call Bayport Officer McPherson. His radio call number is 503. Anne, Manning was at Judge Lord's. He has her stolen boat chair on the service pontoon."

I contacted Officer McPherson and briefed him about Manning and the additional information we now had. That Manning was currently on a blue bicycle stolen from his city.

"It may be time for you to contact your chief and advise him of our updated situation. I will be checking a house where Manning may reside."

I walked the entire perimeter of the fencing and found another padlocked gate at the back of the house. All windows had been covered from the inside. This house was consistent with Buster's description, and it appeared it could have been prison housing of some kind.

While walking back toward the driveway gate, my leg started to throb. I barely felt it. This house had to be Manning's, and I believe I was close to finding Mary. The urgency was the only thing I was feeling at this point.

I wasn't too concerned about going into the house, but the barbed wire on top of the gate was intimidating, especially with my leg. Taking the lock in my hand, I discovered that it was dummy-locked. It looked locked but hadn't clicked closed. I walked through the gate and up to the front door and pounded on the door with no answer. I tried the door and found it locked.

Pulling my phone out, I called LaVonne while attempting to find a window I could see inside.

"I am having lunch with a friend. This better be good, Jack."

"You know I have you on retainer for professional services when requested, and I'll make it quick and hope you will, too," I explained the situation.

"I need to know if my situation qualifies as exigent circumstances. I don't want to compromise evidence or a conviction, but I'm close to not caring right now. This may be where Judge Lord's niece may have been taken or held. I need to know if this qualifies as exigent circumstances."

"Jack, hang tight for a minute. I'm with the County Attorney now. Let me get his opinion. I'll call you right back."

"LaVonne, you have fifteen minutes before I kick this door down." Just as I disconnected, my cell phone rang in my hand. It was Anne.

"Officer McPherson spotted Manning driving a golf cart and pursued him in a low-speed chase. We couldn't find the bike, but it had to be somewhere around the city park. The golf cart has Anderssen Security graphics, but Bayport reports Anderssen Windows is no longer the owner."

"Anne, you probably don't want to get involved in the chase unless requested. I'm ready to enter a house near the Stillwater Prison, where I believe Manning lives and where I may find Mary. What do you know about exigent circumstances and searching without a warrant?"

"Jack, I am no lawyer, but I believe exigent circumstances apply to law enforcement or the government. It involves a police action taken without a warrant immediately to preserve evidence, now or never. But, Jack, you are no longer an officer of the court. You are a civilian. I don't believe that your entering the house applies. You may be sued in a civil action, though. Jack! Manning just flew past my location! I didn't realize a golf cart could go that fast."

"Anne, have McPherson take Manning into custody. Stand by there to see if you might be of some help." As soon as he is in custody, have Bayport transport him to St. Michael's Cemetery. You will see my Jeep. We may need him to locate Mary."

I couldn't wait any longer for LaVonne's legal advice, so I was ready to use force to enter the residence. The only proof I had was my gut instincts. They had never let me down before. I trusted them now.

I suddenly remembered Scott telling me about the keys the divers recovered, which may be a critical clue. I retrieved the keys from my Jeep. I didn't know why I hadn't grabbed them until now. I made my way back to the front door, inserted the key that I had thought looked like a house key, and unlocked the door.

My training would have me unholstering my duty weapon with my index finger off the trigger until I was ready to shoot. Trigger discipline. Today, with only a Kel-Lite flashlight and no other weapon in my tool belt, I opened the front door slowly and shouted as loud as I could, "Sheriff's Office," then slowly walked inside.

It was a tiny living room with all the blinds closed. The trees were now shading the house, and with the setting sun, it was pretty dark inside. I could make out two kennels, side by side, across the room. I could hear the dog better than I could see him. He was whimpering, almost crying. It was a smaller white-brown-and-black dog. I think they are called Cavaliers, but more importantly, in the smaller kennel, I could see the orange face of a cat peering through the kennel door.

It was Tabby! I suddenly remembered Mary's color crayon picture of the green grass and the two images. One was black, brown, and white. The other image was orange. She had indicated to me with a nod the orange figure was Tabby. I had never questioned Mary about the black, brown, and white image she had colored.

The living room and kitchen were joined together with an eerie similarity to Buster's. Several bookcases and shelves contained only children's books.

There was also a children's table with two small chairs. The kitchen table, in the center of the room, had a corncob pipe resting on an ashtray.

Finally reaching the kennels, I saw they were in a type of pantry almost the size of a bedroom. I found miscellaneous clothing for boys and girls neatly stacked on the top of a bureau. I found more boys' and girls' toys on a shelf above the kennels.

No Mary. Tears began running down my face. The drumbeat in my head synchronized with the words, *If you find Tabby, you'll find Mary*. I ran my fingers through my hair and pulled in frustration—no Mary. The dog had quieted down. Both the dog and cat were looking at me impatiently when my cell phone had a text from LaVonne.

It read: *If you enter the house, you are not acting on behalf of the County Attorney's Office or the Sheriff's Office. That's the best I can do without a warrant.*

At this point, it hardly mattered. Mary had been here. The phrases kept going over and over in my head. I felt like I was falling apart. I sank to the floor beside the kennels. The tears were rolling down my cheeks, and I didn't even notice them. The animals did. Both of them were sticking their noses out of the kennels. I reached to pet their noses, and the dog was licking my hand. I started talking to them both. "Do you guys know where Mary is? I wish you could tell me."

As I talked, I opened the door to the kennels to release them. The dog jumped into my lap and started licking my face. For the first time, I realized that I was crying, and the dog was licking the tears away.

Tabby walked across my lap and headed to the back door. My emotions turned from a complete breakdown to fierce determination. I reject defeat, and I will find her.

My cell phone rang. "Jack, we lost him," Anne announced. "Near Anderssen Windows."

"Anne, he is our only hope of finding Mary at this point. Vivian's cat is at Manning's house. Manning knows where she is. We have to find him. Have McPherson call for backup from the Sheriff's Office, Stillwater and Oak Park Heights Police, and get the state patrol chopper up looking for him before it's dark. They are looking for the man who abducted Mary.

"I have concluded the search of Manning's house, and there is evidence that Mary was here. I will secure the home. I'm going to look around outside. Can you come to my location? I could use your help. Head toward the cemetery. You will see my Jeep, follow the path through the woods, and you will see Manning's brick house."

Tabby sat at the back door while the dog sat in my lap, enjoying the petting. "Tabby, come here." She only stood up and pawed at the door. I put the dog down, stood up, and walked to the back door. I saw a beaten-down pathway heading to an old large stone building. The path could have been from a lawn tractor of some type.

The outbuilding appeared to be from earlier times at the prison, with the same stone facade. Possibly a storage building of some kind. There were no windows from what I could see.

I opened Manning's back door, and Tabby immediately brushed past me and headed down the pathway, stopping at the gate. I found the padlock was also dummy-locked, similar to the front entrance. I unlocked the gate, and Tabby ran to the outbuilding, as I followed Tabby with the dog at my side.

I paused halfway to the building and, looking up, saw a very tall blue water tower, identified as Stillwater Prison in bold black letters. Would this qualify as a reservoir or water source? Could this be what the psychic was seeing?

There was a small service door on the outbuilding at the end of the path. Tabby was sitting right in front of the door, looking back toward the dog and me. My heartbeat was rapid as I picked up speed toward the building. Even the pain in my leg didn't stop me from running full out to the door.

Tabby would periodically stand and make a circle, then sit again, as if impatient for me to arrive. I approached the door and found it locked. I promptly pulled the key ring from my pocket and said, "Thanks, Scott."

Tabby was now winding herself between my feet, almost tripping me. The door appeared to have an older, outdated deadbolt lock. I inserted the first of the two MCF keys into the lock, held my breath, and turned. Nothing happened. Not wasting any time, I tried the second MCF key. The lock seemed to spin smoothly, as though it had been in frequent use.

The door opened with a creaking sound. Tabby brushed past my legs as she launched into the building and disappeared. The single upper window that faced west over a garage door was the only natural lighting, piercing the darkness. The building was cold and smelled musty.

Through the upper window, the shaft of light from the setting sun captured moths, dust, and, no doubt, nanoparticles in the light stream, adding movement and radiance to its path. Turning on my Kel-Lite, I added my own light stream to the darkness, stepping over scurrying mice as I called out, "Mary!" I listened and then called, "Mary, it's Jack. Mary!"

I know Mary doesn't talk, but just making an announcement for her to hear was important. My eyes were adjusting to the darkness more and more as I moved slowly into the building. Looking around, I observed old dusty sewing machines and rolls of twine from earlier years at the prison twine factory.

In a dark shadowy corner of the building, I saw a sign above a colorful bookcase that read PETER'S DAY CARE. The sign is decorated with four stick figures in colored outfits of red, green, yellow, and blue. There were both boys in pants and girls that had triangles for dresses.

I could hear the mice scurrying away from the sudden light as I cautiously approached the area. Squinting into the darkness, as I waved my flashlight back and forth, I stopped and focused my light just to my left. I could make out a small body. It was Mary's lifeless body. Tabby lay curled closely beside her as I approached. I rushed the remaining distance to Mary and fell to my knees. I could immediately feel the sutures tear in my right leg.

"Mary, it's Jack." While leaning close and kissing her cold forehead. I started checking for signs of life. I listened for breathing and checked her carotid artery for a pulse. I found both: a faint pulse and shallow breathing. I didn't have time for more than a thank you, God, as I quickly checked for any injuries. I was desperate to pick her up but didn't want to do any further harm. I could find no injuries, but she was freezing. She needed immediate attention. I didn't know how much time I had, only knowing that this precious girl was near death. I would not panic. I never panicked. I wanted to panic.

I had to pick Tabby up if I wanted to lift Mary. Tabby's warm body was helping. Tabby lay alongside Mary and would not move. I had to remove her from this building. She felt so cold but opened her eyes briefly as I began to move her. Lifting her, I wrapped one arm, then the other, around my neck and felt a slight squeeze.

"We are getting out of here, Mary. Jack has you. Tabby showed me where you were. We are getting out of here."

They felt featherlight in my arms. I think the cat weighed more than this little five-year-old did.

I began running out of the building, almost tripping over the threshold and nearly knocking Anne down. My recent leg surgery was now painful and feeling wet.

"We need rescue, Anne. She is barely breathing and almost frozen." I didn't even hear Anne request paramedics on her radio to our location.

Although I have heard of people crying tears of joy, it isn't something I have ever experienced. I had done more weeping in one afternoon than I remember since I was a very young boy. I could taste the salt of my tears in my mouth. My emotions were so intense I felt that I could explode into a million pieces.

I had to keep it together for Mary. *These are happy tears*, I kept reminding myself. I was so afraid I had been too late.

As we walked, almost running toward Manning's house and around toward the cars, I asked Anne for the time. "It is 1754 hours, sir."

"You can knock that sir off, Anne. We are partners. Save time for your report."

I could hear sirens in the distance approaching. I handed the key ring to Anne, asked her to secure Manning's house and the outbuilding, and then turn the keys over to Bayport Police.

As Anne headed back up the path, I punched the number for Children's Hospital into my cell phone while holding Mary and Tabby. I knew the number by heart. I wanted the best for Mary, and that was Dr. Carolyn Engel.

I knew Dr. Engel in a professional capacity. Dr. Engel is an expert and founding physician for the Midwest Children's Center, located at Children's Hospital. She is nationally recognized for her medical evaluations, diagnoses, and case management of child abuse investigations. I need her on Mary's case and only hope she is available tonight.

My heart rate slowed as the Bayport ambulance pulled up behind my Jeep. I met the paramedics at the back of the ambulance as they rolled the stretcher out.

As I approached the first responders, I called out the paramedic protocols. "Five-year-old Mary Hastings, abducted October 5, in a very weakened condition, dehydrated, hypothermic, only opened her eyes once, transportation to St. Paul Children's Hospital, Children's has been advised."

I carefully placed Mary and Tabby onto the ambulance gurney. I don't think these young first responders quickly take instructions from the public. The driver, who was the taller of the two, replied with a tone of contempt, "Yes, sir!"

My commands continued, "I will be riding in the back. Judge Lord, the girl's aunt, and her mother will meet us at the hospital."

The driver's response was, "Yes, sir. We are unable to take the cat, department policy." I dismissed his response as Anne approached the ambulance.

"Have they got him?"

"Not yet in custody, Jack."

"Copy that, Anne. We are taking Mary to Children's Hospital now."

The driver repeated, "Not the cat, sir. It's policy." I continued my conversation with Anne without responding or looking at the driver.

While pointing to Manning's dog, "Would you take care of that dog, keep him safe?" I didn't even know the dog's name. He had been sitting patiently beside my Jeep all this time.

Anne looked over at the dog, patted her leg, and he came right over. "Nice dog, Jack. Is he yours?"

"He is now."

I attempted to call Vivian while the paramedics did their preliminary transport work. No response from Vivian. I was sure the candlelight vigil had started without me, and she had turned off her cell phone.

The paramedic had now started an IV and was administering oxygen to Mary. She looked so small, lying on the life-assist cot, strapped down and ready for transport. I had a flashback of seeing baby Mary, critically shaken and on life support at Ramsey Hospital, who had died.

Tabby isn't a large cat but looks almost bigger than Mary at that moment. Mary barely made a bump under the blanket. Her color was returning, but only once—when I picked her up—did I see those beautiful blue eyes. The skin around her eyes appeared sunken and dark, and her eyelids were puffy.

The driver was going to make an issue about bringing Tabby with us. That was confirmed when he said, "The patient is ready for transport, sir. Would you please remove the cat?" It was declared as a question, but he expected to be obeyed. It wasn't going to happen—no sense in wasting time and trying to plead or coax him.

My response was substantial. "My name is Detective Sergeant Jack Janssen, my partner is CSO Anne Reed from the Sheriff's Office, and the cat's name is Tabby. I have instructed Officer Reed to arrest you for failure to obey a lawful order if you don't have this ambulance moving in the next thirty seconds. Understood?"

Looking in Anne's direction, she looked apprehensive, maybe because she doesn't have handcuffs or has never made an arrest or probably because she wanted her first arrest to be a felony, not a paramedic doing his job.

The driver took less than ten seconds to decide getting his patient to the hospital as quickly as possible was more important than mixing it up with me. He promptly moved to the driver's seat and got behind the wheel as I said to Anne, "I need you to go to Bloomington and notify Judge Lord and Amanda that we found Mary. She must bring Amanda to Children's Hospital, and don't forget the dog. Do you have the Bloomington address for the chapel?"

At her nod of assent, I said, "Let's go, gentlemen. We have a critical patient going to Children's Hospital." I gave another call to Vivian, with negative contact. I was concerned about how Vivian would react when Anne arrived at the chapel.

I hoped she didn't fear the worst when it was all good news.

CHAPTER 23

I had taken this ride a few times before with a victim in the back of an ambulance. Tonight was different; Mary was the victim, and I was so damn scared. She looked so fragile. So weak. She made my heart break. Tabby lay stretched out along her side. As close as the blanket covering Mary would allow her to be. I managed a little smile for Tabby. It was the first time I had ridden in an ambulance with a cat on the stretcher.

As we pulled away from the street in front of the cemetery, I got a call from Officer McPherson. He sounded pretty shaken up. "Detective, your friend Manning is a piece of work. He crashed into my squad and caused a real traffic jam. I'm sorry he managed to escape, but we are still searching for him."

"Thanks for the help, McPherson. The good news is we are transporting Judge Lord's niece to Children's Hospital by ambulance. She should be okay."

"Well, that makes this mess worth it then! I'll be happy to give my chief that news."

"Copy that. You should probably have your chief contact Assistant County Attorney LaVonne Williams for a search warrant of the residence. She is familiar with the case. Let me know when Manning is located, and thanks again for your help."

I tried calling Vivian's phone again, but it went to voice mail. This call wasn't the news you left on voice mail. I figured she had her phone off for the vigil.

Again, my phone rang. "You're a popular guy," the paramedic said as he carefully checked Mary's vitals. He did not like working around a cat, but he was taking good care of Mary.

195

I answered my phone, "Jack Janssen here."

"Jack, It's Bob from Bobber's. That asshole Manning just left the marina heading north on his pontoon. What should I do?"

"From what I hear, Manning is a shitty driver during the daylight hours. I guess we will see how he does at night. I will call Washington County and get their water patrol to search for him.

"Say, Bob, when they locate Manning, would you be willing to pull the pontoon out and secure it in your storage barn?"

"Jack, if they drive it to my marina, I will pull it out and make sure it is secured inside."

"Thanks, Bob, for everything. And, Bob, we found her. We found Mary. We are on the way to the hospital, but I think she will be okay."

"That is the best news I have heard, Jack. I am so damn happy for you and her family."

"Thanks again for everything, Bob. Talk to you soon." Before my phone shut off for lack of battery, I wanted to check with Anne. She was en route to the vigil in Bloomington.

"Hello, Jack. I'm only a couple of blocks from the chapel."

"Thanks, Anne. My battery is low. We are only five minutes from Children's, and Manning is still on the run. Could you contact dispatch and get the Afton Water Patrol heading north to search the river? He is on his green pontoon with white stripes. Maybe have Stillwater put an officer on the lift bridge watching for him. We are just pulling into Children's Hospital. See you soon."

As the door opened to the sally port of the emergency room, standing prominently in plain view was Dr. Engel. White lab coats and emergency personnel flanked her. She stood out in the crowd. Tall, blonde, with prominent Nordic ancestry. I have never seen her in a white coat all the time I have known her. I asked her once why. Her logic made perfect sense. She thought the lab coats were a barrier between her and the children under her care. The coats made the kids nervous and prevented them from opening up to her. She always dressed down. I have even seen her in jeans over the years. Unless she was in court, then she looked like a force to be reckoned with on the stand. Over the years and the many child abuse cases we had worked on together, we had become friends and colleagues. We recognized the same dedication to the young crime victims we served, each in our way.

Not everyone could work these cases year after year without developing a thick skin. We never stopped seeing each child, not as a part of a caseload but as an individual child who needed our full attention. That is what made us unique in our respective fields. It also brought me to the brink of an emotional collapse. Here I was again. Just seeing her there calmed me.

As I limped out of the back of the ambulance, Dr. Engel walked toward me. I reached out to shake her hand, but she brushed my hand aside and wrapped me in a big hug. She couldn't see it, but it made me want to start crying again.

She began to chuckle as the stretcher came out of the ambulance. "Jack, I have had animals on the stretcher but have always been toys. You brought me a live cat?"

"I hope that won't be a problem, Carolyn. They are pretty attached, and that cat, Tabby, saved Mary's life."

"It won't be a problem right now, Jack."

Just then, Mary opened her eyes. Carolyn pulled me close so Mary could see me when she bent down and said, "Hello, Mary, I'm Dr. Engel." Mary looked at me, then at the doctor, and wrapped her arms around Tabby as tightly as she could. Tabby adjusted her head until it was on Mary's chest, right under her chin.

The attendants began to wheel Mary's stretcher through the doors. Mary suddenly looked very anxious.

"I'm coming with you, Mary," I said. "I'll stay where you can see me. The doctor will come too."

Dr. Engel quietly directed the orderlies, "Room 10, gentleman."

I recognized the room number. That exam room has a conference room attached with a two-way glass that enables authorized people to observe the activity in the exam room. Dr. Engel looked at me with a raised brow, and I nodded that I understood.

Taking her elbow to let the orderlies pass with the stretcher, I said, "Carolyn, I have to tell you, Mary is nonverbal. You need to know that before you go in there. She is a smart little girl, though, and I swear that she almost communicates telepathically because I never have a problem knowing what she wants." We had caught up with the stretcher.

"That isn't Mary's telepathy, Jack. That is your heart. It's the biggest I have ever known. Come to the exam room with me so Mary can see you. Let's see if we can separate her and the cat so I can do an exam."

I stood beside the hospital's exam table so I would be beside Mary as they transferred both Mary and Tabby off the ambulance stretcher. I gave the paramedics a salute and a thank you as they wheeled their empty cot out of the room. Mary was still clutching Tabby, but now she was looking at me.

"Hey, Mary," I said as I put my hand on her little head and leaned down. "You're safe now, and Mommy and Aunt Vivian are going to be here soon."

She continued to stare at me with those big blue eyes. First, they wouldn't open, and now it seemed she would never blink or close them again. "Mary, you trust me, don't you?" Continuing to look at me, she slowly nodded. "I trust you, too, you precious girl. Dr. Carolyn is my friend. She came to help you just because I asked her to. She is a special doctor and needs to look you over. You have been so brave. Can you be brave just a little longer and let Dr. Carolyn do that?"

She looked over my shoulder at the doctor, then back at me. I think I was holding my breath, waiting for her to respond. When she gave me a little nod, I felt like I had passed a steep hurdle.

"Mary, I have to leave the room while you and the doctor get to know each other. I have been looking for you for so long, and I feel bad that I have to leave you, even for a minute. Do you think I can take Tabby with me so that she can make me feel good like she does for you?"

I could see her try to tighten her hold on Tabby, but her little arms were weak. Tabby lifted her head from Mary's chest and rubbed her nose on Mary's chin. A little tear ran down Mary's cheek. My heart was breaking. Then she nodded. She kissed Tabby's nose and let her arms drop away.

I carefully lifted Tabby off the exam table and stood with her in my arms for a few minutes. Finally Carolyn moved to the other side of Mary.

"I think Tabby will take good care of Jack."

Mary looked at her and gave her a brief nod and a little smile. The smile didn't reach her eyes, but she was trying. I knew she was still afraid. I hated to leave the room.

"Jack, I think Mary and I will be just fine. You can stay right outside the door. I will get you as soon as Mary and I get to know each other a little."

I leaned over, kissed Mary on her forehead, and left the room, moving to the room next door. Having Carolyn take over was such a relief. I wouldn't have felt like this with any other doctor.

Suddenly I felt my right leg wouldn't allow me to stand for another minute. I sank into one of the chairs. The tension had been the only thing holding me upright. My head was throbbing, and my leg had started to bleed at some point.

Carolyn had an incredibly calming influence over her child patients, which tuned into Mary. In my lifetime, I've never met any person who has this uncanny gift with children. I have seen her work miracles with deeply traumatized children. Carolyn spoke of my heart. I think that is where we recognized alike spirit.

I didn't dare leave the room in case Mary needed me, so I used the hospital phone and called the desk. I explained my phone situation and asked if anyone had a cord I could borrow. The admitting clerk said she would find one and bring it to me.

Tabby and I looked through the glass and watched Mary and Dr. Carolyn. Of course, the doctor was talking, but Mary was listening. I think Carolyn was winning her over.

A young woman came in with a cord for my phone. I was in touch again. I asked her to keep her eye out for Vivian, Amanda, and Anne. And to please direct them to this room when they arrive.

Having my phone plugged in, I received a text message from Anne, who reported being within five minutes of the hospital. I also had a voice mail from Buster Greeley, who said Peter Manning was now at his home. Please call.

The hospital line in the room rang, and I picked up and identified myself. It was the Washington County Communication Center. The dispatcher advised me that water patrol had located the pontoon boat, believed to be driven by Manning, south of the Arcola High Bridge on the Minnesota side of the river.

I asked her to confirm the boat owner was Buster Greeley by registration number and not to leave the pontoon unattended. I then advised her to dispatch two squads to the registered owner's residence on Arcola Trail to search for Peter Manning, who was at the Greeley residence and wanted in the abduction of Judge Lord's niece.

In addition, I advised dispatch that Buster Greeley is the uncle of Manning and has cooperated with law enforcement. I was holding Tabby, who never took her eyes off Mary, through the window during this time.

Feeling like my legs would finally hold me again, I stood up just as Anne opened the door. Vivian rushed past her, straight toward me with outstretched arms. She wrapped her arms around me. There I stood, with my arms around the cat and unable to reciprocate. Vivian was crying, Amanda and I were crying, and poor Anne looked like she didn't know what to do next.

I began laughing through tears and kissed Vivian on the mouth. To hell with letting the cat out of the bag, so to speak.

Then I said, "We're squishing, Tabby."

Laughing, she pulled back. I knocked on the window. A sign we had used in the past to indicate we needed entrance to the room. "Come with me," I said, bringing them to the exam room door. Opening the door, I let them pass through, closed it behind them, and went back into the conference room.

Tabby wasn't happy as she remained with me. Anne and I watched the reunion between Mary, her mother, and her aunt. They were all overcome with emotion. If I had to say who was more controlled, I would have said Mary.

She gave hugs, weak though they were, and her loved ones took turns hugging her back.

Carolyn let the reunion run its course. Then there was some discussion. I didn't have the speaker active. It felt too much like invading a private moment to me. Finally Vivian and Amanda returned to the room with Anne and me.

Grabbing my now-partially charged phone and pocketing it, I asked the three women huddled around the window to the exam room, "Does anyone want some coffee?"

Not taking their eyes off Mary and the doctor, Vivian and Amanda nodded absently, still absorbed by what was happening through the window. "I know I could sure use some."

Anne said, "I'll go with you and help carry the cups."

I passed Tabby off to Vivian, and as we turned to go, I asked Vivian and Amanda if they wanted the speaker on so they could listen to what Carolyn was saying.

Amanda spoke to me for the first time since she entered the room. "Oh, yes, please. I didn't know that was an option. Thank you." I backtracked to the window and flipped the ordinary light switch beside the window. Carolyn quietly asked Mary if things hurt as she examined every inch of her little body.

I walked down the hall to the vending area, and my phone rang. It was the Sheriff's Office Communication. I learned that Manning was in handcuffs at Buster Greeley's house. In addition, the water patrol was standing by at the pontoon, waiting for instructions. "Stand by, and I'll pass the phone to Anne Reed. She has been very instrumental in solving this case. She would be the better person to give directions from here on."

With a wink, I passed the phone to Anne, who muted the speaker and looked at me askance.

"Okay, smart guy, what should I say? Should they impound it as evidence?"

I smiled, my first genuine smile in days. "Right in one. Have them tow it to Bobber's Bait. He has been advised and will pull it out and secure it inside his pole barn."

Anne relayed instructions through dispatch to the water patrol and muted the speaker again. "Jack, what about Manning? What should the deputies do with him?"

"Come on, Anne, what do you think they should do with him?"

"Arrest his ass for probable-cause kidnapping, Minnesota statute 609.25?"

After relaying that information through dispatch, she disconnected and handed the phone back to me. "Easy peasy," she said.

"Now you are talking like a cop, except for the easy peasy stuff," I said. "What about the fact that you are a civilian with the Sheriff's Office? Can you direct a sworn officer to arrest a perp for a probable-cause arrest without a warrant?"

Anne thought about it for a moment, then answered, "Yes. The requirement involves an established basis for the cumulative knowledge of the investigating officers. In this case, a totality of circumstances with the combined information obtained would qualify as probable cause, making this a good arrest."

"Wow! You are a credit to the Sheriff's Office, Anne. You will make a great deputy sheriff."

Smiling at her, I said, "Grab a few of those cream and sugar packets. I don't know what this stuff tastes like." Handing her two cups of coffee, we headed back. "I hope you don't mind waiting awhile. You are my ride home."

"No problem, Jack. We should check on the dog. He may have eaten the upholstery of my car by now."

Holding one cup with my teeth, I opened the door to the conference room. I handed Vivian the first cup and kissed her before she had a chance to take a sip. "How is it going in there?"

"Well, she has gotten those rags off her and into that little gown. She found one with kittens on it. She almost got a smile out of her for that. I only saw a few bruises, but the doctor may have seen more. She is doing a more detailed exam now. She lets Mary look over every piece of equipment before doing anything. Jack, she seems very nice." Taking a sip of coffee, she made a face as she looked into the cup.

"It's not like the coffee that comes out of your magic machine, but it will have to do. I brought these to help, though it still won't measure up." I smiled as I handed her the cream and sugar packets. "And Dr. Engel is the best in the whole country. You can trust her. We will step out and take the dog for a walk, and then we will be back."

Vivian said, "Dog? What dog?"

"I think it's Peter's, but he is friendly with Tabby, so we are keeping him," I said with a smile, as though what I said sounded normal.

She patted my cheek and said okay, then went back to watching and listening to what was happening in the exam room.

As Anne and I turned to leave, I said, "I don't think she even heard me. They must both be so relieved. I think Amanda had given up on finding Mary alive, though Vivian never doubted we would find her. Even after the commander put the case on the back burner."

"They were so lucky to have you, Jack. One more night would have been the difference for that little girl."

"Lucky to have us," I said in return. "I have to make a call while we walk the dog. I hope you don't mind." Passing the security, I told the officer our plans and told him we would be back in thirty minutes.

The cute little dog had waited patiently in the front passenger seat of Anne's squad. He was pleased to see us and gave equal attention to us as we took him out of the car. Neither of us had a leash, but the dog was obedient as we began walking. I pulled out my phone as we walked through the parking lot, looking for some grass.

I called Scott. "We did it! We have her, Scott! Mary was taken by a convicted sex offender, probably from Judge Lord's dock."

I could hear the smile in Scott's voice. "I never had any doubt you would find her, son. How is she?"

"As far as I can tell, she is doing all right. Dr. Engel is examining her now. I know she is dehydrated and probably hungry, but I think she is doing well. When I found her, she was unconscious. She awoke after they started an IV, and we arrived at the hospital."

"Such good news, Jack. What about the cat?"

"Found her too. She was the one that led me to Mary. And I may have inherited a dog."

I went on to explain finding both animals in an old brick house owned by the cemetery or the prison. "Scott, the key ring was instrumental, and the keys were for that property!" I explained how I let them out of their kennels, and we followed Tabby to the back door and then down a path to an outbuilding concealed in the woods.

"Scott, the cat waited at the door and ran ahead of me to Mary. That cat is incredible. She lay beside Mary and climbed on her when I lifted her to the stretcher. The paramedics were unhappy about transporting a cat, but Tabby and I joined forces and didn't give them much choice."

Scott chuckled through my telling of the story. I guess it did sound kind of funny.

"How is Vivian?" Scott asked.

"She is doing great under the circumstances. I had Anne pick them up at a candlelight vigil held in Bloomington, where Amanda lives."

"Jack, I am so happy for all of you. You have no idea what that news means to me. You remember what you promised?"

"What? Okay, I remember, all right? I will take Wanda out for a drink at Grandpa's Saloon, right?" Wanda was hardly at the top of my list, but he would not let that go until Wanda and I had a drink together.

"No, not that one, the other one. You promised to bring the little girl and her aunt to Duluth to see the lift bridge and all the big ships coming into the canal. That is the one I am talking about."

"Sure, Scott. I promise to bring them."

"Good," he said, sounding like he had checked off another item on his list.

"And one more thing, Jack. You have known Vivian for years. For god's sake, you don't need to go through a long get-to-know-each-other phase. Don't screw this up by being shy. I know you are comfortable being alone. Trust me. It's not what it's cracked up to be. She is good for you, son, and your shot at the gold ring, don't drag your feet. Jump in. Ask her to marry you."

"Jeez, Scott, isn't this an odd time for fatherly advice for the lovelorn? You're right. I do love her. And guess what, she said she loves me too. I'm not going to mess this up. I know she is the one. So I guess you give pretty good advice to the lovelorn. Now when is your surgery?"

"Oh, who cares about that right now? I think it's next week. I am so happy for you, Jack, and I always wanted you to find the

204

perfect woman. I didn't understand what the hell was taking you so long. Now I know. When the time is right, I guess the time is right. Jack, on that note, I will call it a night. Love you, son."

I put the phone back in my pocket. I was a little confused. I had stopped walking while talking to Scott, and Anne had continued ahead. As she walked back toward me, she asked, "Everything okay with your friend, Jack?"

"Yeah, I guess. Scott has been trying to put my life in order for a few weeks. I think, being in a care center and not having much control over his, he decided I would be a good project."

"Older people get like that sometimes. Dog and I have taken care of everything. There is a little twenty-four-hour grocery store across the street. I don't know about you, but Dog and I are hungry. Let's get something for us, then head back."

While Anne remained with the dog in the squad to wait for me, I joined Vivian and Amanda in the observation room to say my goodbyes. Amanda was the first to give me a big hug of appreciation. Vivian walked me to a hallway leading to the waiting room and said, "How can we ever thank you, Jack?" She pulled me toward her to wrap her arms around me in a firm hug and a kiss.

I wrapped my arms around her and returned the kiss. "Vivian, do you want me to call Madel to tell her Mary has been found?"

Continuing to hug me, she lay her head on my shoulder for a moment and said, "Madel was at the vigil. I was able to share the good news with her there, but I will call and give her more details. Poor thing, she has been blaming herself for all of this, and it isn't her fault at all. We will be here for the night, and I will call you in the morning." Giving me one more kiss, she dropped her arms from around me. "I Love you, Jack."

Sneaking one more kiss before releasing her from my arms, I replied, "Love you, too, Vivian."

Exhaustion wasn't a strong-enough word for me. I felt close to collapsing.

I felt Ann had parked the squad a mile away instead of in the front row of the parking lot. As I climbed in, I said, "I know it's late, and we are both exhausted, but would you mind stopping at Ramsey

Hospital? My leg hasn't stopped bleeding since I fell to my knees when I found Mary. It shouldn't take long. It probably only needs a stitch or two."

"God, Jack, why didn't you tell me or someone you were bleeding!"

"I just think a suture or two gave way."

We pulled into the ER at Ramsey and parked in reserved police parking. While Dog and Anne again waited in the squad, I walked into the ER and explained the situation. Once they saw my blood-soaked pants leg, I was immediately admitted and escorted to an exam room. Almost immediately, Dr. Denise came into the room. She stopped just inside the door and just stared at me.

"If this is how well you follow orders, your superiors must have been thrilled when you retired, Detective." Walking toward me, she continued, "I'm disappointed you chose to ignore my orders when you talked me into discharging you early."

I decided I had better start polishing the apple soon before she got angrier with me. "Dr. Denise, this is my lucky day! What were the chances you would be on duty and would be so lucky you would be assigned to attend to your favorite patient? I thought you worked days."

Though tired, I was in such a good mood I gave her a big smile. I was just so damn happy. I didn't even care about my leg.

Giving me a fierce look, she replied, "I just bet you did. Let's see the leg. Please remove your pants, and put on this gown."

She had taken a gown out of the cabinet and practically thrown it at me. I stood up and paused, expecting her to leave the room while I took off my pants, but she just waved her hands, indicating I should continue as she continued to chastise me.

"What took you so long to return to the hospital? Your jeans are soaked with blood. What part of forty-eight hours didn't you understand?"

Standing with my pants off, trying to figure out the front from the back of the exam gown while being severely scolded by a female doctor, puts a man at a severe disadvantage. Trying to have a comfortable footing, I said, "Aren't you supposed to leave while I undress?"

With a sigh, heavily laced with frustration, she turned to leave the room and said, "I will have a nurse clean up your leg, then I will be back. God, I hate stubborn men," she muttered as she turned toward the door.

"Denise," I said quietly. I suddenly felt exhausted. The adrenaline that had kept me going through the day had picked this moment to fade away.

She turned toward me, and I thought, *I must look like hell, sitting in my underwear and bloodstained sock. I haven't showered in days, with a stubble of beard.* "I found her," I whispered.

The doctor came toward me on the exam table and said, "What did you say?"

"I found Judge Lord's five-year-old niece."

The doctor grabbed my hand with a look of despair on her face.

I said, "She is going to be okay. She is at Children's Hospital. Carolyn Engel is her doctor."

All the anger forgotten, she grabbed me up in a big hug. Pulling back, she took my hand and said, "My god, Jack, what a blessing. I'm sorry I didn't allow an explanation from you. I am so happy for all of you. Let's get you cleaned up and repair those stitches."

She went to the door, opened it, and called someone's name. A nurse came through the door that Denise held open for her. The stitches were repaired and bandaged quickly, and the nurse cleaned up the table and bagged my jeans.

Denise had left the room for a minute and returned with a pair of scrub pants for me to wear home, surprising me by offering me a ride home.

"My shift is ending, Jack. If you need a ride home, I could take you."

"Thanks so much, Denise. That is nice of you after I have been such a horrible patient, but I have an officer waiting for me."

"Okay then, may I walk you out?"

"Sure, that would be great, Denise."

Denise took my arm as we walked down the hall and stopped near the door to the waiting room. "Jack, we need you back in the trenches to combat the effects of child abuse. Our hospital has seen a significant increase in child patients with permanent lifelong injuries or deaths. One detective can make a difference, Jack."

I was shocked to see tears rolling down her face. She continued, "Jack, what happened to the baby who was shaken and died while on life support was not your fault nor my fault, but I do know how you feel. We both need to put the blame aside. Jack, in our profession, we have emotional needs as we struggle with feelings of despair that the public often doesn't understand. We both work in a culture that upholds an image of being invincible. In reality, we are not. Now get some rest. You look like hell." Smiling at her parting shot, she kissed me and held the door open.

Anne had to wake me up in Bayport as we approached my Jeep near Manning's house. Dog and I climbed into the Jeep and headed to Arcola. Driving through an open gate at Vivian's property didn't even bother me now, and I parked the Jeep inside the garage.

Picking the dog up from the passenger seat where he had fallen asleep, I gave him a hug and a scratch on the head. "First thing tomorrow, Dog, we're giving you a name."

I got out of the Jeep and stood with the dog in my arms, watching the garage door come down on the conclusion of a real-life drama in the *Corncob Jungle*.

CHAPTER 24

The sun shining through the open blinds woke me. I felt disoriented and confused for the first few moments. When was the last time I woke up after the sun had risen? Just reviewing the last couple of days of insanity, my second question was: when was the last time I slept? I need coffee before I can answer all these questions, I decided. Just before I moved, I felt something on the bed and looked down to see the dog near my feet at the end of the bed. He will need to go out, probably before I get my coffee. I better get used to that, I thought, smiling.

Sitting up roused the dog, and just as I thought, he headed for the door. Luckily I still had on the scrubs that Dr. Denise had given me the night before. I reached automatically for my gun and speed loader before remembering the Sheriff's Office had not returned it to me yet. Just as well, I don't have any pockets in these scrubs. Instead, I reached for the shirt I had thrown on the recliner the night before.

The dog and I took a brisk morning walk around the house. I felt wonderful! I can't imagine ever getting used to the tranquility and beauty of the St. Croix Bluffs. The trees look bare, and most colorful autumn leaves have fallen. The branches reaching for the sky, rising above the currently tranquil waters of the river, have their beauty. The sun shining on the river makes the water sparkly like diamonds floating on the surface. It is just a breathtaking moment for me. I could stand here all morning with a cup of coffee. I wish I had one.

Suddenly the sound of a car door slamming alerted the dog, and he went on a run to investigate.

By the time I reached the driveway, the dog had already greeted Anne and looked at me as if to say, *Look what I found.* Anne had parked her unmarked Crown Vic in my usual spot, in front of the first garage door.

"Good morning, Jack. I have a few things I thought you would want back as soon as possible." She opened the passenger door and took out a bag. Walking back around the car, she handed me my gun, speed loader, and cell phone.

"Bless you," I said as I took the items from her hand. "I had already reached for them once when I woke up," I joked, then looked to see her face.

"Anne, what's wrong? What could be wrong on this beautiful day?"

"Jack, Wanda from Superior Shores called the Sheriff's Office when she couldn't reach you on your cell, asking if we could get a message to you."

I was confused and braced myself, not understanding why.

"Jack, Scott McCloud passed away early this morning."

I was stunned. I had talked to him last night, and he was fine. I couldn't react. I stared at Anne and couldn't absorb what she was telling me. I heard the words, but I couldn't believe them.

"I'm sorry, Jack," she said, reaching out to touch me on the shoulder. "I know the two of you were close."

I needed to sit down. I turned, and Anne and the dog followed me around the corner of the house to the downstairs patio, where I sunk into a chair. I set down the stuff in my hand and rubbed my face. I was trying to absorb the information, but I couldn't believe he was gone.

"Thanks, Anne. I knew Scott was aware his time was approaching. He had even had me bring burial clothing to him. I think he was more realistic than I was. I just never wanted to talk about him dying."

"Ah, Jack, another message for you from a Minneapolis Police officer, Erin McCloud, probably a relative." She handed a piece of paper with Erin's name and phone number. Also, Commander Jacobson told me to tell you the communications center wasn't your damn answering service."

"That guy is such a prick," I said, dismissing him from my mind.

"Erin is Scott's granddaughter. She is also Scott's executor. I'll give her a call."

Looking down at the dog, who had found a nice place in the sun to lie, I said, "So, Anne, you wouldn't be interested in a dog, would you?"

"He is a cutie, but I would be evicted from my place if I brought home a pet. My landlady made that very clear in my lease. I thought you wanted a dog."

"I do, but I am not sure Vivian wants a dog. I think she is a cat person. At least, that is the pet she chose. We will see. Do you want a cup of coffee? If I can make that coffee machine of Vivian's work, I want one myself."

"Thanks, but no. I have to get back. Commander Jacobson has me organizing the War Room to close out the Clayton rape caseload. I'll be working on that for weeks.

"And, Jack, there is one more item. I'll be right back." Retracing her steps to the car, she brought back a white cardboard file box and set it on the table.

I looked at the box, then back up at Anne, who was now standing beside the table.

"I hope no one expects me to write a report covering the last ten days."

"No, at least not yet. Jack, a dear friend has been kept out of the loop. I have been in contact with her a lot. I think Ms. Adeline is feeling a little abandoned."

"Shit. I dropped the ball, Anne. I hadn't talked to her in days like I had disappeared. We usually talk every day. She probably thinks I'm dead. I owe her an explanation of the last few days. I suck. I don't know what to do—first Scott, now Adeline. What else have I screwed up?"

"Jack, it isn't as bad as that. I've contacted her numerous times, by phone and in person. She is just a sweet lady that cares for you. In this box are newspaper articles from Ms. Adeline from the last ten days. Everything—abduction, your being shot, the serial rapist, even today's paper reporting finding Mary. It's like a scrap box. And she has been receiving all sorts of gifts from your adoring fans—flowers, chocolates, and even a box of Bullet Bourbon from Judge Magnuson.

Your mailbox is full of get-well cards from your adoring fans. It has been a full-time job for her for the last few days. You are the local hero.

"Ms. Adeline has also been talking to the press. Several reporters stopped by and got friendly with her. I kept her up to date, and she unintentionally gave the information I provided her in confidence to the reporters."

At my look of absolute horror, she rushed on to say, "It's all very positive, Jack. It makes you sound like you wear a cape." She stopped talking after I threw her a glaring look, then continued, "It's all in the box. Go through it. Ms. Adeline arranged them all and highlighted your articles. Most importantly, give her a call, Jack. She needs to hear your voice."

"I definitely will, and thanks for all you've done. And I mean *all* you have done."

"Sorry about Scott, Jack. Give me a call when you have time. See you." With a quick pet for the dog, she returned to her car.

Wow, what a morning. Picking up the box, I rose and called the dog. "Come on, Dog, I need coffee, and you need something to eat. I hope you will eat cat food. I don't know if you will have a choice."

I managed to get the coffeepot working and found some beef and a can of cat food. Who knows how long the meat has been in the Sub-Zero. Sitting down at the kitchen table, I went through my voice mails. There was a message from Erin McCloud informing me of Scott's passing and a funeral service at Fort Snelling Chapel in five days.

There was also a message from LaVonne asking me to call about a formal complaint regarding Peter Manning.

Lining up my to-do's for the day, first, I need to call Buster to see if he wants Peter's dog back.

My mind couldn't stay on track. I kept going back to Scott.

So Scott's expiration date had finally arrived. It still hadn't sunk in, but I was beginning to feel my loss around the edges of my feelings. I wanted to hold off the crushing sense of loss as long as possible.

I had been looking forward to spending more time with Scott. I had wanted to debrief, so to speak, the events of the recent days with him. It had always been so with us. I almost didn't need to say something regarding my cases. He just knew me well enough to understand. We had a kind of verbal shorthand. So much had happened in the last few days, and I had wanted him to hear about it from me. And I wouldn't have minded telling him about my romance with Vivian and my hopes for the future. I guess I just wanted him to be proud of me, as any son would want from a father.

I pushed Scott's death to the back of my mind and decided to call Buster. I could ask him about the dog and volunteer to help him get Vivian's yard back into shape before she returned. After Mary's release from the hospital, she planned to spend a few more days in Bloomington with Amanda and Mary. That would give us time to remove the physical signs of the past few days.

Madel is supposed to be by tomorrow for an inside cleaning and freshening up. That would be a good day for me to meet Wanda for a promised drink in Duluth. I wanted to know what happened to Scott. His death was so sudden.

The second promise to Scott may have to wait. I hope there will be plenty of time to take care of that. Then I have a long overdue visit with Ms. Adeline. I hope she will forgive me for neglecting her. Maybe a phone call would be an excellent first step.

I timidly called Ms. Adeline, not quite sure what my reception from her would be. As it turned out, she was delighted to hear from me, and she proceeded to chronicle the many gifts and thoughts of comfort she had received for me and was enjoying all the delivery people coming to my door.

"It takes me an hour or more to water and care for your flowers, and, Jack, someone sent you orchard apples. I am enjoying all the mums especially. I have them out on the porch. And I have eaten a few apples too," she said with a giggle.

"Jackie, I can hardly wait for you to come home and see it all. I have even brought over a card table for all the flowers. There isn't any more room in your kitchen or the living room."

"Ms. Adeline, what would I ever do without you? You have been so wonderful and supportive. I—"

She interrupted me, saying, "Jackie, someone is at your door. Maybe you could call back later. I have to go."

213

"Okay, Ms.—" She had hung up on me. I chuckled. She was having fun with all this hoopla. Better her than me. I hope there is room between all of her visitors for a chat with me. I got up, knowing I was avoiding that call to Scott's granddaughter and any more thoughts of Scott's death, at least for a little longer.

Freshly showered, with a fresh bandage on my leg, I grabbed my gun, speed loader, and cell phone and stuffed them in my pockets, feeling complete for the first time in days, silently thanking Ann once more for their return.

I opened the door and asked the dog if he was ready to go home and meet Ms. Adeline. He ran up the steps and right to the entrance to the garage. I could swear he knew what I said.

Pulling into my driveway in Bayport brought reality home. *Oh my god*, I thought. American flags, colorful pots of seasonal flowers, and yellow ribbons decorated the trees in my front yard.

Just as I turned off the car, Ms. Adeline came out of her door and hurried down the steps. "Oh, Jackie," she exclaimed as soon as I climbed out of the car.

She wrapped her arms around me. Stepping back, she looked me over with her hands on her hips. "Thank goodness you are all right. I have been so worried. I managed to keep busy with visitors and their gifts, deliveries, and who is behind you?"

The dog had jumped from the car and peeked around my leg at Ms. Adeline. Turning to pick him up, I said, "Ms. Adeline, meet my new friend."

"Oh, you cute little thing. Jack, give him to me. What is his name?" she asked as she wrapped her arms around the dog as I held him. Letting go, I watched her cuddling the dog. It was love at first sight for both of them.

"As you can tell, Ms. Adeline, he loves people, and cats, too, if you can believe that. As far as his name goes, I haven't named him yet. It is somewhat complicated to give him a name, but I'm working on it." I don't think she was even listening. She was in love.

Ms. Adeline had taken control of the dog, and he didn't seem to mind. I almost felt jealous. He didn't even give me a backward glance as she began to walk toward the porch.

"Come with me, Jackie," she said, looking over her shoulder as she began to walk toward the porch. "I want to show you all of your gifts and flowers. I have been to large funerals with fewer flowers than you received. You should feel very flattered."

"It is very nice of people, but I am overwhelmed by everything. By the way, Ms. Adeline, thank you for the scrapbook of news articles. I haven't had a chance to read all of them yet."

"Jackie, you have become Bayport's hometown hero! A celebrity all through the St. Croix Valley. I usually have one or two reporters stopping by for cookies and coffee daily, and they write complimentary articles about you in their newspapers. I think I have made new friends. I don't doubt they will stop by to see me just for conversation after all this dies down."

"Ms. Adeline, I don't doubt they will stop by to see you, but I think it may be about more than your company. Your apple strudel is state fair Blue Ribbon quality, after all."

She blushed a little and just cuddled the dog even more. The dog was eating up all the attention. "Oh, Jackie, I put all your mail on your desk and changed your bed linens. You will like the lilac fragrance I use in the dryer. I hope you don't mind. Please let me know if you need anything, dear boy."

"Thank you, Ms. Adeline." I'm not sure of that lilac smell, but I continued, "I am going to lie down for a bit and rest my leg. It is a little sore. It is good to see you. I've missed you, and I have lots of things to tell you, but let's catch up later, okay?"

"That will be nice, Jackie." She bent over to put the dog down, then looked at me and said, "Jackie, it is so good to have you home." And with that, she patted my cheeks with her hands and went inside.

Walking into my living room and seeing all the gifts, flowers, and apple baskets put a smile on my face. I never even got a thank-you note when I worked for the Sheriff's Office. I guess getting the job done as a civilian made a big difference.

I started a pot of coffee as the dog was sniffing around the flowers and drinking the water from the flower pans. I put a couple of bowls on the floor in the kitchen—one for kibble—and remembered that I need to get more kibble. And a clean bowl for water that hadn't gone through the flower dirt first.

"Come on, Dog, let's take a nap." He gladly followed me back into the bedroom. I lay a folded hunting blanket on the floor near my nightstand. I patted the blanket and said, "Here you go. You can sleep right here." He obediently lay down. Forgetting my coffee, I lay down on the bed and closed my eyes. I never even felt the dog join me on the bed.

*****

Waking slowly, I looked around the clutter. Clutter is not my wheelhouse. I'm not a neat freak, but this was too much for today. I left everything where it was and headed for the porch, hoping for a chat with Ms. Adeline and something freshly baked, if I was lucky.

CHAPTER 25

Perhaps an early start this morning wasn't necessary, but I was sleeping free of nightmares and waking up early refreshed. So this morning, I am trying to enjoy a leisurely ride up to Duluth. It was so weird; I wanted to feel so good about my life right now, but my grief over Scott kept pulling me back. I know he wouldn't want that, and I hope this visit with Wanda will help with closure. I know Scott had prepared for this. His best years had been behind him, and he was tired of going piece by piece. He had said as much to me. I know all that, but I guess I was just sad. Sad for myself and the loss of such a good friend.

Wanda had said she would meet me for lunch at eleven o'clock at a popular downtown Duluth location called the Aerial View Restaurant. They claim they have the best views of Duluth Harbor.

Driving northbound on I-35, approaching Duluth, was always spectacular. Coming down the hill on I-35 and seeing the largest surface freshwater lake in the world was a breathtaking sight. I even spotted the Aerial View circular restaurant, rising above most of the other buildings in the downtown area.

Exiting the elevator on the sixteenth floor brought you to the cocktail lounge surrounded by linen-covered tables for upscale dining. The continuously changing cityscape and lake views out the large windows are made possible by the carousel floor that slowly rotates and provides the guests with 360-degree views as they dine.

I hardly recognized Wanda approaching me at the hostess station just as the young woman asked me to follow her to our table. Indicating Wanda should follow her, I walked behind.

As we sat down, Wanda said, "What do you think?"

I responded, "I think you look great out of your nursing uniform and your hair,"

Interrupting, Wanda said, "Jack, you can cut the compliments. We are both here to honor a request. I am sorry for your loss."

"Thank you, Wanda." Before we could say more, a waitress took our drink order. We both ordered iced tea. I thought to myself, *Scott, a drink is a drink. You didn't say anything about alcohol.* We looked over the lunch menu, and Wanda ordered the poached salmon with capers and dill with a salad. I had planned on the one-half-pound burger special, but I always liked good salmon, so I just said, "Make that two.

Looking across the table with awkward smiles, we both seemed to be thinking, *What now?* Finally, with some hesitation, Wanda said, "Can I be perfectly blunt with you?"

Oh, never a good start to a conversation. Does Wanda need my help or something? Lunch may have been a terrible idea.

"Absolutely. Please go ahead."

Taking a deep breath, Wanda told me that this was a business lunch, and she was here as a representative of Superior Shores Care Center during this conversation.

I shrugged and leaned forward as she began. "Jack, Scott took his own life with a handgun he must have acquired sometime in the last couple of months. While being admitted to Superior Shores, residents have all their property inspected and inventoried. Scott did not have a weapon in his possession nor would one be allowed to enter the facility.

"The night staff heard the gunshot and rushed to check on patients. When they found Scott, the lead nurse immediately called the Duluth Police. Mr. McCloud's death has already been classified as a suicide. I'm so sorry to have to tell you all this."

Her lips were moving; I knew she was talking, but after she said Scott took his own life, I couldn't hear anything else. I sat there, frozen. I couldn't believe it. I never had any hint of Scott being suicidal. Why didn't I see it? Am I so self-absorbed when I visit that I miss the clues? Where did the damn gun come from?

"Jack, Jack, Jack, are you all right?" I came away from my daze, and Wanda had her hand on my arm, gently shaking it.

"I'm okay, Wanda. It's such a shock. I knew he wasn't looking forward to his next surgery, and he did talk to me about dying. God, what an idiot I am. He had been talking about clothes to be buried in and all the good times, but I never once thought he would kill himself."

Wanda continued, "He was starting to act a little depressed. We discussed it at our team conference, and we kept an eye on him. We had scheduled surgery appointments for him, and at the last minute, he would cancel them."

I was listening carefully now, hoping to hear something that would help me understand Scott's actions.

"I was beginning to think something was up. I didn't understand why there was no sense of urgency about the surgery. If part of a leg has to come off, I thought it would be rather urgent, but Scott never wanted to talk with me about surgery. Did he leave a suicide note, Wanda?"

"The police didn't find a suicide note. It appears the firearm came into our care center in a hidden compartment from a Minneapolis Police memory box, according to the police report."

"My god, Wanda, I brought that up to him. It is my fault he had that gun. He asked me to bring his dress browns and his shadow box. I just thought he was reminiscing." God, I put my elbows on the table and held my head between them, as though it was too heavy for my shoulders. Raising my head, I looked at her and said, "We were talking about taking a road trip up the north shore to Grand Marais. We even joked about asking if you wanted to accompany us. Don't you remember?"

"I remember, but, Jack, you never came inside that day. You left the duffel with Scott. He had it in his lap when I brought him back to his room for meds. I even looked at the uniform and the shadow box and commented on both. Jack, you never signed in on that day. There is no record that you were there. The police confirm that Scott was the registered owner."

She reached over the table, touching my forearm. "Jack, I know you would never knowingly have brought a gun into Superior Shores. No one knows who brought it except you and me. Let's keep it that way. Scott died his way. He made his decision. We have to live with it."

The waiter came up to the table with our salads. Wanda took a deep breath and said in a no-nonsense tone I had heard her often use, "Now let's eat our salads. Jack, would you like a stronger drink?"

"Yeah, I could probably use a drink, but I don't want to drink alone, and you have to go back to work. Thanks."

"Okay then, I have a suggestion, if I may. Let's have lunch, then drive to Canal Park and take a walk. We will have a drink at Grandpa's and toast Scott McCloud, a man you thought of as a father. My treat. Besides, this may be the last of the nice weather. I rarely get down to Canal Park and the aerial bridge. I have something in my car for you. The police returned Scott's gun to us for his family. We can't mail it. His granddaughter asked if you would bring it back."

"His firearm." At her nod, I agreed to take it and the lunch tab.

We drove separately to Canal Park and parked alongside each other to exchange the brown evidence envelope. It had multiple dates and initials on the front that I didn't bother to read. I put the brown evidence bag under the driver's seat.

I asked Wanda if she minded if I brought my dog on our walk along Canal Park and into Grandpa's. Wanda said not at all and asked me my dog's name.

I said, "It's complicated. He doesn't have a name yet."

Turning toward the restaurant, Wanda informed me, "We can bring your dog with us on the outside upper deck."

"Sounds good, doesn't it, boy," I said, rubbing the cute little head as I helped the dog down from the car.

Wanda had a cosmopolitan, and I had my usual—Bullet over ice. The dog was well behaved as we watched a laker heading out onto Lake Superior from our table.

We raised our glasses for a toast to Scott. I said, "To Scott. Thanks for everything. I will never forget you," as we tapped our glasses together. Afterward it felt good, and I thanked Wanda profusely as we walked back to the cars.

Wanda gave me a big hug when we got to the car. "We will miss Scott and his rather bizarre cop humor."

Nodding my head, I turned to open her door for her. I stood beside my driver's door to watch her drive away. Getting into my car, I pushed the dog over to the passenger seat. "Good Dog. Hang on just a bit, and we will walk at the overlook on the way home."

The dog and I took a nice walk at the overlook, and it only held my attention for so long before my eyes were drawn back to Lake Superior's incredible beauty. I thought to myself, *I will never forget you, Scott. Every time I see this water, I will see you in my mind—Godspeed, good friend.*

It was a melancholy ride back to Stillwater. I kept going over things I could have done to stop him from committing suicide. Would that have been in Scott's best interest? Why didn't I see any signs? I thought I knew him as well as anyone.

If there had been signs, why didn't I see them? Scott didn't want you to see them and was nobody's fool. He wouldn't have tipped his hat. He was one wily old Irishman. So no clues. Maybe I should have checked out the shadow box. Why would I have done that? There were no clues.

It occurred to me then that Scott had planned this all along. Before becoming a resident of Superior Shores, he had hidden the gun and left it in the Twin Cities out of his reach until he knew he had had enough and was ready to go out on his terms.

He had been ready. I wasn't. But he had left me with a pretty clear picture of how he wanted me to live going forward. He wanted me to have a family; Vivian, Mary, and I would make that happen. I am going to keep his final words with me always. I could see his face as I heard the words again, *Love you, son.*

Suicide sucks. I have had a lot of experience with it. My first experience was just two weeks after graduation from BCA rookie school. A classmate committed suicide with his service revolver after a domestic situation with his fiancée. That was only the beginning. Each year of my career that followed, people made suicide calls to the Sheriff's Office, and patrol deputies would respond to a death scene.

On one quiet evening on patrol, the communications center received a call from a man asking the dispatcher which water towers in northern Washington County were the tallest. The dispatcher told the caller that she lived in Hugo, close to a water tower, and she thought that tower was the tallest in the area. The dispatcher asked the caller why he had inquired, and his response was he would commit suicide. Dispatch gave a call to our squad to call the communications center ASAP.

After an hour of coaxing the caller down from the top of the Hugo water tower, our persuasion was successful, and we saved a life.

The caller was transported to the hospital only to be released before we completed the paperwork on the incident. The intake staff had decided that he was no longer a threat to himself. The hospital classified their patient's behavior as infantile manipulation.

A failed suicide attempt occasionally occurs, as a young Grant City man had learned the hard way. Taking a shotgun blast to his head had only blown his jaw off. After that, he wore a face mask to cover up the results of his failed attempt.

Firearms are the most common method of suicide each year, but occasionally suicide by asphyxiation or carbon monoxide occurs, as well as hanging or overdosing on drugs. Law enforcement would prefer a suicide note, but they often don't find one.

Suicide leaves enormous amounts of suffering for family members, probably all asking the same question I am asking myself now—why?

Sometimes the method or location sends a postmortem message to a loved one, leaving that person to carry the guilt with them the rest of their life. Suicide is no one's fault but the deceased.

Suicide is a hazard of the job for police officers. In the course of their career, one in four officers admit to contemplating suicide, and more officers die of suicide than in the line of duty each year.

Child abuse investigations can be incredibly stressful for law enforcement and child protection workers. I had a youth minister commit suicide by automobile asphyxiation and a blue-collar worker commit suicide by gunshot with a picture of his victim beside him, in one month!

I had been investigating both of them for child abuse. They left a trail of collateral damage, revictimizing the victims they had abused by pointing the finger at them for causing their death by reporting. It had been a horrible month.

Reaching Forest Lake on I-35, I turned off, heading back to Vivian's house. She wouldn't mind if I spent one more night there before returning home to Plant City and further debriefing with Ms. Adeline.

Turning in Vivian's driveway, I saw Buster parked near the house entrance and working on the island by the flagpole. Buster smoked his corncob pipe while raising a bright new American flag.

"Hey, Buster, how are you?" I asked as I got out of the car. The dog got out right after me and ran to Buster, his whole body wiggling at seeing an old friend.

"Doing well, Detective. Ms. Vivian wanted a new flag at the house. She hasn't had one since Charles passed. Looks pretty good, doesn't it?" he asked rhetorically, looking up at his handiwork, unfurling as it caught the light breeze.

Looking back at me, he said, "Detective, you did a yeoman's service to the Sheriff's Office finding Ms. Vivian's niece. We are all very grateful."

"Thanks, Buster," I replied, accepting his compliment. It was, after all, his nephew that was responsible, but pleased he held no hard feelings.

"The property looks very nice, Buster. You do such a great job for Vivian."

Buster was still petting the dog as he wiggled in front of him. "The dog looks happy to see you. I don't suppose you want him back?"

Buster looked up and replied, "He is a great little guy, but I don't want him back if you would be willing to take him. At my age, I don't need anything else on my to-do list. I only accepted him because Peter wanted the dog."

"I have grown attached to the little guy, but I figured you, by rights, own him. Say, what's his name anyway?"

"Folks down the road here had a litter, and Peter could hardly mow their yard. He was so taken with those pups, so they gave him one. I don't know what Peter called him. You go ahead and name him."

"I think I will call him Scottie, after a friend." Feeling good about the decision to keep him and his new name, I told Buster that I would stay the night in the guest suite, and then I would be heading back to Bayport tomorrow. "You have a good night, Buster."

Turning to go into the house, I looked over my shoulder as Buster said, "You have a good night, too, Detective. Madel just left. She didn't know how long you were staying here, but she left a few dinners in the refrigerator for you."

I waved my acknowledgment as I let myself in the front door. I hope there will be many more nights with Vivian here.

Madel had been as busy inside as Buster had been outside. The kitchen and solarium sparkled. Maybe I should grab my clothes and head back to my place for the night so that Vivian could come home to a clean house.

Scottie and I went down the stairs to the guest room. I took the stairs considerably slower than the dog. He sat at the foot of the stairs, questioning my slowness with his big brown eyes. "I'm coming, I'm coming," I said to him. "Give me a few more days, and I will beat you down the stairs."

Downstairs, I stuffed my clothes into my bag and grabbed the box of clippings from Ms. Adeline. Heading up the stairs, Scottie and I headed home for what I hoped wouldn't be too long.

It wasn't late, but I coasted into the driveway, hoping to leave Ms. Adeline undisturbed. I carried the box of clippings and my bag through the door without disturbing Ms. Adeline.

Scottie went right for his dishes. Setting everything on the floor, I dug out the bag of kibble I had gotten the day before, filled the bowl, and then refreshed his water before heading to my room. I had decided to declutter the mess before I went to sleep.

I stood at the door of my bedroom and observed the clutter. The monumental task of putting things in order almost defeated me, but I dived in anyway. Setting the box of clippings on the floor beside my desk, I placed the evidence envelope containing Scott's gun on top of the box, wondering if I would ever open the envelope. I wasn't sure I was ready to look at the weapon he had used to take his life.

I sat down and started wading through my pile of mail. Thankfully most of it was junk and didn't take too long to go through and throw out. To my surprise, I came to an envelope in Scott's handwriting.

I sat staring at that envelope for some time, unsure I wanted to read what was inside. Then taking a breath, I ripped open the envelope and pulled out the letter inside.

> Son, you may be the only person who will understand my final chapter. You know me better than anyone else, kiddo. Remember your promises. Have a drink with Wanda, bring that little girl and her aunt to Canal Park, and watch the ships come in. Please, son, no regrets. Chin up. Always, Scott.

I sat with the letter in my hand. Finally I released the breath I didn't know I had been holding and said, "I'll be damned." Scott didn't leave his suicide note for the cops and strangers to read. He sent it to me for my eyes only. In my experience, most people don't leave suicide notes. Looking now, from this perspective, I thought maybe it was because the person committing suicide doesn't want strangers to read their private thoughts. I will respect Scott's wishes. This letter was only between Scott and me.

Scott and I had many conversations, some of which we would never share with anyone else. Knowing he couldn't be here, he had sent me his message the only way he could and stayed true to his plan. Scott had mailed this letter several days before he took his life. He wanted me to know that he had a plan, and none of it was my fault. He didn't want me to feel guilty about bringing him the gun. He wanted me to go forward with my life.

I sat staring out at the dark beyond my window for a couple of minutes, coming to terms with this information, then thought, I might as well get it over with. Reaching for the brown envelope that boldly read EVIDENCE, I unclamped the thin little clasp on the back and carefully tipped it to slide the contents to the top of my desk. The envelope contained four unspent live rounds of ammunition. One spent cartridge and a stainless steel five-round capacity .357 caliber revolver—a Smith and Wesson model 640, two-inch barrel with a concealed hammer. A concealed hammer makes for a snag-free draw. It is a weapon routinely used by plainclothes personnel, desk officers, or administration.

I sat looking at the gun that Scott had used to end his life. Scott had begun carrying that gun when he was the Precinct 6 inspector. The Model Cities housing project in Minneapolis. He continued to carry it when he came to the Sheriff's Office in an administrative capacity.

It was an ugly gun for an ugly death. I didn't want it and couldn't get rid of it. Putting it back in the envelope with the rounds and getting up from my desk, I put it in my gun safe in the back of my closet.

Scott's funeral will be in a couple of days. I need Vivian to accompany me. I don't think that I could get through it without her at my side. I will talk to her again tonight and bring it up. In the last couple of days, we have been catching up and sharing our days when we were both alone and free to say what was on our minds and hearts.

I made a poor attempt at humor last night when I said it was our version of romantic pillow talk. We both agreed that it was a poor substitute for genuine romance, but we were glad to have each other to share our day.

Just then, my phone rang. I could see that it was Vivian. What perfect timing. "Hey, you," I said as I answered the phone.

"Hi, Jack. How did it go today?"

"Oh, it went okay. I don't want to spend our time talking about sad things, though. I will tell you some other time. This phone call is the highlight of my day. I miss you."

"I miss you, too, Jack, and that makes this difficult for me."

She paused, and I got a sick feeling in my stomach that I wasn't going to like what she said next.

Vivian continued, "I have decided to take Amanda and Mary on a little vacation getaway. The press has been calling nonstop, and some have come to the door. Hopefully another story will have their attention when we get back." She hurried on, "It is only for seven days, and it won't hurt me either. I still have one week remaining in my leave of absence from the bench. Mary and Amanda need it even more. A change of scenery will help to put this all behind us. Jack, I have to do this." Vivian said her last words with regret, but I could tell she was determined to follow through.

I hoped she could hear the smile in my voice when I said, "Vivian, don't worry about me. I support the idea. A change of scenery from where all the drama occurred is significant for Mary. She will learn that her loved ones will be there for her wherever she is. When are you leaving, and where are you going? I know you already have this all planned out."

"Thank you so much for understanding. I agree. We will try to erase as many of those horrible days as possible. It means we won't be together, but this is important for Mary. Our flight leaves Sunday morning for Homestead, Florida. A former partner of Charles has a Key Largo condo in a complex called Moon Bay. It is on the gulf side of the Key. He has encouraged me to use it since Charles died. I have finally taken him up on the idea."

"Sounds perfect, Vivian. Do you need me to take care of Tabby, or will Madel take care of her?"

"Heavens, we couldn't even think of going if we couldn't take Tabby. Those two haven't been apart since we got back here. I have Tabby's travel all set up."

Changing the tone of her voice as the subject changed, she asked, "Isn't Scott's funeral on Saturday? Would you mind if I came with you?"

Before I answered, I closed my eyes and thanked God for bringing Vivian into my life. "I was ready to beg you to come with me. I don't know if I could do it without you beside me. It hasn't taken me long to become dependent on having someone to share life with."

"Jack, Scott was a symbol of professional integrity and one of the most accomplished commanders for Washington County that I

227

have seen in my career. I can see why the two of you developed such a strong bond. You have many of the same characteristics. Your compassion and even your toughness. I would have gone even if we didn't go together, but I am honored to go with you." Vivian continued, "But, Jack, I don't think even Scott was tough enough to sit beside a ten-year-old sexual assault victim and listen to her account of what her family member had done to her over many years. That takes a whole different level of toughness."

"Yeah, tough until the well runs dry." As I spoke, I realized I hadn't had the nightmare since I found Mary.

"Jack, don't say that. I can tell you now that I always loved watching a defense attorney try to poke holes in your testimony and victim statements. You had what I secretly thought of as your Rushmore face. The defense would lob questions, and you fired back your answers, leaving them nowhere to go. Your testimony and confessions were always golden in court. They stood up all the way through appeals. I think the last few weeks have proven that you are as tough as ever, for which I am grateful."

She started laughing and said that Mary and Tabby were playing on the floor. "I better let you go and get this little girl into bed. I love you, Detective."

I replied, "I love you more, Judge." Then disconnected.

*****

Saturday morning, dressed in a dark-blue suit and tie, I knocked on Ms. Adeline's door.

"My, my, don't you look nice, Jackie." She reached up to pick a piece of lint off my lapel, then smoothed it down. "Now don't you worry about Scottie. I will take good care of him."

"Thanks, Ms. Adeline. I will be back after the funeral and lunch."

Suddenly looking past me, she said, "Oh, Jackie, here comes that lady reporter. She may want to talk with you."

I turned to say, "Can I help you?"

228

"I am looking for Detective Janssen to ask a few questions regarding Judge Lord's niece's abduction. It should only take about ten minutes."

"What is your name?" I asked.

"Ms. Scarborough."

"Well, Ms. Scarborough, my media relations spokesperson is this fine lady, Ms. Adeline Hoglund. She will answer your questions on my behalf. I am late for a funeral."

I winked at Ms. Adeline over my shoulder and left the reporter in her care. As I walked away, I could hear Ms. Adeline ask if she liked oatmeal apple cookies.

I picked Vivian up at her sister's home in Bloomington. Fort Snelling Memorial Chapel is only a fifteen-minute drive from Bloomington.

Smartly dressed in a traditional black suit, white shirt, and black heels, Vivian symbolized respect and mourning for Scott's passing.

During our drive to Fort Snelling, Vivian explained that she always kept this outfit at Amanda's in case she had to spend the night before work.

Her conversation continued, saying, "Jack, when I heard that Scott had passed away, it was almost surreal for me, as I had spoken with him two days before he died." I took my eyes off the road to glance at Vivian in surprise.

Vivian continued, "I know Scott was like a father to you. You know you have my sympathies. What you don't know is Scott called my office and spoke with my assistant, Gail, who convinced me to call Mr. McCloud regarding his son, Jack Janssen. It took me a minute or two to figure out who Mr. McCloud was, but when I did, I called him and had an enjoyable conversation with him. He was a very dear man, Jack. He loved you like a son and wanted me to know that he was blessing our relationship and made the following four requests. One, you are a cop to the bone and for me to always treat you like a cop. Two, you lost your parents very young and still need positive reinforcement." She took a minute to laugh at my scowl and the red that was blooming across my face. Chuckling, she continued, "Three, you love me unconditionally and would do anything for me."

Interrupting her, I almost growled, "For god's sake, did he think I was a complete dunce? Maybe the man in question should be able to declare his love himself," I said the last in a near shout. Vivian was full-out laughing now. Putting her hand on my arm as I was driving, she composed herself enough to continue.

"The last one is a curious request. Scott wanted me to take you and Mary to Duluth to see the big ships going through the canal and under the lift bridge. I thought that was strange, but, Jack, I did promise."

"Vivian, the requests are the same as the ones he made of me the last few times I visited him. Let's talk more about Scott's requests someday over wine."

As we walked toward the chapel, Vivian put her hand through my arm and asked me what branch of the service Scott had served in.

"He was in the navy. He served as a lieutenant on the USS *Carter Hall*. When I asked about battles or what his assignment was aboard the ship, he only gave me the ship's name and the motto Working for Peace, Ready for War. That was all the information he ever gave me."

The funeral was a dignified formal ceremony for the life of Scott McCloud. A small group of friends, colleagues, and family had gathered to offer their condolences and honor Scott's naval and law enforcement services.

The closed-casket funeral was brief, and so was the internment. The small number of family and friends who attended disappointed me. The clergy assembled, the funeral director staff, the color guards, the trumpet player for taps, the rifle team, and finally, the piper who played "Going Home" on the bagpipes outnumbered the bereaved.

Bagpipes get me every time. I wanted to remain dignified while the bagpipes added their salute to a fallen law enforcement officer, so I held tightly to Vivian's hand throughout the music, fighting back the tears. Bagpipes are a tradition for most law enforcement funerals. They add a sorrowful yet dignified presence to ceremonies. I have attended far too many services with bagpipes.

Vivian and I briefly stopped by the Fort Snelling Officer's Club for coffee and appetizer-size sandwiches. We were able to have a short visit with Scott's granddaughter, Erin. While Vivian had gone to the powder room, I asked Erin to keep Scott's suicide between us, and she said that she would. Erin also asked me to keep Scott's weapon.

We didn't stay long as Vivian still had things to prepare for the last-minute vacation. On the way back to Amanda's, Vivian told me that Madel had packed a Florida suitcase for her, and Buster was going to drop it by this afternoon.

"Anything I don't have, I will do without or buy it in Key Largo," she said.

As we pulled into Amanda's town house development, Vivian asked me to pull to the side of the road. She released her seat belt and turned to me. I met her halfway, eager for a kiss from her. It seemed ages since we had shared any intimacies, and the kiss ignited a banked fire. Vivian maintained some conscious thought because she pulled away, laying her cheek on my shoulder. "I love you, Jack."

Kissing her forehead, I replied, "I love you, too, Vivian. You go relax and unwind and then come back to me, okay?" Out of self-defense, I gently pushed her back into her seat and started the Jeep. I needed to drop her off now, or it wouldn't happen.

CHAPTER 26

My final phone pillow talk conversation with Vivian before her return to Minnesota made me aware of what I have been missing all my life. I've never looked forward to a telephone call before in my life. Hearing her voice inspires me; if I could only see her smile. I realized that I never felt happiness till Vivian. I didn't even know I was unhappy. I guess you don't miss what you have never known.

I was having fun just listening to Vivian tell me about her day. She was happy and relaxed. Since we were involved, everything had been so tense and scary for her. I was grateful that I could ease her pain during the rough times of Mary's abduction. That is all behind her now, and you could easily hear it in her voice.

"You are going to be so jealous, Jack. We have soaked in the sun, down on the beach. Even Mary has gotten a tan. She loves collecting shells. Mary carries her bucket for them and has begun running ahead of us. She is so much better than when we first got here. Mary was glued to us when we arrived. You wouldn't believe the weird looks she gets walking down the beach with Tabby at her side," she said with laughter. "Oh, Jack, you won't believe it! Mary said her first word! You will never guess what it was. Guess."

"Well, let me think a minute. Okay, *Tabby*."

"What! How did you know that!" The shock was apparent in her voice.

Laughing at her reaction, I said, "I'm a detective. Seriously, Viv, what else would it have been?"

"Okay, but she hasn't stopped saying it since the first time. It's almost like she is trying to connect other words, but the only thing that comes out is *Tabby*. Amanda will take Dr. Engle's recommendation and take her to the specialist."

"If Carolyn recommended the specialist, you can bet she is top in her field. I think Mary is going to be just fine. Everything is looking up, Vivian."

She had so much to tell me, and we talked for over an hour. I have never heard her talk so much.

"Jack, Mary fed the tarpons at this restaurant in Key Largo. Those fish are huge! The restaurant we go to is just a short walk from the condo, called Sunsets. They give you the stuff to feed the fish. She was so cute. She squatted down, feeding them, but turned around to find us. She does that a lot. She saw we were watching her, and she smiled, pointed at the water, and said her second word—*fishy*.

"Jack, we also saw a manatee at our dock. I wasn't even sure what it was. This funny head poked up out of the water, and rather than back up, Mary went closer to it."

"Wow, I've seen pictures but never have been up close and personal with one."

"A young man was on the dock working on a boat and walked toward Mary. She backed up a little, then crouched beside him, and he whispered to her, 'Manatees are friendly and love the fresh water from this hose.' He helped Mary, holding the hose for the manatee, and the manatee came close enough for Mary to pet him. Oh, she just loved it."

As our conversation slowed, Vivian told me she was concerned about Tabby's weight. "She just skimmed under the maximum weight on the way down here, and she has been eating everything since we got here. I'm sure she lost some weight while captive, so keep your fingers crossed we make it home tomorrow."

"I'm coming down to take Auntie Vivian home if you're not on that plane. I can't wait to see you. I will be waiting for you by the luggage carousel when you land. I have enjoyed our pillow talks, but it will be the real thing tomorrow night. I love you, Judge Lord."

"I love you, too, Detective Janssen. See you tomorrow."

I sat with the phone in my hand for minutes after we disconnected. I had almost told Vivian about my debriefing with LaVonne, scheduled for tomorrow, but decided it wasn't a good time during their much-needed vacation. Let her be on vacation for as long as she could. I could tell the time away from here had done her a world of good. And when she came home, it would be different. She wouldn't be coming home to an empty house. I would be there with her.

Going to sleep these days has been a lot easier. I have been more relaxed when I head to bed since the nightmares seem to be a thing of my past. I must say that I miss the sound of the water lulling me to sleep as it did at Vivian's. You can hear the wind rustle the leaves and create waves that lap at the shoreline.

Since I have been back at my place, I wake up surprised and disoriented. I miss the guest suite at Vivian's. It was comfortable, I thought as I stretched and got out of bed.

Walking into the kitchen to make myself my morning jolt of Java, I thought I could make a pot of coffee without looking at the manual.

I was meeting LaVonne at the government center watering hole, Club 36. It wasn't unusual for county employees, current or retired, to meet for a beverage of their choice while they talk shop, present or past. LaVonne called our meeting a relaxed conversation over cocktails. I didn't care what she called it. It was a debriefing.

We were seated in the quiet adult room, reserved for private parties or confidential exchanges—attorney and client exchanges, meeting with a Realtor, client, or sometimes small business meetings. LaVonne arrived before me and must have asked to be seated back here. It was three o'clock and still pretty quiet in the front room.

Oh yeah, more than a casual conversation between friends, I thought. The hostess led us to a table in the corner of the room and asked if she could bring us a beverage.

Lavonne had brought in two expandable legal files and placed them on the table before hugging me and saying, "A glass of Chardonnay, please, and I assume you would like a bourbon, Jack?"

Colette, the server, knew both of us well and asked if I wanted my usual brand. "Sure, LaVonne is buying, make it Bullet," I said, smiling at LaVonne.

Without wasting any time, LaVonne proceeded into the real reason for this drinks-between-friends meeting. "Jack, this is my agenda. I have two separate case files—Kenneth Clayton, deceased, and Peter Manning, in custody." At my nod, she continued, "Let's start with the more straightforward of the two—Kenneth Clayton. First, you have been exonerated by the BCA for all improprieties, including all criminal offenses. The death has been ruled accidental, caused by an unexpected event that was not intended, expected, or anticipated."

"Well, that's a relief," I said with a sarcastic look. "That has been keeping me up at night."

Looking up from sorting through papers in front of her, she noted the sarcasm and chose to ignore it. "Now as for the criminal sexual conduct reports from victims, these have expanded since Clayton's death and the media accounts. For various reasons, we both know that unreported sexual assaults are far too common."

While sipping on my bourbon, I enjoyed watching LaVonne detail the accounts of my retired life for the last ten days, as if I needed LaVonne to document what I had experienced. I'm glad she had a report because I wasn't going to write one. I had done that for twenty-seven years.

Most cops hate writing a report, and for a good reason. Legal terminology used in report writing is a specialized language and is often difficult for a layperson to understand. It can also be dry and dull. The best part of being retired is that this layperson isn't writing any report about the last ten days.

LaVonne continued, "You may be interested in the connection between Clayton and Judge Lord's residence. Clayton's mother, Crystal Boutwell, lives in Somerset and owns Somerset Winery. She had Judge Lord's passcode to gain entrance through her security gate. Boutwell drives the suspicious white VW Jetta seen in the area.

"It seems her son, Kenneth, often used her car. Numerous matches on fingerprints and DNA were made, including the cigarettes found at Lord's vineyard and the letters written to victims after the assaults. It's interesting that in Clayton's young life—nineteen years—he had no juvenile adjudications or adult criminal convictions.

"So, Jack, do you have some questions about this case, or are you bored? You look bored."

I asked her if the tab was going to her expense account.

She nodded and added, "By the way, Jack, you have been nominated as Police Officer of the Year by St. Croix and Pierce Counties for bravery and valor."

"Oh, for god's sake, LaVonne, that is very nice and all that, but I'm retired. I was never even a cop in Wisconsin. I will tell them I appreciate it, but it isn't necessary. Cops are putting on the badge every day in their state that deserves recognition. My bravery and courage are retired. Let's move to Manning."

LaVonne flagged Colette to order another round and an assorted meat and cheese appetizer platter. Famously called the Docket, in honor of a list of cases on a judge's calendar.

"So, Jack, the Manning case." LaVonne looked through her file to locate a document. She continued, "The Manning file has become somewhat more complicated, as you will see. So Manning has been formally charged with kidnapping, 609.25, with an enhanced sentence for conviction because Mary is under sixteen years of age, for a maximum sentence of forty years. It may be difficult to prove malicious intent in Manning's charge of kidnapping. He has also been charged with false imprisonment, 609.255, whoever knowingly lacking lawful authority to do so intentionally confines someone else's child under eighteen without the child's parent or guardian's permission shall serve no more than three years."

LaVonne is good at reading a jury, and she could see that I was unhappy with the charge of false imprisonment.

"Jack, the charge of kidnapping is problematic. The results of Mary's physical exam indicate no distinguishable abuse. However, more updated information may be forthcoming. According to Manning's court-appointed attorney, Manning pulled up to the dock to steal from *Courtship*. Mary came down to the dock and walked onto his pontoon. He heard someone calling Mary's name and got scared and just pulled away from the dock, with her still on the pontoon. Furthermore, Anderssen Windows has a video of Manning operating a golf cart with a passenger—Mary—and the cat heading toward his residence in Bayport."

"Allow me to interrupt with a few questions." Sitting forward from a relaxed pose in my chair, I put my elbows on the table and began, "One question that I would like addressed—Manning has several charges of criminal sexual conduct and was never entered as a sex offender. What gives?"

"Jack, all I can say is it was a data entry error. The correction facility, Stillwater, owns the house that Manning rents, and apparently, the technician believed that Manning was an inmate at Stillwater Prison, as it is on state property. Big mistake. The state of Minnesota realizes its mistake could have adversely affected the outcome of this case. The police went through the sex offender registry list while conducting the investigation. The state corrected the error."

I gave her another withering glance at that statement and a dismissing snort.

"Jack," she said in a placating tone, "we do have a list of stolen property that Manning admits to taking, like Judge Lord's boat chair, a bicycle stolen from Bayport, the golf cart stolen from Anderssen Windows. In addition to an assortment of traffic offenses, driving after revocation, evading the police."

"Oh, for god's sake, LaVonne, you know those traffic and theft offenses are all misdemeanors and, at max, would only add on county jail time. That is just so much BS."

Sitting back in my chair again, I just stared at her. She knew me so well in bed and the courtroom as a witness. She just stared right back.

"So, LaVonne, regarding the kidnapping formal complaint, my takeaway from your summation is that the likelihood of a conviction is not good, and my response is, BS! God, what that little girl went through at Manning's hands? She could have died if everything hadn't fallen into place when it did, LaVonne. He deserves to go to jail for longer than three years!"

Ignoring my outburst except to say, "Speaking of Judge Lord, there is more that we should be discussing. Manning's attorney has requested a change of venue for his client. His request states that you and Judge Lord will likely be called as witnesses in the prosecution. He had a few more points, but that makes a solid case for a change of venue. I'm not going to argue that fact, and I already agreed to the change of venue. Have you ever been involved in a change-of-venue case before? It could be dicey for the kidnapping case."

"I have. Years ago, before you came to Washington County, I arrested a Stillwater city attorney for criminal sexual conduct. We had a change of venue to Pine County. He was rumored to be the governor's next appointment to the bench for Washington County."

"What the hell, Jack? Are you kidding me? You never told me about an arrest involving a lawyer. Who was it?"

"Darrell Cammer."

"Did it go to trial?"

"No, Cammer entered a statement of sorts where the defendant will not contest the charge made by the state. I forgot the name."

LaVonne said, "Nolo Contendere sound familiar or Alford plea?"

"Alford plea sounds like the one. Once the state became aware of the conviction, Cammer's license to practice law was suspended for several years. LaVonne, I have no problem with a change of venue. It usually involves more windshield time driving for the witnesses.

"The problem I had with the case was Cammer's church group that wanted my head on a platter for disgracing the name of a good man. Protesters were positioned at the government center, calling for my termination. It wasn't until a Twin Cities television station, WSTP, did a weeklong series on child sexual abuse and highlighted the Cammer investigation. The reporter had footage of Cammer scrapping snow off his car at his Stillwater residence. An on-camera interview followed in which Cammer made some admissions.

"The reporter interviewed me as well. I declined to answer specific questions regarding the Cammer arrest. I only confirmed what was in the formal criminal complaint. LaVonne, it wasn't to protect Cammer. He was married and had young children. They didn't deserve the fallout of his actions, and I tried my best to protect them. After the weeklong investigative report, the protests and calls for my dismissal ended. The shoe is on the other foot. Now I'm a Bayport local hero. Go figure."

LaVonne looked fascinated, like she had more questions to ask. "Jack, sometime I would love to sit down and talk about the Cammer case. I can't believe we have never talked about it before."

"Lavonne, go into the County Attorney's Office files. You should have all your questions answered. You have all the information you need on the Clayton and Manning cases. If I thought I had any clout in changing the charges on Manning, I would keep hammering, but I know that would be pointless from experience.

"Perfect. LaVonne, my good friend Commander Jacobson just walked in. Probably a good time for me to go. Do you have any more questions for me about the current cases?"

"No, Jack, thank you. I will keep you posted as to the charges on Manning. Convey my best wishes to Judge Lord."

"Thanks for the drinks, LaVonne." And with a nod, I started walking. The path to the door was directly past Commander Jacobson's table in the main dining room. His brows drew together as he spotted me, and he looked beyond me to see where I came from as our eyes met. Including Commander Jacobson, all the men sitting at the table were in plain clothes. I recognized two others at the table—sheriffs of St. Croix and Pierce County in Wisconsin. The men who had nominated me for Police Officer of the Year in Wisconsin. I presumed the other men were detectives. They were law enforcement, you could tell.

I approached the two sheriffs I recognized and stopped beside the table to thank them for the nomination. "I am honored, but we all know that being in the right place at the right time is half the job. I sure didn't know he would start taking shots at me."

That got laughs all around the table, with one notable exception. It seemed that Jacobson hadn't been aware of the nomination until now, and looked displeased.

The table of men stood, and I gave handshakes all around the table. Jacobson remained noticeably seated.

The sheriff of St. Croix County, with whom I was most familiar, said, "Jack, the award ceremony takes place during May. We would like you to attend."

"Sheriff, I appreciate the nomination, but don't you think it is all a little over the top? I'm not even on the job anymore. The officers still wearing a badge and Kevlar vests every shift are the ones to be thanked. I'm sure glad they were there that night."

During this conversation, I moved behind Jacobson's chair and placed my hands heavily on his shoulders. He immediately became agitated. Jacobson is known to be a germophobe. I admit I knew it and was enjoying his discomfort. To rub his nose a little, I said, "I am happy to continue this conversation at a different time, Sheriff. Anne Reed at the Sheriff's Office was also instrumental in this case. Give her a call, and we can all get together for a talk.

"Gentlemen, could I give you some menu recommendations here at Club 36? You can't go wrong with a New York strip steak, my favorite, but you would enjoy the Wisconsin cheese curds for appetizers."

That also got a chuckle from the table. I continued, "But I know Dick's favorite is the Rocky Mountain oysters. He loves them. Enjoy."

My amusement was restrained until I was in the parking lot and had a good belly laugh. I love cop humor.

As LaVonne exited Club 36, she saw me and stopped in surprise. "Jack, you have a smile that has been absent for far too long. I didn't realize until now that I hadn't seen you smile in months. Probably the bourbon, right? Did you talk with Jacobson? I was going to say hello when he suddenly jumped up from the table and rushed into the restroom. He looked flush too. I hope he is okay."

Restraining my laughter, I said, "Maybe it was something he ate."

27

Thanksgiving is three weeks away, and Vivian has returned home from Key Largo. I could hardly wait to see her. Mary and Amanda were at the top of my mind, and Vivian was in my heart. With the colder nights and Minnesota daylight evaporating, I felt Scottie could use an outing on Arcola Trail, his old stomping grounds with new smells.

We walked along the blacktop, gravel, and easement paths near the river. I was getting a kick out of Scottie's enjoyment. I hope someday, this scent walk will be in our future and become routine. Scottie took off after a red fox near the Arcola Railroad High Bridge. Not that he would hurt a fox, I think Scottie thought the fox was kin, another King Charles Cavalier spaniel, and was just curious.

It was two hours before I was concerned he may be lost or just not returning to my whistle or calls. Darkness came quickly, along with the colder temperatures. I started driving through the area in hopes I would see him walking along the roadway. When I was almost ready to call the search pointless and give it up for the night, my cell phone rang. It was Washington County dispatch. "Detective Janssen, this is Elizabeth calling."

"Yes, Elizabeth?"

"We received a call from a Buster Greeley on Arcola Trail that reports finding a dog and believes it's your dog. Would you like his phone number?"

"Thank you, Elizabeth. I'll go directly to Mr. Greeley and pick up my dog. Thanks so much." My thoughts returned to more accessible, laid-back times in the *Corncob Jungle* when a dispatcher could visit with callers.

241

With relief, I drove to Buster's while a light snow was falling. It was only a few minutes away from my location. I pulled into his cottage driveway. As I got out of the Jeep, I instantly got a whiff of Buster's wood-burning fireplace.

I inhaled the fragrance of oak burning. The aromatic smoke was a signal for Minnesota residents. Winter was hastily approaching. While walking to Buster's door, I felt sympathy for him living alone in such a beautiful setting, with only a library of reading material.

Vivian had opened my world to new possibilities and family. Buster had to settle for books.

I knocked at the door, and to my bewilderment, Madel opened the door. "Detective Jack, or Mr. Jack, welcome. Come in."

"Madel, I don't want to intrude. I'm just here to pick up my dog, Scottie. Is he here?"

"No, Mr. Jack, my Buster, he is now dropping off your dog at Ms. Vivian's and going to Stillwater for some baking supplies for me. Would you like coffee?"

"Oh, no, thank you, Madel. I guess I didn't know that you lived here?"

"Yes, Mr. Jack, I have lived with Buster for several years. We had worked together for Ms. Vivian for almost ten years. We enjoyed each other so much we had—what do you say—a ceremonial, at the Historic Courthouse. Ms. Vivian married us. I've been baking cookies and sweet breads for Ms. Vivian's Thanksgiving dinner. She is having a large group."

"Whatever you're baking sure smells good, Madel. I'll go to Vivian's to pick up my dog. He has become a great companion."

"Yes, Mr. Jack." And she wrapped her arms around me with a big hug. "You brought our chica back home. God bless you, Mr. Jack."

While walking to my Jeep, the light snow continued, and I momentarily felt that I had returned to my solitary ways upon the loss of Scott.

Vivian and I have had many conversations; although we haven't discussed Thanksgiving. I found Madel's words interesting. Madel and Buster had been coworkers for almost ten years and enjoyed each other's company, so as Madel said, they had a ceremony.

Along with Scott's paternal advice, I think a wedding proposal may be in my plans, which is an occasion I haven't given much thought. A lovely dinner with wine at a romantic restaurant. A walk along the St. Croix now seems too frigid of a setting. Do I ask Vivian to join me for a destination weekend getaway at a beautiful log cabin on Lake Superior? No, that sounds presumptuous. My only resource seems to be LaVonne or Ms. Adeline. I know this cop will call for officer assistance for this monumental occasion.

The much bigger question: is she prepared to begin a new life with me? Is her love for me as strong as my love for her? Is Vivian prepared for marriage? Am I prepared for marriage?

The snowfall became steady, which always made the temperature feel colder than it was. I paused at the front gate and entered the code to open. Did Vivian continue to share her love with me, or will this be a one-sided romance?

Thoughts of Vivian bombarded my mind. As the snow fell, I pulled around the circle entrance and looked up at the American flag, aglow with lights. I felt proud, patriotic, and grateful.

Vivian opened the door and greeted me with the most beautiful smile and long glistening auburn hair. The inside warmth of Vivian's home from a glowing fire in the fireplace radiated like opening an oven door, which immediately warmed my body.

Our eyes met, and Vivian said, "Jack, please come in. You must be chilled." I could sense her love for me and my passion for her.

Vivian wore an emerald-colored silky blanket kind of thing with a hole for her head and armholes. As her body under her clothing moved, it was the sexiest thing I had ever seen. The sleeves moved up and down with her arms as she opened the door wider, exposing the beautiful, delicate movements of her arms. The velvet blanket clung to every curve she had. Who knew a blanket could be so sexy. Whatever that material was, it was hot. It made me smile. It was suddenly my favorite material.

She was more beautiful than any time we had been together. My typical awkwardness and queasy stomach around her disappeared, replaced by love and happiness.

"The warmth feels nice," I said in my Carhartt jacket. I was distracted by the chemistry I was feeling toward Vivian.

I had momentarily forgotten the purpose of stopping when she asked, "Are you missing someone?"

"Oh yes, yes, I am, Vivian. Madel said Buster would be dropping him off. Is he in the garage?"

With a smile and snicker, Vivian looked toward the fireplace stacked with logs, glowing red from the fire, and sounds of crackling and hissing.

Lying in front of the fireplace hearth, Tabby stretched out with Scottie beside her. I don't think either cat or dog saw me. I said, "Hey, boy, come here."

Scottie lifted his head momentarily, stretched out a little closer to the fire, and put his head back down.

"Jack, Scottie is probably tired from his extralong walk. He feels right at home and enjoys following Tabby wherever she goes. He will eat all of Tabby's cat food if I'm not careful."

"Scottie eats cat food? Really?" I said with a sheepish smile.

"Jack, please have a seat. I have something to discuss with you."

Suddenly I felt underdressed and a little uncomfortable. I hadn't shaved today and looked grubby, like I had just returned from a two-week hunting trip. Sitting across from Vivian, she looked beautiful and comfortable in front of the fireplace. I was back to comparing us to *Lady and the Tramp.*

"Jack, I have a confession to make."

"Do I need to inform you of the Miranda warning?"

"Jack, I'm being serious. When Buster found your dog this afternoon and called me for your telephone number, I was feeling a little off, like something was missing. Sort of woe is me. First Charles, then cancer, Mary's kidnapping. I was feeling very sorry for myself and was deliberating—no, thinking—what makes me truly happy. Instantly I visualized Mary. She makes me feel young again, gives my life purpose, and makes me feel incredibly blessed. The only other person that can equal my affection for Mary is you, Jack. I know our relationship could have complications, pending court, conflicts of interest, so I have requested the chief magistrate to have me recused from your arrests and pending appeals. What is important is what I feel for you."

I could dialogue with the most clever criminal types or characterize a defendant's demeanor before a jury. Right now, I didn't know what to say. Wherever she is going sounds serious. I just hoped I didn't say anything stupid. Just listen, Jack.

Suddenly Vivian stood up, walked toward me, and knelt on the carpet directly in front of me, taking my hands. I looked at her in surprise.

"Jack, I want you to pay careful attention, as if you were under oath and seated in the witness chair."

With a somewhat puzzled look, I nodded in the affirmative.

"Jack, my court reporter cannot record your answer."

I chuckled and replied, "Yes, Judge, Your Honor."

"Madel has made a lovely Swedish dinner for us, and I have chilled a bottle of champagne for a celebratory toast. What I am about to propose is voluntary. Dinner, however, is an order from the court.

"Jack, my world collapsed around me four years ago when I lost Charles. My first love, the center of my life. One month ago, I almost lost the second love of my life, Mary. Someone whose love has carried my spirit and blessed my life with purpose and fulfillment these last years. I had been lonely until I made that first call to you. I waited for you until I was ready to give love again. I didn't know it, but it makes sense now. And here you are, the man I love. You have been my trusted courthouse friend, guardian, and protector, and now, will you have me as your lover and wife? Remember, Jack, you are still under oath."

Sliding out of the chair onto the floor, with my knees touching hers, our hands still joined, I looked deeply into those big gorgeous brown eyes. Mine started to water. How did this happen? I asked myself. Thank you, God.

"Vivian, I love you. Maybe I always did, but first, you were married, then after Charles, I guess I never thought I was good enough for you. That phone call has changed our lives, and I am so glad you made it. I want to go forward in our journey of life with you at my side. I can't wait to see what tomorrow holds. Let's not waste time, Vivian. Let's get married."

Vivian laughed loudly and threw her arms around my neck, toppling us onto the carpet. A perfect position for my way of thinking. Our lips met, and we kissed for all our tomorrows.

Suddenly we were joined by Scottie, who thought all the kissing looked fun and wanted to play. Jumping between us, he began offering his kisses to each of us.

Tabby looked on with disdain and disapproval.

Epilogue
Thanksgiving Brunch

The Honorable Federal Judge Magnuson held open the elegant doors to the river bluff home, allowing Vivian and me to enter before him. Vivian took hold of my hand with a loving squeeze and walked me over the threshold and inside. Smiling at me, she continued to lead me into the house. Vivian stopped when we reached the opening to the living room and pointed to the wall above the piano. Vivian had replaced the portrait of Charles with a photo enlargement of Mary and Tabby shelling on the gulf beach. I looked at my beautiful bride with the love I felt for her displayed in my eyes.

I whispered, "Where is our little flower girl?" Then I heard the pure playful giggles of Mary. She cheerfully repeated *Tabby* as her cat pranced close by, and Scottie followed.

The fragrance of pumpkin spice permeated the air. The fireplace glowed, heating the room and adding an occasional crackle or pop to the soft piano background music.

I have been blessed. My life is suddenly full of family and friends, who are all here: Bubbles; Anne; LaVonne; judicial assistant Gail; Wanda; Dr. Carolyn; Dr. Denise; foster brother, Doug; Madel; Buster; Amanda; Ms. Adeline; and even Josie Magnuson, wearing her red cowgirl boots. There were several guests I haven't had the opportunity to meet as well. I was a happy groom.

Vivian looked incredible. She was wearing a classic ivory-colored pantsuit that symbolized love, grace, and elegance. Vivian wore her thick auburn hair with a messy twist in back, which enhanced her natural beauty. Her autumn flowers accented her sleek braided sandals.

I had proudly donned a cream tuxedo with *tabby*-orange accessories, my color choice for an autumn wedding ceremony.

Vivian and I held hands and faced our family and friends. There was a pause in the conversations as we came into view.

Judge Magnuson raised his voice and asked for everyone's attention. "We have just returned from the Washington County Historic Courthouse Rotunda. It is my great honor and privilege to introduce to you, Jack Janssen and Vivian Lord, *husband and wife*."

The celebratory kiss brought out applause, cheerful shouts of joy, and no tears from me, as I had promised.

Outside the windows of *our* river bluff home, winter was approaching, changing the scenery yet again. The warm glow of autumn was fading away and welcoming in the solitary colors of winter. Whatever the season or the colors, I will always cherish the view.

The Arcola High Bridge looked even closer now that the branches were bare. I will never look at that bridge the same way ever again.

The Arcola Railroad High *Bridge Over Troubled Water* of the St. Croix River, with the *aid* of friends, family, and criminal justice system, has *calmed* the water. Mary is back in the nurturing arms of our family.

The final puzzle piece and closing chapter of a missing five-year-old girl and her orange cat. The puzzle is complete and everything is right again in the *Corncob Jungle*.

About the Author

L.C. Simon is a retired Sheriff's Office detective sergeant with twenty-seven years in law enforcement. He investigated child abuse for seventeen years and has interviewed hundreds of suspects and victims of child abuse. Simon participated in the formation of the first statewide training program for child abuse investigation in Minnesota. Simon was a contract law enforcement instructor for ten years in the child abuse curriculum course presented by the Bureau of Criminal Apprehension.

CornerHouse is a globally recognized training institution that provides professionals with forensic interviewing. Simon has not only attended the training program, he provided CornerHouse with leading-edge written strategies for children and family dynamics, now included in their teaching program. Simon had been invited to the Sally Jessy Raphael show with a perpetrator of Munchausen by proxy, who he had arrested.

A true pioneer of child abuse investigations who will captivate readers with mystery and romance. Law enforcement and child protection workers will find proven techniques and strategies sprinkled throughout this novel. Throughout his career, Simon has always maintained the child-first doctrine and comports to the do-no-harm approach.

Printed in the USA
CPSIA information can be obtained
at www.ICGtesting.com
JSHW022106280723
45564JS00001B/5

9 798888 513804